# Equilibrium

Isaac Diaz

# Equilibrium

Published in the United States.

First edition.

ISBN 978-0692440285

Pure Publications.

To the ones who kept me on my toes.

# Forward

You look out in amazement as you watch your accomplishments. No, this isn't anything you created. No. It's something far greater. This was something you fought hard for. You pushed and ran. Battled and fought. You used every part of your energy for this. Every dream of yours consisted of this.

What the heck am I talking about? What you just read was my life in the past couple years. A desire deep within me for something I didn't even know was vital for my wellbeing.

Corrupted without it. Sent to Oblivion using my desperation. Hatred brewed and I was a mess.

And it's only because of what I gained that I can say thank you to the specific ones who brought me out of what I was in.

What you're about to read is a mirrored image to what I went through. It's the journey that took me to the place I'm at now. It's what lets me fall asleep at night. It's what makes me pure. It's what makes me…

**EQUILIBRIUM**

# Prologue

Buildings reflected the bright rays of the afternoon sun making everything look like a beam sticking out of the ground. It was the norm for everyone. These large metallic buildings were everywhere. No matter where you went, they were there.

A small child pondered while aimlessly staring at them. Never before had they been this bright to him. Who made these buildings? What were they for? He thought to ask his mother, but went against it when he saw that she was immersed in the television.

He picked up the see-through device that he set on the balcony railing. He knew this device to be his entertainment and way of learning before he started school. It went over the basics. It would go through the alphabet and make sure you pronounced the letter correctly. Next it taught numbers with the same process. Everything from colors to basic fundamentals of learning. It was his goal to accomplish everything it laid out for him.

Determined to finish what he started, the small child picked back up the precious device and held it with a firm grip, tapping the clear glass-like material to continue on the next lesson.

A gleaming smile spread across his face as he heard the computer voice talk to him about his progress. He wanted to continue on but he'd finished all the lessons for that day. Even if he wanted to work ahead, he wasn't allowed to.

His zeal for learning was put on halt for a brief moment. He set the device back on the railing on the balcony. Despite his love for it, he often was careless with it. It never really occurred to him that it had the potential to fall the hundreds of feet down the building they lived in with a single gust of wind.

The child was now stuck with the task of finding something else to occupy himself. No matter of what he thought of, it always involved his mom. He never enjoyed playing by himself. He never had a dad or siblings to play with. All he knew was his mom. She meant everything to him. But at the moment, he wasn't so sure why she was crying.

That wasn't the only thing out of place that he noticed. She usually sat comfortably on the couch when she watched television. Now, she stood and had her hands clamped over her mouth as tears strolled their way down carelessly. He could hear the little spurts of sobs that managed to escape her hands, muffling her misery.

He turned back around once again knowing that it wouldn't be a good idea to bother her. With nothing else to do, he resumed his gazing out at the marvelous city. The child eyes widened at the sight of the city. There was now a large ship that hovered over it, casting a shadow down on the area it positioned itself.

He'd never seen one that big before. It looked to him like the ones he saw in pictures of the army. He was sure of it when he saw the cannons and guns that revealed themselves to the world. He decided to finally give up and let his mom know. Surely something of this stature was worth telling her about. How often did you see a military ship fly over the city?

"Mommy! Look!" he yelled as he pointed out towards it.

Her head immediately turned at the sound of his voice, letting him see her tear stricken face head on. He watched as his mom's eyes did the same as his when he first saw it. A ball of joy exploded inside him. She must be just as amazed as he was. He did something to make her happier.

Just as he thought he accomplished something, her sobbing turned into a scream. She pleaded at the world for salvation and he knew no reason as to why.

"No!" she sobbed. "No!"

She kneeled down to her child and hugged him tightly, not letting him go.

He felt her tears drip onto his neck but it didn't matter to him. He was watching a real military ship for the first time. His face continued to brighten as he watched the bottom of the ship open up.

His eyes followed a small black dot that was barely big enough to actually see descend and make its way towards the spotless city.

Falling.

Falling.

Falling.

It must have been the happiest moment of his life. Whether it was or not didn't really matter. It was to be his last.

A blinding light brighter than any glare of the buildings burned through his retinas only to clear and reveal the rolling fire that hurled towards them and encased him and his mother.

It's known as the bomb that started the war. People tell of the impact it had, completely clueless about what really started everything. It was the choice of the person inside the airship to drop it that decided this fate. They clearly had a plan. They clearly wanted something. And part of it included wreaking havoc to the home of the Equilibrium.

# Chapter 1

Equilibrium. I've heard that word many times before in science and math but it never meant anything more than it was supposed to. It was just supposed to be a word, never having any value to it.

Well, that could be said about a lot of things. Names, for example, have more meaning than you really think. You may have wondered why your parents gave you the name you have. Sometimes it was just because the name sounded right. It fit the ugly and disgusting baby face that they loved so much. Other times, it was because they knew a certain person with that name. A person who had a lasting impression on them. Whether they changed their lives, helped them through the hard in life, or was just overall a good person, it was because of them that you have your name.

Now, Equilibrium isn't my name, but it does have special meaning to me now. The past couple years were what made me *me*. I've always wanted to be in a crazy situation you see in movies where you are randomly thrown into some massive conflict. I wanted to be the one who everyone looked at with sparkling eyes. Yes, I'll admit, I wanted fame and drama. The typical high school student. But never in my life did I ever think that something like that would actually happen, and in a way that I would have never thought.

Now that I look back at it, I always think of ways it could have gone better. Choices that would have benefitted everyone as a whole.

Yeah right. Like I could have changed anything. Nothing could have prepared me. There is no person in the entire universe who could go through this and be ready in the slightest. A soldier could train all his life for fighting wars, but nothing will ever be like fighting in the actual war. That war will change him. Change his mind. His soul. His intentions. Change his whole being. Seeing horrors will always change a person. And it's at that moment when you realize who you really are. It's at those moments of stress and others relying on you that you find your true feelings.

So, let me ask you a question.

Who are you?

\*     \*     \*

My eyes had already gotten used to being open long enough that they lost any sign of grogginess. The sun hitting my face didn't help either. The summer's rays were still beating down on the earth. It would soon start to lose its strength in the coming months. I felt a little piece of my joy chip off when I realized that summer would be ending pretty soon. It's not like I did anything during summer anyways. It mainly consisted of laying around all day and playing video games.

"What about going and doing things with friends?" you may ask. Well, that's the thing. I've never had any. Yeah, I had the few people I would hang out with at school, but I wouldn't necessarily call them friends. More like fat nerds who would spend most of their time talking about video games. I didn't mind any of it, though. We would actually get into some pretty good conversations about how to strategically beat a boss in a game.

Well, great. Now you see me as no different from them. Just another fat nerd. I'll have you know I'm not fat! And we could debate on what is considered a nerd. Not completely saying I'm not one—but, I'm pretty average. Just a regular high school boy. No particular talents or unique features.

Oh, and it might help to tell you my name. Name's Mark Anderson. Yes, I know. It's as boring as you can get with a name. Don't blame me. Blame my mom. I had nothing to do with it. But I guess Mark isn't that bad. I've heard some pretty weird names over my life so I shouldn't complain about my name being so generic.

At the time, I was walking to school. This whole walking to school thing was pretty new to me. I was pretty fortunate to move into a house that was about ten minutes walking distance from it. I didn't have to rely on my mom to drive me to school or bother spending my saved money on a bike.

We had recently moved from my house across the city when my previous school burned down. No one ever found out why or how it happened. I personally think it was those dirtbags who would always set traps and wait for people to trip them off. Like that one time I—never mind. That's a whole other story. Anyways, we woke up to charred buildings with a smoky stench in the air. Good thing was, it was on the last week of school. So that meant being on break a week early. And a whole seven days really makes a difference when you have nothing to do at home.

My mom got a new job on the other side of Springfield and we got a house out here. It's not like it mattered anyways. There wasn't going to be anyone or anything to miss besides the perfect view of downtown. My window now looks out to the mountain behind us but I actually like the change. And distance wouldn't matter either way. We are pretty much still the same distance from everything since Springfield is just a huge circle surrounded by mountains, or what other people would call a valley.

The street was crowded with cars going to drop their kids off for the first day of school. I could imagine what was being said inside the cars, especially with the freshman. Mothers would be asking their kids if they had all their things and would force them to look in their backpack for the fifth time even if they said yes. Overprotective mothers galore.

I let out a small chuckle and looked forward. I could see the school building clearly now and was able to make out the big white letters that hung over the double doors.

**SPRINGFIELD HIGH SCHOOL**

Once I read those words, my stomach fell. I was pretty good at not being nervous, but it was always last second when it would set in. My heart rate started to increase and my breathing became more jagged. I wanted to stop and take a breath but I knew if I stopped now, I wouldn't want to start walking again.

"It's just a stupid school, Mark. What the heck are you nervous about?" I said to myself.

Once I crossed the pavement line for the school boundary, I saw tons of new faces I have never seen before. I knew none of these people and they knew nothing about me. But that was my advantage. They didn't know anything about me. My stomach fell even further and continued its descent. Dang it. That just added to the pressure; knowing that I had a clean slate. If I screwed anything up, they would remember that and continue to remember it. It would be the first impression I give.

I shook my head as hard as I could. What the heck was I talking about? Who cares what these people think of me. It doesn't matter. They could make all the assumption they wanted. All that mattered is how I view myself.

Right?

"Ugh. You're so useless," I muttered under my breath.

I was surrounded by the chatter and piercing screeches of teenage girls reuniting with their friends when they just saw each other the day before. Idiots. All of them. I could feel the intensity of my glare, staring them down. If they looked over at me, they would meet my brown eyes beating into their skulls. Yeah, harsh isn't it. Since I've never had friends, it annoyed me when I saw people like them. They acted like everything was fine when there was obviously more pressing matters in the world. Can't they be a little more…normal?!

I walked through the barricade of students at the entrance of the school. I would constantly look down to make sure I didn't step on anyone's new shoes. I noticed my new shoes have already started to scuff up at the edges along with the stain of the freshly cut grass clinging to my foot. I felt sorry for the grass. Hundreds of people have been trampling on it when it just went through a massacre of a haircut.

I finally made it inside and was greeted with even louder shouts and screams. Several students stood in front of the front desk with a stack of papers in their hands. They welcomed people with bright smiles and a cheery voices that somehow was able to speak over the chant of students.

"Hello!" said one of the girls. I was actually grateful for her bright natural contagious smile. It made things a whole lot better. Whoever chose these people to stand out here was pretty smart in choosing her. "What's your name?"

"Mark Anderson."

She shuffled through the papers, searching for my name. She stopped on a dime and yanked the paper from its pile of friends.

"Here you go."

"Thanks."

I took the paper, not really knowing what it was.

"Mark, welcome to Springfield High."

I said my thanks and slowly shuffled off, knowing that I wouldn't get far even if I took long strides because of the crowd. I looked down at the paper she had handed me and stared at the faded ink. At the top of the page was my name and below was a chart. The more I studied it, I realized it wasn't so much of a chart, but rather a list of the classes I would be taking over the next couple of months. I started to read off the names of the teachers in my head when a force that of a bus whacked me in my side. The pain was delayed due to the fear of the floor getting closer to my face. Making a disgusting face, I flinched and braced for the feeling of hitting the cold hard floor to combine with the hit. I followed my papers decent to the ground and heard a thud as my head made contact with it.

I stood up as fast as I could and dusted myself off. To the left of me lay a blonde haired girl with pigtails. She clenched with pain and bolted up to her feet. In one full movement, she used her momentum from getting up to push me with her arms.

"What the heck?!" she yelled. When she stood on high, I noticed how short she actually was with the top of her head coming to about my chin.

"What are you talking about? You were the one who ran into me!" I protested.

"Oh don't give me that. There's tons of space in this school and you had to be standing in the one spot I was going. So, technically, *you* were the one who ran into *me*!"

I was immediately annoyed with this girl, especially because her arguments made no sense whatsoever. Her appearance made her even more annoying. Those big golden pigtails just went to say how stuck up this girl was.

She rolled her eyes and let out an obnoxious groan. Her head turned and her gold clumps of hair whipped around and gave me a good slap in the face. I watched her make her way down the hall. She had an incredible amount of bounce to her walk that made me want to jab her in the back with my foot. But I noticed something in front of her, towards the way she was walking. There was a girl standing there, giggling at me. Although I couldn't hear her, I could easily put a voice to her giggle. It played in my head as she looked at me almost slyly.

Who was this girl?

Her brown hair came down just to a perfect length, stopping in the middle of her neck. Short hair fit her perfectly. Granted, this was the first time I'd seen her, I couldn't picture her with any other style but the one she had. As to what she wore, casual school wear. The plain red T-shirt she had on slightly pulled under her arms and revealed her slim body. Throw some jeans and some Converse on top of that and you have someone who stood out from the rest of the girls there wearing their best of the best. For some reason, her casualness made her attractive.

Once the pigtailed brat made it to where the short haired girl was standing, they started walking together. I could try and describe to you the disgusting sensation in my chest but there's no way to do that. These two apparently knew each other and because of that, I took back all I thought of the short haired girl looking attractive and simple. As much as I wanted to see her as a pretty girl, I knew I couldn't. Why? Because it's my rules. Why the heck would I ever want to be attracted to someone like her? So I went ahead and shifted my mind to thinking that she was just another one of those "groupies" to convince myself that she wasn't worth anything. She made one more look back and gave me a small smirk before walking off with her friend.

Well, this was gonna be some school. I looked above the entrance to the hallway and saw a poster on the wall. "Welcome to Springfield High School". I read it in the voice of the girl who handed my schedule. It was like it was almost mocking me, telling me how hard things were going to be.

I pushed forward through the hallway, ignoring everyone.

"Stupid poster."

\*       \*       \*

The piece of paper was now covered in footprints of people carelessly stepping on it when I fell. I tried making out the names of the teachers and classroom numbers through the dirt stains. My homeroom teacher was apparently named Violet Harper. I stood off to the side to not congest the traffic any more than it already was and looked for her class. I eventually found a pattern in the numbering of the classes and saw which room it was from down the hall.

My eyes met up with the back of the heads of the two girls. It wasn't because I was looking for them. I mean, they were practically impossible to miss. Gold pigtails and a short haired girl with her neck exposed. Pretty obvious. They started to get closer to my homeroom classroom when I started to panic. It looked like they were actually heading there.

"Please please please. Don't go in," I pleaded under my breath as I hugged the wall for some sort of help.

I watched as their two heads disappear behind the door frame. Great. Just when things couldn't get any more worse. I have to be in a class with them, when they both witnessed me tumble to the ground. It wasn't just because it was going to be embarrassing too. People like them think too much of themselves. With them in the class means more time I have to be around that attitude.

I walked even slower than before, hesitating to walk into class. It felt like everyone in the hallway was watching. They could probably all hear my heart thumping. It felt like it was practically inside my throat. I just wanted to spit it out. Now why the heck was I being so nervous? I never met these girls and I'm practically afraid of them. It wouldn't matter. It wasn't like I was going to talk to people who judged me that quickly.

I stuck out my chest farther than it was and walked in the class using a lame excuse of a confident walk. I didn't bother to look at anybody. My eyes immediately focused on an empty desk and made it my mission to make it there without anything else stupid happening. As I made my way to it, I could see with my peripheral vision that they were both staring me down from the tables they sat at. I made no sign that I even knew they existed and let them fall behind my shoulders. My backpack slumped against my desk and I sat down in the chair.

I could see that the desks were wiped down clean for the new school year. This class was occupied by last year's sophomores. No doubt these desks took a beating. Now this year it will be trashed by a new set of sophomores. I looked more closely and I could see engravings in it that tried to be concealed. Teenagers could be brutal. And this is just with a desk. Imagine how they could be with each other?

I looked around the classroom without ever putting my vision near the two. In front of the whiteboard was a lady sitting at a desk. So this was Ms. Harper. She was sitting at her desk, clacking away at her keyboard while simultaneously sipping on coffee and eating a bagel. I got to give it to her. She was pretty good at multitasking. Her eyes never moved from her screen. She hadn't even acknowledged that there were people in the class.

The clock above her head read 8:10. School started at 8:15 so we had five more minutes. I checked my phone to make sure the clock was accurate. To be honest, I was basically doing anything to occupy myself and not just sit there with the two girls staring at me. Were they even still looking at me? I didn't want to bother checking.

As it got closer for class to start, people poured in the class, the chatter following them in. There were obviously no seating arrangement so people were picking seats to sit with their friends. With the blur of the crowd, I decided to go ahead and look where the girls were. They were sitting next to each other near the window, letting their voices get mixed in with the pool of noise. Ms. Harper still never budged despite all her students. It was as if she was programmed to wait exactly until the bell rang to say anything at all.

While I was focused on watching the teacher, the seat next to me pulled out. I lifted my head up and was immediately consumed by a sea of darkness. There was a girl standing there with the longest black hair I have ever seen. Every article of clothing she wore was black. She set down her *black* bag on the desk and sat next to me.

I was still trying to comprehend all the black and kept my eyes planted on her. Was it a new style I never heard of? Or perhaps she was into the gothic look. Well, I wouldn't necessarily call it gothic. It was just all black. Nothing more to it.

"Was someone sitting here?" she said in a soft and unpleasant voice.

"Uh...no," I replied.

"Then why are you looking at me?"

Darn it.

I immediately looked away. She never even bothered to look at me when she talked. Her head remained locked in a fixed position looking at the board. Her voice was completely monotone and bland. She had a way of instantly taking control of you without even having any form of authority. Half of me wanted to talk bad about her in my mind but she was so innocent looking that I wanted to forget everything that she said.

I couldn't help it. I turned to look back at her dark aura. Her head was still fixed in the same position but I noticed her eyes were looking to the side. From where I was sitting, all I could see was the whites of her eyes. The small amount of color on her surprised me. It was subtle but it made her eyes glow. But what was she looking at?

I followed her eyes to the two girls sitting across from us. Both of them were looking back, but not at me. They were in some sort of stare off, though there was no sign of aggression in any of them. Brunette still had a sort of natural smile to her face and Blondie gave a coldhearted sneer. That was probably natural for her. They had to have known each other from last year. There must have been some type of argument between them because they were clearly not pleased to see each other. Ooh. Maybe some girl stuff went down and they fought over a guy. You know. The usual high school girl drama. Pathetic.

The bell rang with the same tune you hear in every school. It was no different from my last school. For some reason, it let me down. There could have been a little more variety. I was hoping for some more change between schools, but what did I expect? They're schools and it was just a stupid bell. What have you come to, Mark? Really? You're at a low where you complain about school bells?

Ms. Harper jolted up from her desk and interrupted my thinking. She walked towards the front of the desk and sat on it, letting her legs sprawl out. I felt an eyebrow raise. Now that she revealed her whole body, I noticed that she was a lot younger than I thought she was. She wore a white blazer over a black tank top with some denim pants. Completely modern and casual.

"Good morning everyone," she said in a crisp voice, matching her young appearance. "How's everyone doing?"

All she got in return was people groaning. They sounded like a horde of undead rising from the ground.

"Oh, don't act like that. This year's going to be great. I have a really good feeling about it," Yeah right. They always say that. It just turns out to be another regular school year. "I see a lot of faces that I remember seeing last year and also some new ones." Her eyes landed on mine, holding them in place and giving me a warm smile.

"My name is Violet Harper. Those of you who had relatives in my class before or know my daughter, know that you call me by my first name." I was taken aback by her strange request. Never before have I heard of a teacher allowing their students to call them by their first name. "I call you by your first name so it's only fair that you call me Violet. And plus, it makes me feel younger."

She let out a small chuckle that was mimicked by the students. While everyone was laughing, the door to the class opened. A student walked in with ruffled brown hair that came down to his eyes. Great. Another jerk in the class. One who thinks he can get here anytime he wants.

Violet looked over at him with the same smile she gave me.

"And what might your name be?" she asked.

"Will," he said blatantly, without showing any form of respect for her.

"Well Will, you can go ahead and find yourself an empty desk to sit at."

Once he took his eyes off of Violet, they met with the two girls. He constantly switched from looking at them and the girl sitting next to me. He gave a scoff while rolling his eyes and walked to the empty seat at the back of the class. Maybe he was the one they were fighting over. But seriously, who in the world would want some idiot like him?

"Alrighty then. Let's get started. Today's homeroom is longer than usual since it's the first day. And you know what that means. You have to spend extra time looking at this beautiful face."

Violet showed her teeth as she smiled and pointed to her face. She actually brought a grin to my face. Her personality really showed how young she was. It seemed like she was really just a child at heart, and because of that, I knew I was going to like this teacher.

I pulled back out my schedule and saw that right after homeroom, I would have English with her. I went ahead and looked at the other classes I had. Why was I not surprised that it was all the usual classes?

A pair of brown eyes peeking over at me caught my attention. The nameless short-haired girl was looking back in my direction. I figured that she was probably looking at Ms. Darkness over here but when I checked a second time, I saw that she was actually staring at me. When our eyes met, she gave a large smile and slowly turned back around, not showing any hint of cowardice.

I sat there, confused. Any time something like this happens, I always assume one thing. I'm sure you know what I'm talking about. She now had lured me in and I started to admire her in more detail. I noticed her posture was relaxed while simultaneously being formal, unlike Goldilocks who was slouching and leaning against the wall.

"Excuse me, what's your name?" Violet asked, breaking my daze.

"Mark," I said, taking an eternity to unlatch my eyes and look at her.

"Okay, Mark, can you stop making googly eyes at Charlotte and come over here and help me pass out these papers?"

I would usually be embarrassed by something like that but for some reason, I wasn't. I was too focused on putting her name to her face. Hearing her name associated with my own, she turned back around to look at me. But it was different this time. There was no smile on her, not any sign of embarrassment, no hint of emotion.

Charlotte's eyes met with mine and held them in chains, not letting them move. Her mouth was slightly open, adding to the overall sign of trance. I couldn't help but to feel like there was some type of link. It felt like there was a rope that tied us together at that moment. It wasn't just that I was appreciating her, but something clicked. And I could feel it.

Even though it seemed like it was an eternity, our locked stare was only a second or two. I stood up ignoring all the stares in the class and took the stack of papers from Violets hands.

"I need someone else to help pass out the papers," she said.

Violet looked through the class searching for a victim. She ended up picking a random someone from the back of the class who she said was secluded. I didn't bother facing the class, so I couldn't see who was coming up from behind.

When I turned to see who it was, I saw a delightful but creepy smile on some girl's face. She wore a purple long sleeved sweater despite the summer heat. That wasn't the thing that stood out the most. She had black lacing around her neck and arms that added a large amount to her goth meter.

"What's your name?" Violet asked.

"Eris," she replied confidently, almost as if she were bragging.

"Hm, never heard of that name before. Can you help Mark pass these out please?"

When she turned to face the class, it revealed the other side of her head. Her, obviously dyed, black hair was awkwardly cut. On one side of her face was long hair and the other was like Charlotte's, revealing a little bit of her pale neck.

Eris sneaked me a small look, adding a subtle tilt to her head. All of her screamed crazy, but I know I shouldn't judge people. That is just their preference. She likes the gothic and dark style. But Eris took it to a whole different level. It made me want to squirm.

A wide smile spread across her face.

"It's a pleasure to meet you, Mark."

$$* \quad * \quad *$$

We had started to pass out the papers to the rest of the class. Naturally, Eris and I split the room apart and each took a side. Without even giving me a choice, Eris took my side of the room and left me to the side with people I wanted no interaction with.

She was doing this on purpose. I looked over at her and saw that same smug smile.

Her eyes would occasionally dart over to see the reaction on my face. The more I realized she was doing this for her enjoyment, the more I would feed her.

If I had to give any credit to this school, it had to be personality. All the people here were unique. Already from the fifteen minutes I'd been there, I could tell that. I'm not necessarily saying that's a good thing, but it is different from what I'm used to.

I made my way down the aisles, handing out a paper I didn't even know what was for. I kept my head down the whole time, knowing that the two were watching me. With each table I got closer and closer to them. That same feeling started to pound on my chest. It was obvious. I was nervous. But why? Because they saw me fall? Or was it that stare?

Once I made it to their tables, I made no eye contact. I did my job and handed each of them a paper. Just as I thought I was off scot free, the paper slipped when I put it in Blondie's hand. I followed the paper with my eyes and watched it land next to her feet.

"Pick it up."

I stopped myself mid step and turned to face her.

"What?"

"You heard me. Pick it up."

All sense of nervousness went out the door. This brat thinks she can just say that to anyone, and nonetheless when it's right next to her.

I didn't say anything but kept my stern face fixed on hers and nodded towards it.

She crossed her arms and returned my look back at me.

"Piiiiick iiiiiit uuuuup."

I ignored her remark and walked right past her. Yeah, like I'd listen to her. She has arms. She could get it.

The common noise of the bottom of a chair scraping against the floor filled the room. A small smirk appeared on my face, knowing that she actually got up to get it. Because I finished passing out the papers, I turned around to head back to give the extras to Violet. I was expecting to see the stuck up girl getting the paper but was surprised to see Charlotte on the floor picking it up.

My hand crumpled the papers I was holding. I wouldn't let Charlotte be a slave to someone not even worthy of that type of service.

I stormed over to her desk and stepped on the paper she was trying to pick up.

"What are you doing?" I asked, already knowing.

She looked up at me with her hand still on the paper, pressed against the floor.

"Picking up Wendy's paper."

I was in the heat of the moment and had an anger burning inside me to collide with the brat. Only for a second did it subside. It was the first time I heard Charlotte's voice. It was a pitch, a distinction, a clarity I had never heard of before. You might be thinking that I'm talking out of my butt right now but you have no idea what I'm talking about when I say that her voice was exalted above any other.

My foot slid back to get the paper out of her grasp and flicked it away farther.

"Don't let this idiot tell you what to do!"

"But she didn't tell me to do it."

"Even more reason not to! She should get her butt off her seat and pick the dang thing up herself!"

My eyes met with Wendy's. I could tell she was upset but obviously shocked. I felt somewhat victorious inside. No one probably ever stands up against her like they should. And Charlotte? She didn't even seem swayed in the slightest by this.

"Mark. Don't make things worse," Violet said, still waiting in front of her desk. "If she wants to be stuck up, then let her. Don't stoop down to her level."

"Hey!" Wendy darted up from her seat. "I'm not stuck up! If you want to see stuck up, then I'll show you stuck up!"

"Oh will you just shut up!" Will shouted from the back of the class, slouching in his chair. "You guys are fighting over a dumb piece of paper. Who cares!"

Just when Wendy was going to shout something back, all that came out was laughter. Not from her mouth, but from Eris's. She was clearly amused with our bickering. And who could blame her? Will had some degree of reason. It's just a stupid paper. But what was worth arguing over was the fact that Wendy couldn't get it herself.

Wendy walked over to the paper on the floor and picked it up with extra flare, so as to please me.

"Ha-ppy Mark?" she said poking my chest to every syllable. After the last poke, she slid her finger down and smacked the papers out of my hand. The look on her face switched back over to her deadly smile, pleased with her dirty work.

This girl had issues. They should have been dealt with earlier but there probably isn't a psychologist good enough to take her on. Half of me wanted to be the one who would do it, but like I'd seriously have the patience to do that. And who would? Oh wait. Apparently Charlotte does. And to her I tip my hat.

I sat back down at my desk after picking up the mess Wendy made. I was expecting the girl next to me to have some sort of change in her expression after I practically broke the ice for everyone. By the way, you're welcome! To my surprise, it seemed like she never even moved a hair since she sat down. Her blank stare continued for miles ahead, almost as if they were trying to find an end to the white in the board but never could.

Violet started to explain whatever the heck the paper I was arguing about was. I drowned out her voice and filled it with the voices from my previous conversation. I found that was something I did a lot. After I had an encounter with someone, I always break it down. I think of people's intentions, what they said, why they said it. I find things that are out of place. That way next time I do interact with that same person, I have an advantage. I know more subtle things about them than they think.

Now, about Wendy's intentions. I would say they were obviously stupid. She cares too much about her own pride that she didn't want to grab a dumb paper that fell out of her hand. That could all be a ploy. She could really just be hiding her real self behind a thick wall of concrete, but let's be honest. We all know that there are real jerks out there like her who actually do exist.

Then we have people who we want the world to be filled with. The ones who are kind and willing to help despite what others say or do. People like Charlotte. I don't know much about her, but I do know a lot more than I did in the hallway. I'm not saying that my views of her being a "groupie" changed, but I see that she's a better person than

I thought. Not to mention that she's attractive and that we had our weird little connection. That out of the way, she seems like a nice person.

Wendy looked back at me and gave me a huge wink followed with mischievous snickering. It's because of people like her that I hate coming to school. It's because people like her that I hate society. It's people like her I hate to be around. And little did I know how greatly they would affect my life, and I would affect theirs in the coming days.

\*       \*       \*

Never have I thought myself being the type that follows the crowd. Everyone usually likes to think the same about themselves. They all want to be unique. But when I'm forced to do the same thing other people are doing, I can't help but to feel the need to rebel. You may not consider walking with a crowd of students to lunch the same as what I was talking about, but I consider it no different.

I looked around and read the many different expressions. Most of them were the same. Clearly, everyone was happy to go to lunch and talk with their friends. That's if you even had friends. To me, lunch was just another sign that the school day was getting closer to an end.

Once I walked outside, my ears filled with the screams of a normal school yard. Despite everyone here being a sophomore, they still acted so much like children.

The tables were already filled. All except one. I walked closer to it, kind of glad that there was still an empty one. Maybe people considered that one cursed or something. Either way, it was mine.

As I got closer to the table, I noticed one person sitting all by her lonesome. The black consumed all the light in her area like a black hole. I stopped in place and contemplated whether I should sit there or not. It's not like I was going to talk to her. I'm just gonna go over there, sit down, eat and then leave.

"Oh what the heck."

I carefully set down my bag on the table, so as to not startle her, if that was even possible. Her eyes slowly moved up and met mine. I tried to look her in the eye but the longer I looked, I felt like I was going to fall into their bottomless abyss.

"Uh…hey," I said.

Not a word.

Her eyes moved back down towards her food. She had a thermos sitting on the table with steam coming out of it. Whatever was in it, it smelled amazing. The fork she held so delicately slowly moved into the thermos and out came noodles clinging on to the fork for dear life.

"What?" she asked coldly.

"N—nothing."

Ugh! I was looking too long. I still wasn't even sitting. Stumbling over the seat, I quickly sat down not to make things anymore awkward. The aroma of her pasta made me even hungrier. I watched as another forkful of pasta made its way towards her mouth. Just as she was about to eat it, she made direct eye contact with me. The fork was held in place, waiting to be consumed. She waited for me to look away. Apparently, she was one of those people who hated to be watched while they ate. But I wasn't looking because I found her attractive or anything like that. It was because she was so different from everybody. The way she expressed herself with all black. The way she was polite and proper while speaking her mind ever so silently you'd need a microphone to hear what she was saying.

I thought of looking away in defeat, but I wanted to see who she was. I wanted to start my dissection. I continued to press my hard stare. Either she had to take a bite, or she would look away. The choice she makes says so much about her despite it being subtle. It expresses what kind of person they are and breaks down those barriers these kinds of people fortify so well.

I could see she was annoyed with my persistence and her face started to change. Her eyebrows curved just enough that I could tell. Her eyes started to squint, expressing to me that she would take on my challenge. Although I could notice the changes in her facial expression, they were still hard to tell. And so the unspoken challenge continued.

Her eyes eventually rolled back in irritation and moved to the side so she could look away from my face and could take her bite. The fork lingered in her mouth. She knew she lost, and she was affected by it. I started to slowly chip at her wall that she puts up and overtime, I would eventually break my way through.

After looking away from her, I noticed that everything had gone quiet. The chatter of students had disappeared. All I could hear were silent murmurs. I lifted my head up and looked around at the other tables. I was instantly struck with confusion when I saw that everyone was looking over at us. All the attention was on me. There were no smiles on any of their faces. Most of them looked just about as confused as I did. The normal talk slowly resumed and regained its momentum. Everyone went back to eating their lunch and doing the usual.

"Why were they…?" I asked, looking around.

"I'm the only one who sits at this table," she answered.

"Yeah? And who made that rule?" Her mouth opened to quickly respond but was just held open. Her blinking sped up while she tried looking for an answer. Her mouth then closed and her posture shrunk down a bit. "What's your name anyway?"

"Monica."

"I'm Ma—"

"I know your name," she cut me off.

Of course she knows my name. She was there in the class when I was bickering with Wendy. And the fact that she's quiet means that she probably takes in information easier and could remember things a lot quicker than most people.

Even though I've never met Monica, I felt that I knew her well. Although we were different personality wise, we are very much alike. We both seem to hate society. I could see it in her eye every time she looked up. You could see the disgust resonating in the soul ripping pupils. She also stood out with her all black wardrobe. Now that I looked at it in more detail, it was just casual wear. No fancy clothes like Eris. Just a plain T-shirt and black pants. There were no sign of frilly accessories.

Or was there?

It was so obvious, I was surprised I didn't even notice it. At the top of Monica's head sat a black bow. Despite her dark appearance, it didn't seem out of place, but went on to compliment her outfit. It sat silently, firmly locked in the strands of her thick hair.

Monica noticed me looking at her bow and had enough of my awkward staring. She quickly covered up her thermos and stood up. Her movement sped up with her angered state. She shoved it inside her bag and started to walk back towards the main building. Without another word, she was gone. I'm not an annoying person, but when you do small things like that with people like her, you tend to irritate them. Some are affected by it and some aren't. And her reaction just went and ruined her plans. She tries hard to hide her feelings and emotions, but I got her to react. It makes all the difference, especially when you're like me and want to conquer over others, proving them wrong in any place you can.

I sat still at the table, watching her leave. Her walking was just as stiff as her face. I never noticed before how much someone's walk tells about their emotional state. Seeing her lackluster walk made me question my own walk. But that didn't matter right now. I won. I beat her. And I wanted to continue to win.

A smile peeked out of the side of my cheeks.

"I hope you plan on having a fun year Monica, because this one's gonna be an interesting one."

\*        \*        \*

I couldn't help but feel satisfied with my interaction with Monica. So when I was walking in between the tables, I was able to easily ignore all the stares people gave me instead of talking bad about them in my mind.

Clearly, Monica gained a pretty big reputation. It may not be the best one, but she had one nonetheless. I almost wish I was there last year to see what made people stay away from her. It could have been nothing really. Maybe it was just her usual face that made people keep their distance. And who could blame them. When someone looks about as dead as a pansy in the Sahara, you wouldn't want to get near that person.

Despite already gaining a reputation of my own, I still had the new school feeling. I didn't know the place, so naturally, I wanted to walk around and familiarize myself with it. The main building of the school acted as a big backdrop to the whole thing. Other buildings were scattered about. Looking at it as a whole, it was a lot nicer than my old school. Now, for the people? I can't say the same.

What can you expect living in one of the biggest cities in the country? You're gonna have snobs who think they know everything. As to whether you can avoid them is dang near impossible. And it's not something you get used to either.

While I was creating the mental map of the school, I was met with a clump of cheering and shouting. They were all huddled around something, watching with great intensity. I would usually walk away from something like this but my curiosity got the better of me. It couldn't be a fight because it's barely the first day of school. Then again, with the type of people here, I could be wrong.

The closer I got, the more I started to realize that my assumption was wrong. The usual chant was enforced, egging on the contenders inside the circle. The wall of people was so tightly interlinked, I couldn't find a way in. Being too awkward with my movements of trying to get through and find out what was actually happening, I laid down my inquisition. It wasn't like it was any different from the countless fights there were in a school year. I started to walk away when I heard a scream. Not just any normal scream, but one of a girl.

I immediately turned on my heel and quickly made my way back in their direction. If it was a guy, I honestly wouldn't mind if he got his butt handed to him, but I wouldn't let a girl get hurt. Something about the higher pitched voice made me care for the poor soul. All that goes through everyone's head when they see this sort of thing is that I just want to get any chance to wow a girl. But that wasn't the case—at least for the most part.

29

I tried pressing my way through but to no avail.

Another scream pressed at the air biting singe of the afternoon sun, begging for a savior.

My quickness matched the movements of an upset Monica and I trudged through people, not giving a care anymore to if it was polite or not. Like I'd even care when there was someone who was hurting for who knows what reason. Slowly, the wall broke apart as I tore arms off and I made my way through to the center. I finally made it out and was met with the open air of the earth. I took in a large breath of fresh oxygen rather than the sweating body odor of all the teens I was encased in.

I refocused my attention to the reason I fought my way through them. The sight wasn't seen that often. Usually when you saw two girls on top of each other was when they fought over a boy. Rarely did rumors amount to this.

The one on top had a fully developed body that showed through her skin tight tank top. Her clothes were no matter to her anymore, though. After all, they were covered in what looked like someone's lunch.

The one pinned down, having her hands held against the stubbly asphalt, was not as "matured" as the other. Heck, she looked half her size. Uh, I am talking about body size here.

She would turn her head every time the one on top would shout her words of rage and carelessly shove them down her throat. Her face scrunched up as she flinched with every word all while she whimpered like a lost puppy.

"Get off of her!" I demanded.

The girl ignored me and continued her yelling.

"What the heck's wrong with you?! Look what you did to me! You call this an accident?!"

"But it was," whimpered the other girl.

The one on top shrieked in frustration and raised her fist. Words weren't going to stop her and I'm wasn't going to let her hurt her again. I ran over to her and reached out, grabbing a firm hold of her wrist before making an indent in the smaller one's face. Her hand started to shake due to the pressure of her forcing it downwards.

As if on cue, more trouble exposed himself as a bulky guy came out into the middle of the crowd. All 6 feet of him set his sights on me and came at me full force, not even saying a dang word. I had no time to react and was left to the helplessness of watching a freight train wack me. The next thing I knew, I was on the floor. There was a throbbing pain at the back of my head pressing into my skull. My hearing had a ringing to it now but I could still make out the cheers from the crowd. The gladiators had begun their battle and the crowd now wanted a victor to it.

What have you done now Mark?

"Don't you *ever* touch my sister!"

Oh great. Now I'm the bad guy.

"Get him Eli!" people screamed.

I tried getting up but the pain dragged me back down. Couldn't I just stay there? Did I really have to stand up to this guy, especially when there's a crowd watching?

My mind stopped in its tracks.

There's a crowd watching. They're watching me groan in pain on the floor. They saw me as insignificant. I'm the wimp who fell in the hall. The idiot who argued with Wendy over a piece of paper. The person that sat with Monica.

That's right. I'm the one who stood out. The different one.

I mustered up all the strength I could to get myself up. My vision continued its display of a black curtain, darkening my vision. I straightened out my back and locked my feet in their position, standing my ground.

That's right. I'm gonna show everyone. I'm gonna show them who I am. They'll know I'm not one of them. There's no point in trying to make a good impression if it's already been demolished. I'm not going to hide myself in the crowd of society. And what's a better time to do that than in a fight.

Eli looked me in the eye and then went on to size me up. I now realized how hard this fight was going to be. Eli must have been almost six feet tall. What's worse is that he had tons of muscle stacked on him. Then again, he was wearing a tight shirt so he was practically cheating. But that's not the problem. Problem is he's going to pound me to a pulp.

I raised my hands and made them into fists. I've never been in a fight before. I didn't know the first thing to staying up and not ending up with a mouth full of sand. That didn't necessarily matter though. The reason for me fighting was not to win, but to prove myself to all the people watching. You hear that everyone? I'll show you. I'm only going to do this once, so you better be watching.

My heart started to pick up its pace and I felt the drug-like adrenaline course through my body. I ran full force at Eli not really knowing what to do when I got to him. My arm extended to make impact with his face. I was expecting to feel his cheekbone against my knuckles but instead my hand stopped moving. Eli grabbed my hand and started to squeeze it, straining my wrist. With nowhere else to go, I pulled my arm back forcing us both to the ground.

I quickly seized the moment and got on top of him, starting to throw some punches at his face. I was met with the unsatisfying pain of the other end of a punch. The more I hit him, the more numb my knuckles felt.

From behind, I heard a grunted groan. The force of the tackle knocked the wind out of me and left me breathless on the floor. I scrunched up on the floor, clenching my stomach. A shadow covered the sunlight from hitting me. A girl with food all over her stood with a deadly frown, casting all amounts of hatred towards me.

"Get away from him," said a calm but stern voice from the crowd.

I tried my best to turn my head to see who the voice came from. I was pretty sure who it was since I considered that particular pitch of vocal cords to be unique and relay cuteness on all sorts of levels. My hazed vision barely allowed me the pleasure of sight. The lack of breaths didn't help either.

What I was able to make out was four figures. Once I pivoted on my elbow, keeping myself up with it, I laid back down to gather my bearings and allowed myself time to finally see who these people were. As if with an increasing sense of courage mixed with calmness, my sight problem was quickly fading.

To my surprise, my guess was right. Short hair was held on in display with the rays of heaven peeking in through little gaps in her hair. Sure, why Charlotte was here is a good question, but one that made me put that question to death was the one that raised more suspicion and curiosity. I said there were four people there. Who would the other three be? They consisted of a brat, a snobby pretty boy, and the silent residue of death. They all stood in the middle of the circle facing Eli and the girl standing over me.

Why the heck were they trying to protect me? I never did anything nice to them. In fact, I did the opposite. They had no reason to be here. I would tell them to leave, but I honestly wouldn't have mind the help. Monica walked casually over to me and lend me a hand. Eli's sister backed off just for a second, not knowing what to do with this sort of interference. I reached up and grabbed her soft cold hand. I stumbled to gain my balance and leaned on her as she walked back to where Charlotte, Will, and Wendy stood.

The feeling of having myself pretty much draped over her was quite strange. Her soft silky clothes smelled of the light amount of perfume she wore. It brought me back to reality as I realized that she was actually helping me out of her own accord. No one had told her to come over and help me up.

Out of the other side of the circle stepped two other girls. One blonde and one with bright red dyed hair. Their faces were matched, expressing the same subtle smile. They took their place next to the Eli and his sister.

Monica walked me over to where the others were standing, still holding my hand. So there we were, standing there in a little standoff. My head buzzed with total confusion, not knowing at all what was going on. Was I about to be in a group fight? Well, I tapped out. Someone take my place because I was done here.

Eli started towards us in a fit of anger. I watched as the others braced themselves for a fight, getting in their stances.

"Eli."

The redhead called him back. Her tone of voice merely called him back over. Not once did I mistake it with her being afraid of him hitting us. Without hesitation, he walked back. It was like she had total control of him. After making sure Eli walked back to where she was standing, she looked at me. Her face lightened instantly. She gave me a soft smile followed with a nod sending a shiver down my spine.

I couldn't shake the feeling I had at that moment. It felt entirely new. All I did know about it was that it somehow intensified when I stood next to my saviors.

"What's going on here?"

The bright and fresh faced homeroom teacher walked in between us.

"Nothing but a small scuffle," Charlotte told Violet, still looking at the redhead.

"Doesn't look like that to me." She gestured towards Eli's face. Now that I got a clearer look of Eli, I noticed how much I actually did to him. I couldn't help but feel proud of myself. He was a display to everyone of who I was. Now that's some first impression. "Really Eli? You can't contain yourself for one day? Get out of here, all of you, before I decide to give each and every one of you detention."

The group of four turned around and dispersed from the human "arena". The redhead sneaked me one last quick look before she followed her friends off to wherever they hanged out at.

Violet walked over to the girl who got brutally terrorized. Being engrossed in my own fight, I had forgotten all about her.

"You alright?"

"Um, yeah. I think," she said, brushing off the dirt on her clothes.

"I doubt it was Eli who was messing with you, right?"

"Yeah."

"Sarah again?" Violet said, acting like this was a thing that happened often.

The short girl gave her head a small nod. She reminded me a lot of a bunny. Her whole appearance along with the way she acted made her so adorable. To be honest, she didn't even look like a sophomore.

"Now why are *you* guys here?" she asked us.

"I tried to help her out," I said.

"Alright. Well, you should know Eli doesn't like anyone messing with his sister."

"Well that would've been helpful to know a couple minutes ago."

Violet completely ignored my smart remark.

"If you came to help her, that still doesn't explain these guys." She crossed her arms and gestured with her head to the people standing behind me.

No one answered. I expected Charlotte to give one but she just stood there without saying a word. Will wasted no time and after rolling his eyes and letting out a groan, walked away. The others slowly followed him without ever saying anything and I was just left there with Violet. When I turned around to face her, I saw that she looked just as confused as I was.

"You guys, uh...friends?" she asked.

"No. I honestly have no idea why they helped me."

Violet already seemed to lose interest in what had happened and just shrugged it off.

"Eh, who knows what they were trying to do. Just make sure that when there's a fight to let me know. Okay?"

"Sure."

She turned back around and walked towards the main building to go do whatever teachers do when it's lunch. I kept my sight in her direction. I decided to do the same thing I did with Monica to her. Her walk looked confident, stepping with firm steps. She didn't wear high heels like all the other female teachers. Her feet were slipped into regular sneakers. More casual wear. If you looked at her first glance, you wouldn't think she'd be old enough to qualify to be a teacher. If she didn't have developed features, she'd look like she could be a student in this school.

I would ask her how old she was but she would probably give me a good one in the face. I'm serious. I don't care how old any girl is, it's like they inscribe that written rule of not letting a man ask for her age into their hearts. Seriously, we just ask because we're either curious or you look extremely young, which is a good thing.

Suddenly, my "everywhere" hurt. The adrenaline finally wore off and the pain settled in. My hands immediately went towards the areas of pain and tried soothing them.

Was it really worth it? Was it worth helping her? I wobbled over to the table and ignored my brain's interrogation. My skin was now tattered with various marking and scrapes. Proof of my handy work. I traced over the scrapes that the floor gave me. It's funny how I didn't notice these until now.

How ironic.

\*　　\*　　\*

The sun still scorched the earth with intensity. This was one of the reasons why I hated summer. I suppose that it's the least favorite for everyone else too. Then you have the weirdos who actually like to be cooked alive. But to each his own.

I started on the long straight road home. This feeling was new, being all by myself at a time like this. I felt like somehow my mom was probably at school in the car, furiously driving around looking for me, even though I knew she was at home.

With nothing to do besides die of heatstroke, I went over the day. Nothing went like I planned. I've been thinking the past couple days how things were gonna play out. I had precise things I was going to do and say. I even went to the extent of a possible argument and how I would make sure that I showed off. Never did I plan for the type of arguments I would have today. Fighting over a paper, trying to break a silent pit of darkness, and fighting a bulky protective brother never even crossed my mind. Out of all that happened, there were two specific things that I couldn't stop questioning.

The first was the strange but enjoyable locked gaze between Charlotte and I. The way she confidently looked at me without a hint of doubt of what she was doing. It was like nothing I've ever experienced before. Just looking at her like that was comforting. Usually, when a girl looks at me like that or I look at her, we end up looking away in embarrassment. Although, yes, Charlotte is pretty, it was almost something more. I'm not trying to get all sentimental, but I have to say, it was one of the best feelings I've ever experienced.

So there was that, and there was also the mysterious appearance of Charlotte, Wendy, Monica, and Will. They were there to help me when I did nothing to have them do that for me. At least I don't think. Let's see. I got upset at Wendy, annoyed Will, irritated Monica, and Charlotte? Well, I never did anything bad to her. But still, I never did anything that would make her want to help me and risk her getting hurt. Whatever the reason they had for being there, they were all there together. It seemed like they all knew each other from the way they acted when they saw each other in the classroom.

They better have not wanted something from me. That would be the only logical reason for them to help me. With the way the snobby people at school act, they're bound to only care for themselves and want something in return. There's no way they would do this sort of thing because they're all good Samaritans. Either way, it didn't matter. I wasn't going to be talking to them.

# Chapter 2

"Mark! Get up! You're going to be late!"

I could immediately tell the voice came from my mom. Then again, I was half asleep. It could have been anybody.

Someone was climbing the stairs. I could hear the hollowed out wood echo the constant thudding of footsteps. Anyone trying to sneak in my house at night would instantly wake us up. Although, sometimes it did get annoying. I guess you could say it was a curse and a blessing at the same time.

Whoever was walking up the stairs was now running towards my bedroom door.

"Mark!"

My door flew open and standing there was a woman in pajamas. Yup, it was my mom. Her hair was still ruffled up from her beauty sleep and carried around a scar-like indent from a crease in her pillow on her face.

She ran over to my bed and started to pull my bedsheets off of me.

"Come on Mark. Get up!"

"I'm going, I'm going." I responded in a groggy voice.

"Hurry up and shower. Or do you want to go to school looking like that?" she said.

"You're not looking too good yourself, mom."

Her eyes widened and looked in the mirror positioned next to my bed. Almost instantly, she started to fix her hair. In a scolding manner, she looked back at me.

"Ugh, just hurry up and get dressed."

With that, she stormed out of my room. My mother was never too strict with me. She would, of course, occasionally need to correct the things I did, but she was generally casual about everything. Nothing stood out in her; just an ordinary single mother raising a high schooler.

I went about my normal routine and got ready within a couple minutes. I would constantly check the clock even though I checked it several times in the same minute. Being late was not on my list of things to do. As the clock got closer for me to start my trek to school, my heartrate would pick up. Despite all that happened yesterday, you'd think I'd be far past the point of being nervous. That was hardly the case. I think the fact that those things happened made it ten times worse.

I ruffled through the pantry to find something to eat but was quickly losing my appetite. It got to the point where I wasn't even looking for food, but was wasting time zoning out looking at bags of chips.

"What are you doing?" my mom asked.

"Uh, I was just…"

"Staring at food."

40

"How long were you watching me, exactly?"

"About a minute. Do chips really look that interesting?" She walked over to where I was and picked up a bag to closely examine it. "I mean, they're good, but I wouldn't go to the point of having an "intimate" moment with them. You all right?"

"Uh, yeah I'm fine. I was just, you know, checking to see if all of them were organized correctly."

She raised an eyebrow and let out a weak laugh.

"Yeah, good save. You better get going now."

"Yeah. I'll see you when I get home."

I walked out the door and left her in the house. The morning coolness was short lived. Heat started to pierce through the atmosphere, striking the earth's surface. Ugh! I had to live through this for a few more months until it would finally start to cool down. At least it allowed me to do things.

Psh. Like I ever did things. I would see groups of teens my age all over downtown doing whatever it is teenagers like them do. I had never experienced the feeling of having close friends like that. I always would convince myself that I was better off accompanying my mom to the mall and the movies since she didn't have anyone besides me.

My dad died when I was two. I have no memory of him. There's nothing left but pictures of him holding me and feeding me with a bottle. Every time I see pictures like that, I can't help but to feel like he's just a stranger that doesn't belong in those photo albums. Rarely does my mom ever mention him. She never grieves over him, though. Whenever she looks at those pictures, it's followed with a faint smile and maybe also a hint of regret. I can't be totally sure though.

There's been times where I ask her questions but she immediately derails our conversation into something about how she learned that a new restaurant opened up in town. It's not even subtle. She just jumps over to another topic. I've completely given up on trying to ask her anymore questions and accepted the fact that she doesn't want to talk about it.

*Grrr.*

I was interrupted by the emptiness of my stomach. Now I started to regret not eating.

"Shut up stupid stomach. I'll feed you later."

"You always talk to your stomach?"

I quickly turned around to face the direction the voice came from. My feet planted firmly in the ground. I knew this person. With bright red hair like hers, it's impossible to forget. I saw her at the fight yesterday when she called back Eli. The more I looked, the more her hair overpowered her appearance, drawing my eyes away from the rest of her. It had a strange way of dominating people. You were drawn in like her prey and she suddenly would have control over you. Or, maybe I was just overthinking her stupid hair.

"Well, do you?" she asked, putting a hand on her hip and slowly starting to bring a cute smile to her bright face.

"No, I just...I just was hungry," I responded, trying not to speak awkwardly.

"Do you mind if I walk with you?"

"Not at all."

Liar. You know you didn't want her here. I fell into her trap again. And plus, how can you say no to someone with freakin' red hair. Now, you're probably thinking that I've never seen red hair by the way I'm acting. But let me tell you. You've never seen red hair like this. I'm talking bright red. Not just the cheapy hair dye you get at the dollar store. This stuff was legit.

"Great!" she said with a cheerful voice. The sunglasses that were covering her eyes were pulled off. "I'm Penn."

To this day, I still remember myself standing there, struck by shock. When she pulled off her sunglasses she revealed her eyes. Not just any eyes, *red* eyes. Red eyes! Was red her thing? At least she wasn't wearing red clothes, then she would have been exactly like Monica, wearing all one color.

She apparently noticed that I was surprised. "Oh my eyes, right. I sometimes forget I have this color eyes and wonder why people stare at me," she said while chuckling.

"So, do you wear red contacts all the time then?" I asked.

"They're not contacts. This is my real eye color." Okay. I've seen some weird things in my life, but someone who has red as their natural eye color? Was this some kind of stupid prank someone was trying to pull? "I know, it's not natural to have this color, but the doctors checked it. They said it was a rare mutation that occurred. So yeah, I have red eyes. Oh and my red hair, that's natural too. A little too bright, huh?"

I didn't know what to say. A mutation that made her have bright red hair and red eyes. Why have I never heard of these mutations happening before? I looked down at the sunglasses she was holding in her hand.

"So, you wear those so people won't see your eyes?" Penn's face pulled at her cheeks as she smiled.

"Of course not. It's just bright out. C'mon, let's go." Penn rested her sunglasses back on the bridge of her nose.

"It's not nice to have someone introduce themselves and the other person not do the same." she said as we walked towards the school.

"Oh yeah, sorry. I'm Mark."

"Mark, huh."

"Yeah, I know it's boring."

"No." She started to giggle. "I like simple names."

"Really?"

"Yeah, what's wrong with that?"

"Nothing. It's just that I know a lot of people who tend to like names with greater meaning than Mark."

"Well I like your name, and I think nothing's wrong with it."

"Thanks. And what about you? Why did your parents name you Penn?"

"Um...I honestly don't know how I got my name," she said as she looked down at the floor. I could see her eyebrows starting to bend underneath her sunglasses. Was she mad? Oh no, I guess I hit a touchy subject. Her head randomly picked back up as if she remembered something. "Oh, and I'm sorry about yesterday. Eli and Sarah tend to both have a short temper."

"Yeah, I could tell."

"They're really good people once you get to know them but they're always so aggressive towards everyone else. Personally, I think Eli is the most polite person I know."

"I find that hard to believe."

"I'd say the same thing if I was in your shoes, but it's true."

With every good conversation, comes awkward silence. Penn never decided to say anything and neither did I. I took this time to further take in her appearance and I had to admit, she was quite pretty. The feeling of walking alongside a girl was nice. It was somehow enhancing the mood I was in that morning. The way she walked reminded me of Wendy's but with less annoying little brat. She seemed very uppity and it rubbed off on me. The nervousness I had was slowly fading away.

With the time I had, I reevaluated why I was nervous in the first place. It sure wasn't the fact that I had to see Eli or Sarah. I could easily ignore them. I typically found that I had problems with people who had more control over me. When someone was able to dominate over me, is scared me to death. It meant I was under their command without even choosing to. I knew Penn had that same ability with the way she "controlled" Eli. The thing is, I never felt like she controlled me. She was just, there.

The image of Charlotte staring at me in class popped up in my head. She also seemed like someone who could do the same. And when she's with Wendy it seemed like she was invincible. To show you that she does, take for example the fight yesterday. She controlled the situation and was able to settle things. Never have I been able to do anything like that. It just seemed like I made things worse.

Speaking of, it reminded me that I needed to continue my interaction with Monica. I wanted to break her front and find out her true self. The fact that she hides herself and is avoided pushes me even more to deny the social norm and talk to her. Either way, she's bound to show some of herself. Not everyone can hold up a front for that long.

The school was in clear sight and we had broken through the sound barrier. We could hear the usual schoolyard hollers and screams.

And there it goes.

The little confidence I had was now gone. The nervousness found its way back into me and firmly latched on this time, refusing to let go. My walk became awkward and my heart raced with its furious thump. Penn faltered in no way. She kept her same stance. As much as I hated to do it, I decided to break the silence.

"Hey Penn. This may sound very out of the blue, but, I was thinking. What makes you confident?"

"Confident? Hmm. That's vague. Confident in what exactly?" She turned towards me, allowing the sun to reflect back into my eyes.

"Everything I guess."

A huge grin spread across her face.

"A big factor is knowing what's going to happen."

"You mean what's going to happen in your day, right?"

"Well, just in general."

"But what if you don't know what's going to happen?"

"That's an easy one. Just make things happen the way you want them to. Control the situation."

"Easy for you to say."

"Another one is having people to back you. People like friends. They always have a way of giving off an aura that makes you feel a lot better in anything you're doing."

Well that one wasn't going to happen. With no friends and the sure fact that I wasn't going to make any made that impossible.

We finally made it onto the school grounds. People covered the grass chatting away having no sense of time. It was dang near impossible to pick out a conversation without mixing it with another one. It was all compiled into one continuous hum.

Penn turned around and faced me.

"Well, Mark. I'll hopefully see you around."

"Yeah, I'll see you later."

"And remember, confidence isn't found, it's created."

She gave me a wink and turned to walk into the double doors. I stood there taking in what she had just said.

What the heck was that supposed to mean? Wouldn't that be the same thing? I checked my phone for the time. Oh, I don't have time to be thinking about this.

I followed the same path Penn went and made it inside. For some reason, I expected the hallways to be a lot less full. And with my usual expectations for anything, they were crushed. They were just as packed as yesterday. My last school was mainly outside so the idea of this school mainly being indoors sucked. I'll be clumped together with all these sweaty and sticky teens for three more years. Can I just kill myself now?

I slowly trudged through to Violet's class, making each step as firm as I could just in case Wendy decided to run me over again. Thankfully, I made it to the class without injury. I went about my same procedure. I didn't make eye contact with anybody in fear of what I might see when I look at them. My peripheral vision picked up both Charlotte and Wendy sitting next to each other. They did the same and followed me with their heads. Monica was already sitting in the seat next to mine. I dropped my irrational fear of eye contact with her and stared at her. I knew she wouldn't return the look with her head locked in the position of looking at the board.

She looked no different than yesterday. Black still encompassed her whole body and the same black bow sat on her head. As I walked behind her to my seat, I noticed that her back was as straight as a wooden plank. That combined with the way she softly sat her hands in her lap made her look like an English schoolgirl in a manners class.

I took my seat and gave her a smile knowing that we were similar in some way.

"Hey Monica."

Nothing followed my greeting besides her silence. If there was no one else in the room besides us, I could probably hear her blink. That's all that stood out apart from her bow. The way the whites of her eye would disappear then reappear in a monotone like state. I decided to try another greeting.

"So, how was your morning?"

Her head turned ever so slowly towards me. There was no sign of anger or annoyance in her face. She was simply looking at me. I could read in it that she didn't want me talking to her. With no emotion in sight for miles ahead, it made me feel a sense of accomplishment knowing that I could read her quite well. She stayed like that too, allowing her eyes to burn into me. I couldn't help but laugh inside and relayed my smile to her, almost giving her a slap in the face with it. I found it enjoyable to see her try desperately to get her dark glare to work on me as it does others, knowing that inside it burns; stings because she doesn't control everyone.

Once more, she turned her head back in defeat and stared back at the board for condolence, forgetting she ever saw me.

The bell rang and the usual flood occurred. I was able to pick out some faces that looked familiar. Will, Eris, and the girl who handed me my schedule were some of them. Violet was already standing, waiting for people to settle in before talking. She went on and gave the boring usual greeting and explained some of what we were going to do.

"Before we start taking attendance, we actually got a student from another class. Or another way you could put it was that I stole her from another class." The door to the class opened and in walked a girl I had just talked to that morning with mutations running along all of her DNA. "I know many of you might know my daughter Penn from last year. For some reason, despite my request, they still didn't put her in my class. I did a little work arounds and got her in."

Wait, did I just hear her say daughter? I tried putting Violet's face over Penn's to see any resemblance. No matter how many times I tried matching them up, I saw none. There were no physical features that looked the same. I looked for distinct shapes like her jaw and nose, but neither of them looked similar.

Penn caught my eyes and her face immediately lit up, singling her eyes out on me. She walked to the middle of the room and filled the empty table that I just noticed. I would honestly probably continue to question Penn being Violet's daughter, but with the pace Violet was talking, I decided to let it drop.

For now.

\*　　　\*　　　\*

It was at times like this that I wished we were already doing actual work. Usually, the first couple days of class consisted of explaining what you were going to learn and with what material. I mean seriously, could we just start already?! How much do we need to look over the big block of a textbook before we start reading out of it? I stopped my train of thought and thought of it from the other point of view.

When it's around the middle of the year and we're doing an essay for every sentence in a Shakespeare play, I'll be begging for it to be how it is now. I guess I shouldn't complain as much, then. You can't really beat the system. It always worked out that way. Not just for schoolwork, but for everything else. Face it. Humans are stingy. We want one thing and once the thing we didn't want was taken from us, we want it back.

Charlotte gave a quick look over her shoulder and was eyeing me. The dark brown stood out among everything in the room. I tried to ignore it at first but couldn't help but look back. When our eyes met, we exchanged quick smiles. Nothing more than a friendly gesture. Or so I thought. She continued to sneak her little peeks at me throughout the whole class. Any doubt that was left escaped my mind. I knew she liked me. Either that or I had something on my face. I knew it was the first because every time I looked at her, her eyes would light up in a way that made me feel good about myself inside.

I looked back over at her direction hoping to see her look again, but instead, she was looking down in her lap. I tried my best to scoot up in my seat and sit up higher to see what she was looking at. I almost gave up but then noticed Wendy was doing the same.

The middle of my forehead scrunched up in a confused frown. Confusion was frustrating. And when it involved girls it ticked me off ever more than I should've been.

My eyes searched around some more in the room to see anyone else doing the same. To my surprise, which I know I shouldn't be, Will had his phone out on his desk not even giving any concern of Violet seeing. He slouched in his chair and let his thumbs away at it. Something about his face this time was different. He seemed to be frowning, even though that was probably normal for him. It was amplified to say the least.

All the while he was doing that, Monica's head was dipped down as well. Since she was closest, I looked and saw she was also looking down at her phone. She was furiously typing away on the digital keyboard, texting in a group chat.

My thinking quickly assumed that it was about me; that Charlotte was telling everyone how we were staring at each other. Of course that was never it. But it had to involve me. I knew it. Somehow.

The four lifted their heads up and looked at each other. They silently spoke to each other using subtle body movements, signaling to something. They then all simultaneously nodded their heads, gave me a quick look, and faced the board with straight back, ready to move.

I was confused the whole time as to what they were trying to tell each other. My head continued to spin around the class to see what each of them were doing. What was out of place?

Will then reached out and lifted his arm in the direction of the hallway, slightly moving it downwards. Out of nowhere, the alarm screamed as it shrieked in pain. Everyone, including myself jumped up in surprise. To make things worse, the sprinklers on the ceiling ticked, releasing little spurts of water to put out a fire that wasn't there.

All the students grabbed something to cover their heads to prevent themselves from getting wet. With everyone busy tending to themselves and freaking out about there being a possible fire in the building, the four got up out of their seats and headed out into the hallway, unsuspected. They showed no form of surprise or curiosity from the situation at hand. Without Violet even noticing that they were gone, she tried to calm everyone down and contain them.

Out of nowhere, my phone vibrated. I pulled it out and covered it carefully so as to not get it wet.

*Follow them.*

I stood there wondering who the heck was texting me. Everyone in class was either screaming and complaining about the water, or laughing up a storm while acting like children. There was no suspicious activity from anyone. No phones to be seen. I felt it buzz again in my hand.

*Now!*

I decided to go ahead and submit to the direction of whoever this was. With the random explosion of chaos, there was no reason not to. The condition of everyone wasn't going to change anytime soon, so now was my chance.

The constant blaring followed me into the hallway. Teachers were already starting to go into their regular fire drills and gathered all their students into the hallway to head outside. I searched for any sign of the others amongst the forming students. Great! Where the heck did they go? How the heck was I supposed to follow them?!

My hand buzzed again and looked to see that this time it was a call. I couldn't recognize the number. I went through the list in my head of all the numbers I knew. This one was nowhere on there. Whoever it is, it was no coincidence. It was obviously going to be the person who was texting me.

"Who is this?" I demanded.

"That doesn't matter right now, Mark."

It was a girl's voice. One that I've never heard. It sounded somewhere around my age. Maybe someone in the school?

"How do you know my name?"

"Mark! I'm serious! That doesn't matter right now."

"Yes it does! How do you know I wasn't following them? You're obviously watching me. Who are you?!"

"Just listen to me." Her voice was now more firm. "There are people coming for you. Now, I'm not planning on you dying and I know you're not either, so you need to shut up and listen." Dying? My heart worked in sync with my mind as the fear started to spread. "You need to get to the computer lab."

I was flustered, trying to think of where ever that would be.

"I'm new here. I have no idea where that is."

There was a small pause.

"Right. Follow the hallway down until you see some stairs to your left."

I held the phone firmly against my ear. Suddenly everything that the girl was saying was extremely important. There was no hesitation in my walk. The girl on the phone was right, I didn't plan on dying today. I wasted no time and started to climb the flight of stairs as fast as I could.

"Where now?" I asked.

There was no answer. A beeping followed the silence, letting me know that the call ended. I fumbled through the chain of calls that I had received in the past couple days, searching for her number. How does she expect me to know where to go after that? Up the stairs and what?

I was reaching the end of the stairs and the uncertainty of what to do was increasing. The second floor of the school was something I've never seen before. To my surprise, it was mostly empty. There should've been a mass of students due to the fire procedure but it looked entirely barren.

My quick thinking was put to the test when I heard thudding footsteps coming up the stairs. Without a doubt, the people coming up the stairs were the ones she was talking about; the ones who were coming for me. There would be no need for teachers to come up here when there was a fire procedure was taking place.

Wait.

They wouldn't come up here right now. Why else would she send me up here? Why else would the fire alarm have gone off? With his strange hand movement and the following of the alarm, Will had to be the reason for that. But, how could he have pulled it if the fire alarm was in the hallway between about an inch thick of ply wall. However he did it, they were all in on it. They were involved with this girl I didn't know. They were involved with the people who wanted me.

I had no other choice but to create distance between me and the people coming up the stairs. I sprinted down the hall, darting my eyes at every class, checking to see if it was the lab.

What I ended up running into made me stop in my tracks, completely forgetting about whoever was following behind me. Charlotte and the others stood in the hallway next to an open door that looked to be a supply closet. There was a duffle bag opened in between them. The whole picture of them made me start to realize the severity of the situation.

Charlotte, Wendy, Monica, and Will carried guns in their hands, loading magazines into them. Big silencers were twisted on the front, ready to suppress any sort of sound that came out of them. I took a step back in shock of what I was seeing. These people were carrying guns! In a school!

"What's going on?!" I yelled.

Everyone stopped what they were doing and looked up at me.

"Well, it looks like she was right," Wendy said, resuming to load her deadly weapon.

"I'm assuming you got a text from someone, right?" Charlotte asked.

"Yeah. Who was she?" I asked, still standing in place, completely frozen.

"No idea." Charlotte noticed me looking down at the gun in her hand. "Here. This one's yours."

My hand wobbled as I reached out to grab it. Wait, Mark? What are you doing? I was about to grab a weapon that I had no idea how to use and what we would need it for. The girl on the phone said that there were people coming for me, but did she really mean they were deliberately trying to kill me?

Out of nowhere, Charlotte's face started to shift into a stern cold stare. I was afraid for a half second that she was doing that to me, but soon realized that it was meant for the footsteps I heard behind me.

She shoved the gun into my stomach, making me hold it. I held it so awkwardly, I was afraid I was going to accidentally shoot someone.

The others took their place next to Charlotte in confronting the people behind me. I didn't want to turn around and face the people who so desperately wanted me. I had no qualms with anyone that would make them want to hurt me. So, who could it be?

I gave in and turned around. I was met with four people I had just seen yesterday. In fact, the same face off occurred, just surrounded by a crowd.

Penn was standing in front of Eli and Sarah. The dirty blonde who was at her side yesterday was also there in the same position. What made it even more disturbing was the smile on her face; on all of their faces. All of them except Eli's. They seemed just as equipped for a battle as we were, carrying weapons on their waist.

"Hi Mark," Penn said with a smile.

I didn't know what to say. What the heck do you say when there's a group of people in front of you with weapons and they say hello? You don't just say hi back. No one in the right mind would ever do so.

"So, what's with the funny business?" Penn asked, looking at the guns in their waists.

"To be honest, I'm just as confused as you are," Charlotte replied, not letting down her guard.

"Confused?" Penn let out a chuckle. "Who said we were confused?"

A bright light flashed for half a second and in her hand appeared what looked like a sword. The thing is that it didn't necessarily look solid. Looked like a chunk of light that formed into this glossy sharp edged sword. The fact that it just appeared made me question my eye sight.

The dirty blonde stepped away from the others, giving her enough room to perform her magical show. A crackling noise echoed through the hall as her hands cupped balls of fire. Her shirt slowly started to fall apart, creating a pile of ash around her. All that was left was a tank top that firmly gripped to her body and the glimmer aura of the fire.

"Wendy, now!" Will yelled.

Wendy reached out and grabbed my hand, firmly holding it. There was a swooshing noise that made my ears pop. When I opened my eyes after a blink, I noticed we weren't standing in the hallway anymore. Instead, we were in a room full of computers. Will, Wendy, Monica, and I looked at each other before Wendy disappeared following that same noise.

My chest started to cave in on itself. The fear was too much for me to handle and started to take a physical toll on my body.

The room was dark. The lights that were built into the ceiling were dormant, waiting for someone to flip the switch to bring them back to life. There was also a window that looked out to the hallway where Charlotte and Wendy were. I staggered over to it to try and see them. They were already in a ball on the floor with knives in hand, guns being completely disregarded and thrown on the floor for the close combat.

Will was standing next to me with his hand up towards his face. He would move it ever so slightly and I would notice that one of them would follow the same movement. Telekinetic.

There was a ringing of a phone. I reached into my pocket to answer it but saw that it wasn't mine.

"Hello?"

I turned around to see Monica still standing in the same place she was when we came in with a phone to her ear. There was a pause of silence while she listened to who was talking. She then walked over to a random desk and turned on the computer.

"Mark. Come here."

I looked over at Will, almost asking if it was okay for me to go. Still concentrated on helping Charlotte and Wendy, he jerked his head in Monica's direction.

"Put it on speaker," she said, handing me her phone and setting the bulky hand gun to the side.

I tapped the speaker and waited for the person on the other end to start talking.

"Alright Monica, plug in your flash drive."

I watched Monica the whole time, waiting to see what she would do. I was shocked to see that this time, there was emotion. She had her eyebrows raised and her eyes widened. It was the face of someone being caught.

"I don't know what you're talking about."

"Oh don't give me that. You know well what I'm talking about." Her hand slowly moved into the pocket of her black jeans. She pulled out a slim flash drive that she held so dearly. "Go ahead."

Once she plugged the drive in, the normal looking desktop went black. All that appeared was a small green cursor at the top left hand corner that blinked continuously.

"How'd you know about it?"

There was a sighful laugh in the speaker.

"I know a lot of things. Sometimes I think a little too much."

"No. That's not something you can just know. I check my room for any type of surveillance any time I go in there. There's no way that something can just slip in."

There was no answer from the girl. We could just hear her subtle breathing. Monica looked over at me with one of the most confused and uncomfortable faces ever.

Her voice was more firm this time.

"I need you to get me a list of names for the Japanese Oblivion project."

"So you're essentially asking me to hack into Japanese National Security?"

"It's not like you haven't done it before."

I then witnessed a phenomenon. A smile appeared on Monica's face. The everlasting emotionless face was gone for a split second.

The furious clacking on the keyboard was something I'd never heard. Nothing to that extent at least. Her fingers were nothing but a blur. She input a bunch of codes I could never decipher even if I was given an eternity.

The blocks of codes went on to clear and appeared an interface. I was amazed at how fast Monica would navigate it, clearing on to the next page of information, not even needing to think twice about what to do.

"Mark, set the phone down and get over here!" Will yelled.

I set the phone down and hurried back over to him. Charlotte and Wendy were still in a furious battle with Penn and her "comrades". Knives were being swung at one another's face. I could already see the blood that trickled down from the small slices that were made.

"Don't just stand there." I did the exact thing he told me not to do. I can't just go out there and help with no fighting experience. What did he expect me to do? "Help!"

"Help with what?"

Will glared me down.

"Don't act stupid."

My fear started to turn into anger. I've just witnessed things that I never thought were humanly possible, and now he expects me to know what the heck he's talking about?

"Your powers."

Monica stopped her tapping and looked over at me. They were both waiting for a response. Yeah, well I had a response for them. They had the wrong person. I knew for a fact that I wasn't freaks like them. There must've been another Mark that they were supposed to be talking with and putting *his* life on the line.

"I don't have any."

Monica quickly stood, pushing back her chair. Both of them stared me dead in the eye.

"You better be joking, Mark," Will said.

"And tell me why I would joke about that."

Will dropped his hand and ran over to me, pulling me by my shirt.

"Because we all got a text from that girl on that phone telling us you did!"

"Well, I hate to break it to you, but I don't have any."

There was a loud bang at the door. Will extended his hand towards it and locked it, keeping his eyes fixed on me. The banging didn't stop. It kept getting louder with every pound.

There was another one but this time it sounded different. It sounded like the cause of someone being rammed into it. I heard Wendy grunting behind the door. I ran over to the window to see her holding her own against Eli. I wasn't surprised knowing how prideful she could be. Her sheer pride could make her win any fight.

The same swooshing sound that I heard when Wendy brought us into the room blasted through it once again. Both Eli and Wendy were inside the room on top of each other. Both of them looked as bad as can be. I couldn't imagine the amount of punches they had taken.

"Wendy!" Will yelled at her.

"Sorry!" she yelled back, just barely allowing her voice to travel before disappearing with Eli back into the hallway.

"Monica. I need those names," the girl on the phone said.

She quickly sat back down in the chair and continued her furious typing. All the while, I stood there trying to interpret what I was seeing. The fear and anxiety came back without hesitation.

"Monica, hurry!"

The girl's voice sounded panicked. Wherever she was, something was going on.

Monica's eyes moved faster and faster looking for the files she needed. Of course someone like her would be good with computers. Not to mention be able to hack into Japanese National Security. Now that was some feat.

"I got them. Where do I send it to?"

"Yourself."

"You mean…save them?"

"Yes."

Monica reached up to the tower of the computer and put her hand to it. There was a cracking noise as electricity left her fingertips into the computer. The purple glow illuminated the dark room.

"But, I thought you needed it."

There was no answer from the phone. The same beeping I heard when she quickly ended my call came from the speaker. Monica, looking confused as ever, tapped the end call button and nodded at Will. He gave a nod in return and opened the door without even using his hands.

I barely realized that the alarm wasn't ringing. It seemed that the staff had gotten everything under control for the most part.

I didn't know whether to walk out into the hallway or stay where I was. Monica made up my mind by forcing me out there, holding my hand. I would normally complain about how she thought I was a child by doing that, but to be honest, in that situation, I was a child. I hadn't a single clue as to what was going on.

The hallway revealed a battle I didn't really get to see. The results looked brutal. Charlotte's and Wendy's hair was all ruffled up and streaks of sweat rolled down their face. They stood facing Penn and the others. The blonde's hands still sparkled with bright embers. What surprised me the most was that Eli was shining. His whole entire body was the same material that the handle to the door was. It slowly started to fade, uncovering his skin.

Each of them were panting, trying to regain their breath. The fire girl's eyes met with Monica and she gripped my hand even harder. In anger, fear, who knows. The little strength I had was quickly diminishing. I never thought that sight would have a physical effect on my body as much as it did then.

"That was something, wasn't it?" Penn said, somehow able to express her cheery voice. "First time I fought someone else with powers. I got to say, it was pretty fun."

Fun?! That's her form of fun?

"What do you want?" Will asked, still flexing his forehead as if it were a muscle to be exercised.

"What do *I* want? I think the question is what do *you* want?" Penn held a subtle smile the entire time she talked despite just finishing a fight. "You want answers and you know it. You have no idea why you have powers and why *he* was thrown into it all."

Penn jerked her head towards me.

Oh, believe me. I knew why I was there. It's because of an accident. I wasn't supposed to be there. I can guarantee my life that I didn't have powers.

"Meet us behind the diner on 4th street later this evening. We'll be waiting for you."

Penn allowed the sword to fizzle away in the air. She extended her chest as she took in a breath while focusing on me. A smile was given and the four of them walked off down the stairs like nothing even happened.

"That's it?!" Wendy yelled in frustration. "We hold them off for you guys that long and that's it? I nearly got stabbed like fifty times!"

"Either way, we're still going," Charlotte said.

"But—" I tried saying but was immediately cut off by ringing.

Monica pulled out her phone and pressed the speaker button for us all to hear.

"Thanks for the help guys." It was the same girl. "Sorry for freaking out at the end there Monica. I know there's a lot you guys don't understand but let me assure you that you'll have the answers you need soon enough."

"Why did you want me to keep those files on me?" Monica asked.

"Including that. I'll hopefully repay you guys in time. Oh and by the way, take care of the Equilibrium."

Everyone's eyes were on me. I felt the pressure finally hit me like a truck. I couldn't take all the stress anymore. I had seen too much. These were things I had never seen before and never thought were possible.

The middle of my chest seemed to be pierced with something sharp. My legs started to wobble and my breathing increased exponentially. Their faces seemed to fade away while my sight started to darken. I gripped my chest hoping to make this feeling stop only to make things worse. I didn't know what was happening or what to do. Everything was slipping away. I tried my hardest to fight it but couldn't take it any longer. I decided to let my body go into the pit where it was falling. It was at that moment when everything went black and I collapsed.

# Chapter 3

My whole body ached and a cold feeling chilled me. I had no idea where I was. All I remember was seeing an unthinkable series of events. Or, was it all a dream?

I mustered the energy to sit up. The entire room was mostly white with some counters that held jars of multiple items. I patted the material underneath me. It was a futon with the same color scheme as the rest of the school.

I was in the nurse's office, no doubt. I've never been in it but they all looked the same in every school, mainly being used for the aftermath of the usual fight and the occasional person who was actually sick.

"Oh, you're awake," a cheery voice chirped from the other side of the room.

I tried looking over in the direction of her voice but stopped halfway. There was a nasty kink in my neck that I couldn't fight. I resorted to take the struggle of turning my entire body.

Charlotte sat quietly in the seats provided. With her relaxed position, it looked as if she was sitting there for some time now. There was a delicate smile that lightly touched her face. It could've been her normal face but I wasn't so sure. This was only the second day of seeing her. I cursed in my head about how I should've known by now. I liked to notice things like that in people. Small things. Small things that counted. And plus, I thought she was kinda cute so it gave me even more incentive to find out. But then again, every time I really saw her, she was smiling. So did she always smile?

Like always, I didn't look in the right places when I thought I had it all along. All I did was slightly shift my eyes upwards towards her eyebrows and noticed the position of them. Going against and standing with my current argument of hardly knowing her, it was still funny to know that all it takes is one look to notice if someone's eyebrows were out of place. It's as if there was some ingrained mechanic that evaluated them automatically. Hers barely slanted at the ends and were raised higher than normal. Nothing more than a precious touch on her face.

"Why am I here?" I asked, realizing my voice was groggy.

"Because you passed out cold," she said, almost laughing at the fact. Her hands were placed carefully in her lap. I focused on them as they fiddled with each other, wondering how soft they must've been.

"I did?"

I had no memory of that whatsoever. The last place I was at was in the hallway with the others. Penn had said to meet her downtown and that was it. Did I really pass out?

"Mhm. That was the first time I've seen someone faint like that. Do you have some type of condition?"

"Not to my knowledge," I said, now leaning over the edge of the futon and rubbing my eyes.

I looked around to see if anyone else was in the room with us. It was just the two of us.

"So, what was your excuse for my passing out."

"You were afraid there was a fire in the school and didn't know where to go."

"Really? That's the lamest excuse ever. No one ever passes out over something that stupid."

"Apparently you do. They bought it pretty quickly. I didn't have to elaborate at all."

How stupid are the people here? For someone to get into a fight on the first day of school and then pass out because of not knowing what to do was not something that was likely to happen. I wanted to thank her for helping out, but knowing that she was involved with whatever Penn wanted made me hold it back. She was one of them, and who knows what they are.

"It just turned lunch. You wanna come eat?" she asked.

"Yeah, sure. Shouldn't we let the nurse know that I'm going to be leaving?"

"Nah. She just left for lunch herself. That's why I came here."

She did wait. I stopped for a second and thought about what she did. Yeah, whatever. She just waited for me to wake up. You might see it as something insignificant but it meant something. She chose to wait for me. No. She kept me company as I was unconscious, watching me stay in the dark slumber.

She opened the door and held it open, waiting for me to walk through. I was just about ready to join her, but the question kept nagging on my brain. I didn't want to ask after knowing that she waited for me to wake up but I needed to. The matter of lives were on the line just a few moments ago. That relayed more importance than the feelings of others.

I let out a larger sigh than needed to express my distress to her.

"Charlotte, what are you?"

She looked down a little. The bright face of hers was now replaced with dejection. Seeing her like that made me instantly regret my question.

Her eyes were the only thing that looked back up towards me. Her eyebrows now bent the other way and let a nasty frown smother in itself.

"The others are waiting outside. We have some things to talk about."

\*     \*     \*

Boy, did I feel awkward. The five of us sat at the same table I sat at yesterday; the one that was "forbidden". Some were eating their lunches and others were just sitting there, spacing out. I was among the latter. I had so many questions as to what happened earlier that morning but didn't know how to say them or where to start.

With all of us sitting there, we got so many looks. That was Monica's table. No one sat there but her. I broke that rule yesterday and now today three others joined me in the abnormality. To them, it must have been the strangest occurrence.

I could tell it really was messing with Monica. She was used to being all alone with no one to talk to. People stayed away from her and she seemed to like it. Now that we were all here, it made it seem like she was one of them. Like she was part of their society. I felt for her. I would hate it if I were in her position.

"Alright, I'm just gonna come straight out and ask. What exactly are you guys?" I asked. I didn't realize it at the time but my face must have displayed how serious I was. It took me aback for a second when I heard the tone of my voice, speaking with a solid volume but having a way to spit them out in their face, making them eat it without a moment's notice.

They all looked at each other, seeing who would be the first to answer. I already knew it would be Charlotte talking since she was the one that had that sort of dominance I was talking about.

"We don't entirely know. We've all had our powers for a couple years now. No clues as to how or why we got them." She paused and let out a sigh. "I guess I should start from the beginning and that involved Wendy. I met her in middle school. It was sixth grade and I remember how annoying she was."

"Please. Me? I was annoying?" Wendy said sarcastically.

"You know you were too," Charlotte responded, giving her a small glare.

"And that's why you love me."

A miniscule chuckle left Charlotte's mouth before she suppressed it to conform to the tension of the situation.

"Anyways, in time we became friends. She went from being just a regular friend at school to being my best friend. There wasn't any secrets between us and it was together that we found out what we had hiding inside us."

"It was the stupidest thing." Wendy laughed. "We were walking past the boy she liked at the time. Of course, being Charlotte, she's all nervous and stuff. She goes on to blabber asking me if he was looking at her and next thing you know, I can't see her. I mean, she was still talking but she wasn't there anymore."

"So that's your power?" I asked.

"Yup. I can turn invisible."

"And yours is teleportation?" I asked Wendy, remembering being transported into the computer lab without even having a second thought as to what was happening at the moment.

Wendy gave a big nod.

I thought about Charlotte meeting Wendy for the first time. I wondered how this charmed person could have the mind to take up a conversation nonetheless a friendship with her. Or maybe she ran over her too. It seemed to work on me. I hadn't stopped talking to her since. Granted I hated every moment of it, but for some reason it still held.

"What about the rest of you?" I asked, looking around the circular table.

"I can bend electricity to my will," Monica said. I thought back to earlier when in the room she touched the computer tower and electricity came out of her fingers and traveled into her. "I can also store data inside me along with communicating with technology if my body-made electricity is inside it."

"Is that what you did with the computer then?"

Monica's head moved up and down ever so slightly. With a power like that, she's practically a living artificial intelligence that can interact with the outside world. I gotta say, the more I listened and thought about the powers they had, the more it seemed to appeal to me.

"And you have telekinesis?" I asked Will, being somewhat sure of it.

"Yup." He was still somehow slouching at the table when there was nothing to slouch on. The little tufts of brown hair that covered his forehead dipped outwards as he tilted his head. "But a thing you need to know about our powers, Mark, is that we can't just use them anytime we want. It's used from our body energy. Well, that's at least what we found out. Let's say I wake up in the middle of the night and to add some emphasis, I'm sick. I can't just open all the doors without touching them. If we're tired or physically weak, then we can hardly use them."

"So as long as you have some form of energy in you, you can use them?"

"Yes. That and there's another thing. We don't work very well under stress."

"There's a limit to everything pretty much," Wendy butted in. "It sucks. I can't just go to France, get a croissant, and come back. If it was like that, then I would never be spending my free time here is this pothole of snobs. Going back to what Will was talking about, I can't travel that well under anxiety. It limits my distance and I have the chance to get stuck in walls."

"Same goes for me," said Charlotte. "It's harder to make other things invisible under the same circumstances. Only myself, and even then it's kinda choppy."

I looked over at Monica who has hardly said anything. She sat staring at her thermos, almost like she was waiting for the food inside to find her a way out of the situation. Although I wanted to break her front, I couldn't bear to watch her suffer like she was. It was enough.

I reached over and uncapped her thermos, allowing the steam to billow out and fill the table with the scent of the fine cooking. I stuck the fork in and handed it back to her.

Her head continued to stay down but her eyes followed me. They had a silent way of thanking me. Any type of communication with Monica was strange. It was like I didn't really need to talk to her. She had a unique talent of talking with her body.

A smile found its way to my face. I felt like the only one who understood her. And because of that, I felt like a good person. Although she might not have felt the same way, our interactions were something I enjoyed. It was pretty much the first time a person and I connected in the way we did.

My eyes scanned the table. These four people weren't freaks. They were humans just like I am. They have feelings and ideas just like I do. Powers make them no different. If anything, it made them more special. I envied their abilities. My dreams have always consisted of their reality. If only the claim of the girl on the phone was true.

"Do you guys know who the girl on the phone was?"

They all simultaneously shook their heads.

"No. We just got a random group text in class that said you had powers like we did. We already knew that each of us had powers. It was our freshman year when we met each other. I found out Monica had powers when we had a power outage in computer class and her computer was the only one on. Will's was an accident. It was in P.E. and there was a football going straight towards his head," Charlotte said.

"Of course I was gonna stop it! What did you want me to do? Let it hit me?" Will said, now sitting up.

"Maybe you should've. Then it would've smacked your jacked up face and made it look better," Wendy said.

"Shut up before I hurl one at *your* face!"

"Anyways, we talked for a bit and found out a little more about each of our powers. Again, we didn't have a clue why we had them. To be honest, we didn't really care all that much. Yeah, we should've, but heck, we had powers. It got to the point where we were just happy to have these gifts. But, of course, we learned what limits we had with them and we're more disciplined with them now you could say."

"Charlotte being Charlotte wanted us to all join together in a cult of mysterious people who lived underground and wore hoods. Ooh! She also wanted us to shave our heads. We'd all be brothers and sisters and fast," Wendy said, sneaking a look at her to see her reaction. It fed Wendy the same way I fed Eris. Charlotte threw her a look and she could only shout inside about her accomplishments even though you could clearly see she was jittery.

"I just thought we could do so much more if we worked together or just were around each other more often. Will didn't want to though."

"I didn't want to feel out of place even though I guess I would've been with people who were like me," Will said. "I wanted to stay normal. Not accept what I had and that I was different from humanity as a whole."

Who could blame him? If you had powers like that, you'd practically feel like an outcast if people knew about it or not. You weren't considered the same as them. I guess that thinking is better than the other form. Someone could think of themselves higher than the rest of the world because of being unique. I personally thought Will would be that type of person, but that just goes to show you not to judge a book by its cover.

"About the girl, she just told us to make a diversion and pull the fire alarm, then to go up to the computer lab. The only reason we listened to what she said was because she told us you had powers, and to be honest, we felt it. Just like the same feeling we got with each other."

"What the heck are you talking about? I have no powers," I said, raising my voice and scrunching my forehead.

"Look. We all got our powers when we started to go through puberty. We think it was secreted as some kind of hormone."

I looked at Charlotte confused.

"Are you claiming I haven't gone through puberty yet?"

"Aww, look at Mark. It's okay. Some people go through it at different times. You were just a late bloomer," Wendy said in a baby voice.

I wanted to punch her square in the face. She fearlessly smiled her deadly smile. There was no shame at all in her. I couldn't do anything really to counter her stubborn ways.

"I'm not saying that at all, Mark. I'm just saying that we knew each other had powers before we found out for sure, or at least had a feeling. Yesterday, after school, Wendy and I were talking about how we thought you had some."

"What's your birthday?" Monica said quietly, barely speaking loud enough for us to hear.

"What?" I said, confused at her random outburst of a question.

"What's your birthday?" she said with a hint of irritation, clearly not liking to repeat herself.

"January 9th. Why?"

They all looked at each other and let out their own little remarks of assurance.

"Yup!" Wendy shouted. "You're one of us."

"We all have the same birthdays. Something happened on that day. It had to. Monica's done a bit of research on it she's told me but she came up with nothing," said Charlotte.

So, I had the same birthday. For a second, I didn't care all that much. But when I started to think about it, it was some sort of proof. They all had powers because of being born on that same day and I was linked to them in some way. I wasn't liking what I was hearing one bit. Being frustrated, I reverted the subject back to what happened earlier.

"Well then what about the computer? Why did she have Monica hack into Japanese National Security?"

Charlotte's eyes widened with the thousand yard stare. Her head turned in the direction of the dark creature, leaving her mouth open in shock. She stared at Monica trying to comprehend what I had just said.

"You did what?"

"I just did what she asked." Monica said, defending herself. "She said all she wanted was a list of names for some Japanese Oblivion project. But don't worry. They won't track us. I covered up everything. I'm currently patching up the last little bit right now."

I was taken aback again by her ability. While we were speaking she was controlling and interacting with a computer with her mind! I had no doubt that what she said was true. If someone had the capability to hack into that type of security, they surely could cover up their tracks without a problem. Now, the question is how. Even if she tried to explain it, I probably wouldn't understand.

"Monica," Charlotte said sternly, trying to make her realize what she'd done.

"She said she was gonna give us some answers and pay us back later. Lay it off, Charlotte," Will said.

"Even if you don't have powers right now, I still think you do." Charlotte reverted her focus back towards me still keeping her darkened face fixed with frustration. "And by the way," she looked around at the rest of the table, "I want all of you to come and meet Penn later today. I don't know what she wants, but she obviously knows some more about us having powers, and any little knowledge about it can help."

Bright red hair was sitting calmly at another table along with her comrades in combat. She caught me looking at her and she gave a shy smile. I couldn't help but think how creepy she was. They just fought each other with deadly weapons and she can just smile at the very people she fought. I'm no psychologist, but that's one messed up mind.

That wasn't all she did. She waved a hand in her direction, calling me over. I personally didn't want to go over there, and why would I? But, with the way she looked at me, my sound thinking hesitated. The way her teeth showed as she mouthed for me to come over was almost enough to convince me.

The others noticed her calling me over and didn't bother to tell me not to go. They went on to continue eating and ignore them.

"Um...should I?"

No one answered me. Everyone's eyes were focused on their foods, leaving me to answer that myself. I decided to give Penn another look to see if she was still persisting. Her eyebrow was raised and laughed at my confused look.

I'm gonna regret this.

I got up from the table and sat in front of her, next to Eli and Sarah.

"Took you long enough," she said with a smile. "I just wanted to introduce you to my friends. I know we kinda had a rough morning but that's over now."

Over? No, Penn. You just started. You started something that didn't need to happen.

The dirty blonde who could control fire gave me a small wave.

"This is Brittany, Eli, and Sarah"

"Penn, what the heck is with you guys? Who are you really trying to kill here?" I asked bluntly, getting pretty annoyed with her happy act.

"We weren't trying to kill anyone." She paused and raised her hands up, holding me from saying anything more. "Look, I'm going to explain a lot of things later this evening, okay? Promise to meet me there?"

I didn't really have a choice. I was dragged into this mess. Plus, Charlotte was making us come, so either way I was going to end up going.

"Yeah, I'll be there."

Her smile seemed serious this time and looked more natural. This was the Penn I remembered meeting. For someone to jump out with a different personality with the snap of a finger was terrifying. When we walked to school together that morning, she seemed like a pretty cool person, now, I couldn't look at her without seeing her draw that sword of hers.

I remembered what she told me before she walked away. Confidence isn't found, it's created. Knowing what's going to happen. To bend the situation to your will. Now I know what she was talking about. She was talking about what had happened today. She must've known that this was going to happen.

Gosh! I couldn't help but feel helpless. All of them had an advantage over me. They all had some form of knowledge of what was happening. But me? I was just thrown in with nothing. I had to rely on the things others told me. That leaves me to decide whether what they're saying is true or not. I couldn't believe I was actually trusting what these people said. I'd known them for two days and even then, I didn't know them that well. But the fact that I saw everything made me believe. It started to take over the facts I knew in my mind. I knew these things weren't real or supposed to exist.

I got up and joined the others again, taking my place next to Charlotte.

My appetite was nowhere to be found. It had been lost in the frustration of everything. There was no point in eating. Rather, I looked over everyone in more detail and at least try to learn more about these people.

At the time, no one was talking. The morbid conversation we just had was still lingering in their minds. Another person knew about their powers and they had found out that another group had some too. There was too much to think about.

Even Wendy wasn't doing anything spontaneous. Her body was completely stiff. Now that I could see her in a more mature and "relaxed" state, if you could even call it that, I could appreciate her a little more. Don't think that for a second I'm saying she's a good person. She's still a prideful brat.

Monica slowly twirled her fork around and scooped up some more noodles. I was surprised that she was the only one who wasn't zoning out. Her eyes would actually move around. Every time she would dip her head down to take a bite, it would draw attention to the huge bow on her head—her one little sign of humanity and emotion to the world. I couldn't appreciate that enough. Despite her being the quietest of the four, she seemed the most unique. She kept people in the dark about herself enough to scare them or put them into submission if the time calls for it. I've studied people like her before, but I've seen no one to her extent.

Will slouched in his seat, not giving a care about anything. I used the think of people like him as absolute jerks, almost to the point of my hatred towards Wendy. Seeing him help Charlotte and Wendy back in the lab made me feel better around him knowing that I wasn't sitting next to a selfish twit.

Charlotte seemed like the one who was out of it the most. Her hand mechanically moved the sandwich into her mouth without her even realizing it. Despite the gross movement and stale chewing, she was still looked pretty doing it. I hadn't had much time to look at her besides the beginning of English when she was eyeing me. If she did like me, I had no idea why. There was nothing unique about me. Nothing that stood out. I wasn't complaining, I was just confused.

I sat back and took them all in. Each of them were something special. They were my first interaction here at this school and I somehow already felt comfortable around them when I knew I was never like this. When I was myself, people thought I was weird or some kind of creep. With them, I never got that kind of vibe. Despite all that, these were the people I would be relying to help me through the mess I had gotten into. I could only hope that they would do a good job at it. That I'd do a good job at being what I was.

*       *       *

Tall buildings filled my eyes. No matter where I looked, they were always there. It would reflect the evening sun off of the thick glass panes that covered them to the point of giving you a massive glare if you were in the right position. From the hills that surrounded the center of the city, everyone could see these buildings. Although no one really knew what purpose they served, the only thing they did was make downtown feel like downtown.

In the middle of Springfield was downtown and surrounding that was the suburban homes. Basically everyone in Springfield goes towards the center of town on the weekend. The overbearing mall we have usually draws a lot of people in. It had two stories littered with stores. I guess what I'm trying to say it that downtown Springfield was the place to be.

I tend to have mixed feelings on it. I felt so small there. Being overpowered by those buildings was a creepy feeling. Then again, I often found downtown to be enjoyable. It was a perfect place to study people. When I say study people, don't think of me a psychopath for doing so. The only reason I do so is to better understand society and why they do the things they do. It was usually the only thing that entertained me when I wasn't wasting time playing video games.

The amount of people in downtown who expressed themselves freely was quite amazing. It had a way of dragging out your true self without needing to try. I remember coming across certain individuals who went to my previous school. In school they would act shy and seclude themselves from everybody else, but when I saw them somewhere like the mall, they would be the loudest mouth on the planet. Even I did the same. It made me want to often show off to the crowds of people I didn't know.

With that thought in mind, I couldn't imagine the true person that is inside Monica. She stood to my right as we walked down the sidewalk along one of the busiest streets. Her face had no change to it. The only thing I noticed different about her was her walk. It wasn't as rigid. It seemed more lively and confident. Where she found that confidence I had no idea.

The smell of various foods from the stands and shops forced its way through my nostrils. I couldn't help but to crave some of whatever I was smelling. But there was no time for that. Although Penn didn't give us an exact time, we didn't want to keep them waiting.

After school got out we all walked home together. I found out that the five of us all lived in the same area. We have to walk in the same direction for most of the walk so we discussed what we were going to do.

The plan was to meet up an hour later at a bus stop to make our trek into town. We were going to listen to whatever they had to say and if things got dicey, we leave. Wendy wanted to choose to stay and fight, of course. It took some convincing, but we finally got the idiot to agree, mostly by Charlotte's charm.

Usually at a time like this, I would consider why we weren't talking and how it would be awkward, but with all the noise of the city, it didn't bother me all that much. That and we were all focused on wondering what Penn was going to say. Apparently she had some answers to why they had powers so naturally they would be curious, including me.

The place where Penn wanted us to meet was close by a famous diner in town. It was crowded as usual. Strangely enough, it was located next to a building that we have all seen before. The weird thing about it was that it didn't have a sign on it. It seemed like no one was using it but there would be the occasional time the lights would be on inside.

There were a few buildings like this throughout downtown that no one questioned. They would mainly be on the top of businesses that bordered the sidewalk. The common thought was that they were all storage for the stores but no one really knew.

Our directions were to go behind it into an empty lot. When we walked past the wall, it revealed the four of them. It seemed like they were there for quite some time. Great! Just what we needed; aggravated hormonal teens who can use god-like powers.

Penn's face was as cheery as ever but it seemed to somehow brighten up some more when she saw my face. The others behind her wore a casual look on their faces. Faint smiles were on all of them besides the living monster. Eli's biceps seemed to bulge out of his shirt. I couldn't stand but to look at him with disgust. I don't mind if anyone's a bodybuilder or wants to keep fit, but when you go and put yourself on a display like that, you look so desperate for attention.

"You made it! Thanks for coming guys." Penn said. "I know this was unexpected but it's kind of important."

Kind of?! If this was kind of important, then I wonder what was moderately important.

"All I ask is that you listen and don't talk or ask questions unless I ask. Things will go a lot smoother if we do that."

She looked over us, checking to see if any of us opposed to her plan. Even though no one spoke up, I noticed Wendy was clearly not happy about it. A crooked sneer was slapped on her face that would carve through any stone.

"Okay, good," Penn said, letting out a small sigh. "You have no idea how long we've been waiting for this. We've always been watching you guys very closely. It's nice to finally talk to you."

"Watching?!" Wendy yelled, not restraining anything.

"Precisely. It was actually quite difficult to not be seen at certain times. We had to make ourselves seem like ordinary strangers, but for me it was extremely hard." she said pointing at her hair. "We were pretty excited when we heard you were going to be transferring to Springfield High. I have to give it to Brittany for her hard work on that."

Within microseconds I linked what she said to the incident at my old school. I knew the reason why it now lies in ashes. She was standing before me, without any form of regret or guilt. Just her alone changed people's lives.

I wanted to hold back from talking but my frustration was getting the better of me.

"You did that just so I could transfer?" I asked, glaring into Brittany's eyes.

Her head gave a big nod, taking great joy in her achievement.

"Once that was done, it sent things into motion. It gave us a chance at close interaction like right now."

"Penn, why'd you fight us? What's the reason behind all of this?" Charlotte said.

"Right. About this morning, it may seem like we were trying to hurt you but I can assure you that was not our intention. I'm sorry about it too. I know it's not the best way to give an impression of who BloodLip is."

"BloodLip?" Will asked.

I knew immediately that Penn's request for us to remain silent was not going to be followed with the current tension between us. There were going to be things that we didn't understand such as what the heck BloodLip was.

"Yeah. BloodLip." Penn gestured to all of them. "The first group of ones with special abilities."

"And what kind of name is BloodLip?" asked Wendy in the most disgusted voice she could possibly utter.

"We didn't give ourselves this name." She stopped and gave the others a look. "Someone very dear to us did. Don't look at it with the view of the actual name itself. It has real meaning to it."

Penn gave a pause to look at us, taking in our expressions towards what she was saying.

"Oh, you guys don't need to be so tense. Consider yourselves lucky. You have the Equilibrium," she said pointing at me.

That was the same name I heard on the phone.

"Equilibrium?" I asked.

Penn chuckled.

"You guys really don't know anything do you? Let's just say Mark is a very special person, one with greater abilities than the rest of us."

"Can everyone shut up with claiming I have powers?"

"Just you wait Mark. In due time it'll come. We also wanted to let you in on a little bit about our powers. Basically I found out about my powers when I was ten, at the start of puberty. Ever since then I've been practicing with it."

The same shiny sword appeared in her hand that I saw this morning.

"I have the ability to bend the natural form of energy in my body. The easiest thing to make without using that much energy is this sword. It's not all I can do, though." The sword disappeared and in front of us was a wall of light that looked like the same material the sword was came into view. "I can make domes and walls of the same energy. You guys like it?"

There was no response. No one was impressed. We all still held the grudge from the fight and she thinks that we can just drop it like nothing.

Penn cleared her throat, knowing we wanted her to continue.

"Brittany, as you all know, can bend fire just as Monica can bend electricity."

Her mentioning Monica made me remember she still existed. With her not talking, I forgot she was even there. She didn't seemed swayed by any of this. Her face was as blank as ever. Knowing that she was normal made me feel more comfortable.

"How'd you know?" Monica asked. "I've never used my powers in the open."

Her random comment seemed to surprise Penn. She still held her smile but she messed up. There was a tug at the side of her cheeks and her eyes widened just barely enough for me to see. She completely ignored her question and went on.

"Sarah has...well, it would be better to show you."

Without hesitating, Brittany pulled out a pistol from nowhere and cocked it before my brain could even register what was happening. She aimed it at Sarah's arm and fired it, making a blasting noise that was lost in the shout of the city. Sarah instantly fell to the floor and clenched her arm. I've never heard a more bloodcurdling scream before. All five of us took a step back in fear of them shooting their own friend.

Eli did nothing to help his sister who was in agonizing pain besides watch her. The sound of her scream was brutal. It made me forget all the bad thoughts I had about her. I couldn't stand to simply just watch her. I was about to run over and help her but she started to get up herself. The hole in her arm was getting smaller and smaller by the second.

"Gosh, Britt. You could've at least given me a warning," she said with a strained voice.

Sarah was now standing on her own and the sign of her injury were nowhere to be found.

"Pretty self-explanatory, right?" Penn asked. "It was actually hard for her to practice using her power. After all, when all you have is regeneration, the only time you're going to use it is when you're hurt. We started off with small things like cuts with a knife then went up to breaking fingers. We thought it'd actually make her tolerate the pain if anything, but as you saw, it still stays the same. All the practice was really good for was the readiness of pain."

"Now, Eli's is—"

"They already saw it," Eli interrupted.

"Yeah I know that, but why don't you show them again?"

He rolled his eyes in arrogance.

"Like they deserve me to do it just for them to see it. This isn't even helping us in any way. It's just making us fall behind."

"Eli."

Penn's firm voice found its way to her throat again, regaining her dominance. Eli had no choice but to listen to her. His hand touched the brick wall behind him and he took the form of the same material. All his skin was replaced with red brick. His bulging muscles were still present, they only were increased in mass because of the material.

Brittany lit her hands on fire and started to expel it on Eli. He seemed unaffected by it, like it was something she usually did. He gave her a playful push, clearly enjoying the stark defiance that Brittany showed, continuing her fiery storm.

But then there was a flash. Everyone's heads looked in the direction it came from. And there stood a man, a man with a camera. His face showed that he knew instantly that he had made a mistake.

Penn broke the silence with a command.

"Get him."

Without hesitation, Eli, Brittany, and Sarah charged after the man. They looked like wolves closing in on their prey and moved with incredible speed. The man could barely react before they caught him. Eli picked him up like he was nothing, but the man squirmed like a child that knew they were going to be punished.

The man amazingly managed to escape Eli's grip, but that didn't faze Eli in the least. He snagged the man's collar and the man reeled back as though caught on a hook.

The man struggled helplessly to escape Eli's gorilla grip, but to no avail.

The corner of my eye caught Penn, standing so deviously and maliciously. Her eyes full of disgust and her body half-looking at the man as though he were beneath her. My focus returned to Eli, who was already halfway down the alley, dragging the struggling man.

I had no clue as to what they were planning to do with him. My question was soon answered as they all dragged him over to a shed that I somehow didn't notice. It was tucked away in the corner of the back lot. The wood on it looked like it had been dead for centuries. It added another layer to the creepiness of the useless building.

The five of them, including the man, filed in the shed. Penn stood at the entrance to it, holding the door open. She signaled us with her hand to join them. We didn't oppose to her direction. There was enough of a problem already and if we decided to bail, who knows what they would do to him.

As I walked through the entrance, I noticed Penn's face was burning with irritation. It was something I would never imagine she had the ability to do. It was not meant for that usual cheery face.

The inside of the shed surprisingly had a lot more room than I had thought. It perfectly fit all of us with a little room to spare if there weren't useless supplies in it.

The man was slumped up against the back wall, gazing up at us in fear. His eyes easily displayed his emotions openly. I could see the whites of his eyes more so than the dark.

Penn walked over slowly to the man and grabbed the camera from him. With the way she went about taking it was obvious she was a different person. Her walk looked deadly. It spoke out to anyone that looked at her to back off. The way her hips moved expressed her continuous dominance over the situation; a way she kept her confidence.

The whole room was silent. All we could hear was the beeping of the camera as Penn looked through the photos.

I gave Charlotte a look. She looked back at me with a concerned face, silently telling me that she didn't like the situation. The face wasn't needed to tell me that. You could feel it in the air. It had a thickness that formed a lump in your throat, forcing you to constantly swallow. No one was comfortable.

"Here."

Penn tossed me the camera. The others huddled in to take in the picture. It was clearly there. Eli was a walking totem and Brittany was a fountain of fire. We were all in the shot, every single one of us looking at their talents.

"That's us alright," Sarah said.

All the attention was shifted back over to the unnamed photographer.

Penn immediately took control and asked questions.

"What's your name?"

"Uh—I…"

"Spit it out."

There was no anger in Penn's voice. It was calm but stern, kinda like when a mother corrects her child.

"Trent Willis."

"Alright Mr. Willis, what's this?" She snatched the camera back and showed him the display. "Hm?"

"It's…uh, you guys."

"Really?" Penn turned it back around to examine it. "It's not like I see myself in a mirror every day and not know what I look like, right?" She leaned in closer so they were just a few inches apart. "Of course it's us. Why'd you take the picture?"

"How could I not take a picture? You guys were doing some crazy stuff and I thought it would be good for my blog."

Penn stood back up and looked back at her friends.

A blog only meant one thing. Everyone would be able to see it. Once something was on the internet, it could never get taken down. Unless, maybe Monica could probably fix that.

Brittany nodded her head and their series of movements were again too fast for me to react.

The camera was given to Eli to be crushed. The crunching noise seemed to break the bloggers heart. But that was the least of his problems. Brittany pulled out the same pistol and pointed it at his head.

"Let's make this quick," said Penn.

We all made the same reaction. There were shouts and pleas from everyone including the man who was held at gunpoint.

"What are you doing!?" Charlotte yelled.

Charlotte ran over to Brittany but Eli simply walked in front of her. With the small space of the shed, there was no way she could get through him.

"I'm not gonna put any of it on there! I swear! Just put the gun down!"

Brittany looked to her leader for direction. Penn seemed troubled by this. Her face, still stern, was intensely phasing out at the floor. I was actually starting to think she would go through with her initial plan and exterminate the man. All because he was curious. All because he happened to have a camera.

"Penn."

I looked at her with a troubled look. I made sure it would affect her. In school, her face would light up when she saw me. I clearly had some influence on her. I could change her decision if I chose the right words, the right expression.

She let out a sigh and walked back over to the man.

"Family. Do you have one?"

"Kind of. I was adopted but both of them died in a car accident not that long ago."

Penn froze in place by his words. Eli, Sarah, and Brittany all did the same. They waited for a reaction from her. The stern face was dropped and a calm set over her as she took the gun from Brittany and put it away.

Mr. Willis' face expressed so much relief knowing that he had the chance to live another day.

"Oh my, you're letting me go?"

"Get out."

"Thank you so much! I'm sorry I ever took the pi—"

"Get out!"

The random frustrated shout shocked me. It came out of nowhere. Matching expressions was probably not a thing for Penn. Her face was still calm, it seemed impossible for someone to yell like that and still look normal, if you'd call it normal.

The man wasted no time and was out of the shed in an instant, leaving behind the crushed remains of what was a possibility for murder.

BloodLip walked out of the shed after not saying anything for a straight minute. All of them were upset, completely aggravated.

"Well, I guess you could say that went wrong," Penn said.

"You guys are sick! You weren't going to actually shoot him were you?" Will asked. "He was just a blogger and plus he said he wouldn't post anything about it."

Penn made sure her voice was firm for her response.

"That's what the last guy said."

With that, they left, walking back out into the main street of downtown. The last image we saw of them was the reflection of the evening sun off of Penn's bright red hair.

BloodLip.

I didn't know much of their intentions, but I did know one thing. They were not our allies.

# Chapter 4

I was about to do something I have never done in my life. I was about to go to someone's house from school. It was something I heard countless times before. Girls having slumber parties or big house parties that I wasn't invited to. To me, they almost seemed like a myth. Having never been in any type of situation like that, it was kind of a weird feeling.

I would probably describe it as a form of nervousness and excitement. I could feel the usual racing heart with nervousness but I also felt the twirling of my stomach that came with excitement. To be honest, I didn't really know if I liked the feeling or not. I wasn't used to it.

Whose house was I going to?

I could just tell you the answer to that question right away, but I'd rather marvel at the fact that this person would never be the type to hold a gathering like this. The fact that she took the initiative and was the one to invite *us* shocked me. No. It impressed me. I was proud of her. For her to make a step like that must have been a big feat. Many people would think of her as the person who was the outcast, the nobody, the creep. Me? I thought of her as the one who understood my thinking, the one who was amazingly good at computers and was able to hack into a National Security, the real person she was.

Monica.

The day after our first encounter with BloodLip, we hung out with each other at school. There was actually some conversation that didn't involve our problems with unnatural powers. It was then that Monica invited us to her house after school. Although, it wasn't for recreation, it was still out of the norm for her. She had told us that she found out some things about BloodLip that she wanted to show us.

After seeing another side of Penn yesterday, I was curious as to what she found. Her actions showed that she was not the person I thought she was going to be at all. I mean, pulling a gun on someone. Really? I would never think a situation would ever come up like that. Someone's life was on the line and I practically did nothing.

I did my best to avoid her that day. When she walked in class, I kept my head down. I followed the same plan that I used with Charlotte and Wendy on the first day of school. If I even gave her a quick glance, it would mean that we were on good standards when we clearly were not.

The address Monica had given me was coming up. Her house was just as plain and suburban-like as the others. I thought for a second that it would be black and maybe even have a bow on it.

In front of the house, Charlotte, Wendy, and Will waited. I thought about how far I've come to know them over the past couple days. I felt I pretty much knew them pretty well despite how little I knew. The feeling was pleasant.

"So, are we not allowed inside?" I asked.

"Nah. Charlotte texted her that we were on our way and she said to wait to come in at exactly four. I don't know why but we're doing it anyways," said Wendy. "She's probably doing whatever the heck Monica does. I'll bet five bucks she's hacking something else right now."

Charlotte kept her eyes on me while Wendy talked. I noticed how big her pupils were. I remembered reading somewhere online that if a girl looks at you and has huge pupils it means she likes you. I'm not sure how true that was, but for that moment, I chose to believe it. Having someone look at you like that was incredibly satisfying. I didn't mind if someone who had the ability to stop time did it at this exact moment.

Everyone was still wearing the same clothes they wore to school. Will had his arms crossed but still managed a smile. The way his brown hair blew in front of his forehead made him look like someone from a cologne commercial. I was surprised he didn't have a girlfriend or was constantly surrounded by girls. He was naturally good looking. Knowing that he wasn't like everyone else at school with a new girlfriend every week increased my respect for him. Although he could act like a jerk at times, he was starting to warm up to me.

Wendy, like always, had her devilish smile as if she was ready to ruin someone's day and enjoy it. I still couldn't understand how this small petite girl could muster up all the courage she had. I bet there are countless amount of people who wish to have her determination. But having all those smart remarks and stupid accusations that she has; I would never accept that for any amount of courage.

I checked my phone to see the time. There were three more minutes until four. We stood outside and waited for the clock to tick down. Right when the nine turned to a zero at the end of the clock, the door opened. Monica stood in the doorway with comfy looking clothes. What looked like yoga pants stuck tightly to her perfectly formed legs. A black tank top was accompanied with a black bra strap that carelessly dipped over the side. The same bow that sat continuously still on her head hadn't moved from its spot.

Her face was as blank as ever.

"Hi."

She guided us through her home and introduced us to her parents. They were both very hospitable and well mannered. I didn't have a clue as to what kind of people they would be before I met them, but I was just glad they weren't blank slates like her. Not that there was anything wrong with that of course.

After introductions with her parents, she showed us to her room upstairs. Everyone else entered her room without hesitation but I stood at the entrance. I was going deeper and deeper into her home. I felt like I was invading something precious to her. From where I stood, I could see her bed and a desk where she probably worked hours and hours on it doing whatever a living AI does. For me to just walk in on that felt like a crime, especially with Monica.

She was about to walk in behind us but noticed I was lagging behind. Her head turned as her body stayed glued to the carpet and didn't bother to look with her eyes. All I could see were the thick natural eyelashes that flared out. She stood for a second and gave a miniscule gesture and signaled me with her head for me to come in.

All of this was new to me. I've never been to someone else's house that wasn't family. She had a life just like I did despite any of her powers. This was her abode and I was intruding. Even with her telling me to come in, I didn't want to. Now that I saw her outside of school, she seemed way more *her*.

Everything from her clothes to her posture. They all screamed Monica. As I've mentioned multiple times, I didn't know her. I could claim that I did all I wanted but in reality I hadn't the faintest clue to what type of person she was. Every second standing next to her like this was revealing what was hidden. But knowing that I had her acceptance, I decided to go ahead on in through the door.

Once we were all in, she noticed everyone was standing uselessly taking in her room.

"You can sit on my bed."

When I thought of Monica's room, I never thought it would be anything like this. It was so…normal. I was thinking maybe some black walls and a couple of coffins on them. Instead, all that was there was a simple room for a teenage girl.

She closed the door and secured the lock on it. Her hand went through the motion to lock it several times over again just to make sure it was locked even though it already was. Her arm then lifted up to the wall and shot out a bolt of electricity into it. The sound of the bolt seemed quieter than the first time I heard it. None of us had any idea what she was doing.

After standing in place and intently listening for a good minute, she loosened up.

"Sorry. Just checking for surveillance. It's a habit now."

She pulled out the rolling chair that was pushed in her desk out to sit on it. I took extra consideration into the way she carefully placed herself in her chair. She couldn't help but feel cautious. It was almost as if she was expecting someone to pull the seat out from under her. But yet, she was way more relaxed than she ever is at school. I just couldn't get this girl.

"The reason I brought you here was because I found out some things about yesterday."

Without even looking or touching her computer, it turned on. No boot up process or anything. She must have been connected to her computer at all times, then. That would mean that she could access it at any time she wanted.

"There was something that made me curious above all the other things. Penn mentioned 'that's what the last guys said'," she said, barely lifting her hands to use air quotes, "obviously meaning there was another person they had come into contact with. I was thinking it may have been similar where someone saw them use their powers. So, I did some research."

"Did you break into some place you weren't allowed, Monica?" Wendy said, placing her hands on her hips while trying her best to make her react.

Monica, completely ignoring her remark, made a page pop up on the computer with a list of information.

"As regards to the man that was captured yesterday, Trent Willis; he's a famous blogger. Thousands of people go online to read his blogs daily. Pictures litter it on crazy and weird things he find out in the world. We were a perfect match for him."

"What does this have to do with BloodLip?" Charlotte asked.

"He was found dead last night in his apartment," Monica said without hesitating.

The room fell silent.

"What?" Charlotte asked again. Her expression completely changed, being the only one to openly react.

"The news article said there wasn't a trace of fingerprints or anything like that. They only know that he died because of a bullet in his chest. The thing that ties everything up, though, is what they found on him. His lips were smeared with his own blood. BloodLip."

I couldn't help but feel cold. A person I had just seen yesterday was now dead and I knew the reason for it. These people were murderers. There was no doubt that it was them too. A bullet to the chest is not gonna make blood magically appear on his lips and there was no way it was a coincidence that the murderer does that kind of thing.

"That's not all. I looked up other cases of the same mark of blood smeared on the victim's lips. Turns out, there were two similar ones like this. But the first one was more interesting. This one involved a journalist. It sounds like the same case as the guy we talked to yesterday, but this guy did something different. He actually reported it to the police."

Another web page came up.

"He wrote this on his journal page: 'I was attacked last night by a group of kids. They looked like they were around fourteen or fifteen. But they used powers! Like the ones you see in the movies. One of them had a sword and another with fire. They threatened to kill me because I saw them use it. After some convincing, I was able to go, telling them I would keep it a secret. But how could I? This changes everything we know. They could be extraterrestrial beings or scientific discoveries from different countries. Who knows! They said their name was BloodLip. We need to find them and run some tests on them or something.'"

"Well that gave everything away," Wendy said, almost looking satisfied that we had confirmed it.

Monica gave a nod.

"There was also a call that he made to the police the night he died."

Monica turned around to face her computer for the first time and fixed the out of placed bra strap, placing it back underneath the tank top strap. She clicked a few times and an audio recording started to play.

>*"911 what's your emergency?"*
>
>*"There's some people trying to kill me!"*
>
>*"Okay sir, you need to calm down and tell us where you're at."*
>
>*"I'm at my home. 2731 8th Street across from the theater. Look, I know you'll think I sound crazy but there were some kids with powers that attacked me and now they want me dead."*
>
>*"We're sending out some people your way sir."*

There was a bang that sounded at the door.

>*"Hurry! They all have powers, I'm telling you! They aren't human!"*

There was a scream and the phone dropped after a gunshot.

I leaned back against the wall. I still was in shock that I was interacting with murderers. They all seemed so normal at first glance, yet, they were living double lives. How could someone smile the way Penn did, looking so sincere, and yet, kill a person.

"I wouldn't be so sure as to say it was them, though," said Monica.

"What?!" Wendy yelled out. "I saw your test scores last year, Monica. I thought you were smart, but apparently not. You heard the journalist. He specifically named them as BloodLip. How can you tell us you don't think it was them?"

"Penn mentioned that someone special gave them their name. Who's to say that they're the only members of BloodLip?"

"So, you're suggesting that there's more of them?" I asked.

"Possibly."

Great. More people I had to deal with. Who knows how big their group could really be? They could be a division of a bigger group for all we know.

"That could be true," Charlotte said, rubbing the back of her neck. "I don't think anyone our age really has the capability to kill someone."

"What about yesterday?" I said. "They put a gun to his head. They obviously had the capability of doing it."

Will propped himself up against the frame of the bed, carelessly messing up her unwrinkled bed.

"Maybe it was a bluff. Brittany hesitated before shooting him. What if there's an assigned killer to their group. I mean, who knows. We could just be overthinking everything. I'd say the only reason we're doing this is because we don't want to accept the fact that they *did* kill someone."

"I don't know. I just don't like the fact that she included me in this. Both the girl on the phone and Penn called me the Equilibrium. I don't get it. Am I supposed to be someone special?"

Charlotte shrugged her shoulders.

"Hard to say. We don't nearly know enough as they do about our powers."

"Again, more proof that they might have more backers. People who have answers," Monica said.

"Are we just going to ignore them, then?" I asked.

"That's one of the worst things we could do, Mark," Charlotte replied. "Doing that'll just make a bigger grudge between us. They're the only ones that we know are like us. To ruin any possibility of them telling us more about our powers would be a bad move. I'm not going to tell you guys what to do, but I suggest we keep our distance while being friendly. We're going to the same school. We have classes with them. We *are* going to see them. There's no way around them. Just keep your interaction limited and try not to bring up any of what's happened."

I couldn't have agreed with her more. Her reasoning brought up a point that I wouldn't usually consider doing. I end up making connections between people very strained when I try to avoid them. She was right. It makes grudges. I accidentally did it all the time. Maybe I would forget to say hi to someone one day and it becomes a regular thing to where I don't interact with that person at all. That was it. I practically ruined any relationship with that person.

But another thing was that I hated being fake with my friendliness. If I was going to be friendly to someone, it was going to be because I chose to. I'm not saying I can't do it. I could actually pull off the fake act pretty well, I just felt disgusting doing it.

Everyone's head nodded in unison.

"Just know that if any of them get in my way, I'm still gonna pound their faces in," Wendy said.

I let a chuckle escape my mouth. She was probably dead serious. I wouldn't be surprised to see her the next day on top of one of them.

It felt kind of good to have Wendy on our side. All that energy needed to be used on somebody. Although I know I'm probably going to be getting hit with it the most, it was still better that we had her. Our one small advantage over them.

Monica stood up from her chair. She held her hands together, letting her fingers interlocked in strange positions.

It was obvious why she was doing this. A small smirk clearly expressed itself on my face before I even heard what she said.

"I made some dinner. If—if you want some, I can serve you," she said quietly, looking at the wall.

She seemed incredibly stiff. It looked like she was thrown out on the stage of a play without even looking at the script. Again, she was doing something out of her element.

"Wait. What kind of food? Is it that pasta that you ate yesterday? Cause if it is, that stuff smelled hella good!" Wendy said.

"It's kind of similar," she said, just now deciding to make eye contact with someone.

"Then why the heck are we still standing here? Oh and by the way, Mark doesn't want any. You can give his bowl to me."

"What the heck! I never said that. I have just as much right as you do to get pasta."

"Ladies, both of your dresses are beautiful," Will said. "Come on."

Walking down stairs I couldn't help but feel proud. The feeling increased as we ate dinner. It took me a while to realize why I was feeling like that. The reason was that I had finally gained something that would've required so much work on my part if I really wanted it. I've gained something that I've never had.

All throughout the rest of the day we were at Monica's house, I kept repeating it in my head; the question I couldn't believe.

"Did I just make friends?"

*   *   *

Time flew so fast. Before I even knew it, it was seven. The sun had started its descent and Springfield shifted into its night life. We all had finished eating some dessert that Monica's parents made. They made so much dang food that I bet I didn't need to eat for a whole month.

When we were about to leave, they pulled me aside, telling me that they wanted to tell me something. My immediate reaction was fear. The same went for when my mom did the same. She would mention that she had something to tell me or she wanted to talk. My brain starts backtracking, trying to remember what I did or think what it could be that I did wrong.

"I just wanted to thank you for being Monica's friend."

I let out a silent sigh of relief. Good, I didn't do anything wrong. But I was taken aback by the fact that they thought I was already her friend. I wouldn't consider us friends, but I was starting to see the potential for one.

"For the longest time, she would never talk to anybody. She would just keep herself tucked away in her room. Even when she was younger, she was this way."

Her dad jumped in the conversation.

"We'd tell her to try and make friends on the first day of school, but she'd just come home with the same look as every other day. No success. Programs did nothing either. We tried so many but they never did anything. And that's when she started to get into computers. Usually we'd tell her to get off when she was on there for hours but we'd never do it. It was the only thing that made her happy."

"When we had dinner after her first day of school this year, she actually mentioned you," her mom said.

"She did?" I asked.

"Yup. She said she met a nice boy that talked to her. She actually went out for a walk after dinner. It was so unlike her but it was a good change."

"Again, Mark. We just want to thank you. Monica's never had a friend before."

Yeah, same here. I guess that's why we kinda got along. First off, we both rejected society. Second, we haven't had any friends and know what it's like to be put off by others your age.

The four of us said our thanks and goodbyes before we walked out. Remembering that we had school the next day put me down quickly. I wanted to keep the good feeling that today had given me.

"Alright Charlotte, let's go," Wendy said.

"Um…" Charlotte blushed a bit. "There was somewhere I wanted to show Mark."

Wendy put her hands on her hips and gave both of us a look.

"You're really gonna ditch out on me like that? What a jerk!" She walked over to me and stuck her face in mine. "You better not do anything stupid. Ok?" Her smile returned from out of nowhere, making her words creepier. "Or else I think it's gonna be pretty hard to hold a pencil when all of your fingers are broken."

I wanted to make a good comeback but came up with nothing. She could probably counter me if I did have one. All I could do was just do my best with a glare.

"Wendy, you're taking me home," Will said.

"How much do you have?"

"Money? Psh, like I'd give you any."

"My teleporting services aren't for free you know! If you want to go home so bad, then why don't you just lift up the dang thing and bring it to you?"

Will held out his hand for her to hold it. She rolled her eyes back in disgust and slowly reached for his hand like it was infested with mold.

"Eww! Let's make this quick."

With that, there was a swooshing noise and they disappeared like they were never even there.

So, apparently Charlotte had wanted to show me somewhere? It seemed sudden. She never even mentioned a place of interest to me at all.

"You wanted to take me to somewhere?"

She had a submissive look when she peered up at me.

"Yeah. It's not far from here. Is that okay?"

"It's fine, but it's gonna be dark soon."

Her eyes widened at the thought.

"Perfect."

She started to lead me to the opposite direction of downtown. We got closer and closer to the mountain that acted as a protector for the whole city. I had only been this far back only once when I was first scouting out the new area I was going to be moving into.

While we walked, I thought about how little I knew about Charlotte. For her to be taking a specific path like she was, she must have been here several times before.

"Look, Charlotte. I'm gonna be completely honest. I'm not good when it comes to knowing what to say."

There was a small chuckle that came from her, making her hair bounce.

"Yeah me too."

"That's not true! You always know what to say."

"Then why haven't I said anything the whole time we've been walking?"

I guess what she said was true. But still. I was referring to conversation as a whole. That's why people didn't really like talking to me all that much. They saw me as awkward for not being able to say anything.

"I guess we could start with the cheesy small talk," she said. "Where you from?"

"I've always lived in Springfield. Born and raised here."

"Same here. Hm...favorite color?"

"Great question, Charlotte."

She gave me a friendly nudge.

"Shut up! At least I'm trying to have a conversation. You ask a question."

"Alright, let me see. How'd you learn how to fight? When I was in the computer lab, I saw you and Wendy holding your own pretty well."

"Ah, that. Yeah, guess whose great idea it was to take self-defense classes once we found out we had powers." Of course Wendy would suggest something like that. For someone who's full of energy, she could master fighting within a day. And then she has her powers on top of that. "I went ahead and agreed. I mean, I guess it was a good idea. We weren't gonna be some heroes of the city like every sci-fi movie does. We thought about it but almost immediately after rejected the idea. We just wanted to be able to defend ourselves. You have to think, Mark. Having these powers that we have, it's practically impossible for us to keep them a secret. Even if you try and hide them, there's gonna be a time when you need to use them."

"Has anyone seen you use them?"

"Not besides you guys. No one knows, and I want it to stay that way. You heard the journalist that Monica showed us. Test them. It's probably something the government would do if they found out. And it's not only that. It would change the way people think as a whole. I know it changed the way I think. We still don't know why we have them. It could be something so farfetched that we couldn't comprehend. All I know is I don't believe a lot of things now because of it."

She looked over at me, studying my reaction.

"What about you? I know all of this is kinda crazy to see in the short time span it's been."

"I don't know. It seems like there's no time to think about it. It's something I would deny even if I saw it, but because of how fast everything is going, I just have to accept it."

Charlotte's face was not smiling anymore and neither was mine. We were on a touchy topic. I would normally not talk like this to anyone. Why was she so special to allow me to talk personally like this?

"I know what you mean," she said, letting out a big breath of air. "It was the same way with Wendy and I. We didn't freak out over it or anything like that. It was just very surreal." She was about to talk but stopped herself before she did, making sure of what she was going to say. "Hey, I know it may irritate you a bit to hear this, but, are you sure you've never used any sort of power?"

"Positive."

She let out a small sigh.

"It's just I feel it so much around you."

"Feel what?"

"You'll understand when we get to where we're going."

We walked through the grassy hills that were at the start of the mountain. I checked my watch and we had been walking for at least twenty minutes. Soon the trees cleared and it was pretty obvious that we made it to the spot she wanted to take me to.

I walked out further into the clearing and found out that it was actually a chunk of land sticking out of the mountain. It was the perfect little perch.

Spreading her arms out, Charlotte walked into the middle and twirled around very princess-like.

"Tada! Isn't it beautiful?"

The smile on my face was enough to tell her it was. It was pleasing to see her happy like that. The way her perfect hair swiftly followed her movement and bounced when she giggled. I just wanted to go over and give her a hug that very second.

Her head looked over her shoulders towards me. The smile on her face had a glimmer to it that could cure any sick man. She was naturally pleasing to be around and she didn't even know it.

"Stop standing there and come here," she said with a snickering smile.

I didn't hesitate for a second. It meant standing closer to her and I would've given up anything for that. I was expecting me to be nervous at a time like this, but again, I was calm. It was just like the first day of school when Charlotte and I stared at each other. It made me feel confident. It was nothing I've ever experienced with any other person before.

"You can't tell me that doesn't look beautiful."

She pointed out to the great view we had of all of Springfield. I'd never seen a view of the city like that before. It was a little overwhelming to think that all of that was occupied by millions of people.

Charlotte looked over at me with that same curious look, tracking the direction of my eyes.

"You're looking at the city aren't you? You're just like Wendy. That's all she looked at when I first brought her up here. You have to look beyond what's in front of you, Mark. Try and see what's been there all along."

I looked as intently as I could. What's she talking about? All there was was the big buildings that were a pain to look at. I wanted to give up but I gave her a look to see her expression. She was lost in a gaze that seemed like it couldn't be broken. I gave it another try and found what she was talking about. Just behind the buildings were two mountains overlapping each other. You could see the little points of trees that covered the whole thing like a thick blanket. That combined with the stars that you could *actually* see and the bright moon; it was perfect.

I must've given a sign that I found it because she let out a laugh.

"Told you." She walked back to the middle of the clearing and laid down on the grass. "That's not all I wanted to show you. Come lay down next to me."

Her eyes widened at the realizing of her choice of words.

"Um...I didn't mean for it to sounds like that. Just come here."

I let some air out of my nostrils in a silent chuckle.

I laid back on the surprisingly soft stubble of green next to Charlotte. I stopped myself from doing anything and thought about where I was at that moment. I was currently laying down next to a gorgeous girl that seemed to like me. We were alone in the middle of nowhere, looking up at the stars. We were so close that I could feel her body heat.

When did this happen?! I was just starting school and getting used to the dumb things I was going to have to deal with. Where the heck did me lying next to a girl come from?

"Okay, remember what I was telling you about when we were walking? I wanted to show you what I was talking about. It's not anything you can see with your eyes, but you just have to trust me."

I didn't know what the heck she was planning on doing. For a second, she sounded like a freaky lady that sold gemstones.

Her hands rested softly on her stomach and she looked up at the white dots in the sky.

"Just focus. All you're looking for is a feeling. I'm going to be laying here trying to get the same one. We're gonna try to do something that Wendy and I couldn't do."

I was convinced that what she was saying was true despite the vagueness of it. My eyes closed and I looked around in my eyelids for whatever feeling this was. For a while, there was nothing, just the skin in front of my pupils. But I kept searching. Searching for the feeling. There was a euphoric feeling in the middle of my chest. It started to spread, infecting my body with the incredible sensation. It certainly was something I'd never felt. It was so pleasant, I didn't want it to stop. But that begs the question; what was it? What was this feeling that I loved so much?

There was a tap on my hand. It was no doubt Charlotte's. It crawled up my arm and laid flat on my chest. What was she doing? I know she's not the type of person to make a move on me.

"Don't open your eyes," she commanded, knowing that I wanted to.

I wanted to fight it but what was the point. This was something entirely new to me. I might as well listen to what she was saying. Everything was true so far.

Her hand stayed still and raised up when I breathed in. I'm not going to lie, I actually liked it. She was resting with me. Or so I thought.

"It worked!" Her voice resonated with an abundant amount of surprise, astonished at whatever the heck she did.

I opened up my eyes and to my surprise, her hand was nowhere on me. Rather, her hand was on her own chest.

"What...?"

"I know, it's weird. You thought I was touching you, right?" She sat up, leaning her hands on the grass. "This is what I was talking about. Wendy and I tired doing this a few years back. We felt this feeling that we were connected. It was subtle and not that strong, but it was there nonetheless."

"Connected?"

"Yeah. We tried to see if we could make it stronger somehow but we got nothing. Then we met the other two. It was the same feeling. At the time, we didn't know what it was. The only thing we knew was that this was our way of knowing who had powers and who didn't. Before any of them showed any signs of powers, we already kinda had a feeling."

She looked down at the ground to collect her thoughts, slowly shaking her head in amazement.

"When I saw you for the first time in the hallway, I knew you were one of us. I got the same feeling and so did Wendy. The thing that was different was that it was so much stronger. When you were yelling at Wendy, I could feel your anger; something that I never felt with her, despite how close we are. I bet she felt it just as much. So did Will and Monica. I guess you could say that's why we easily accepted the claim of the girl who texted us."

If that was the reason, then that must've been why she was looking at me so much. I felt defeated because of that. And I started to think someone had liked me. Man, I was stupid. To think that I believed that.

"That's why you were looking at me then, huh."

"Um…" The same submissive look returned. "Not entirely."

So then she did like me. Or, there actually was something on my face. With the blood that started to rush into her face, the possibility didn't seem so farfetched anymore. I chose not to dwell on it too much. We'd only known each other for a few days. For feelings to be strong in that time span is all story book material.

"So, the connection is always like this?" I asked.

"It'd be kinda creepy if it was. Then we'd all be able to feel what you're feeling all the time. It's only at certain times that the connection is as strong as it is. I laid down and looked up at the stars, remembering the time I would be alone up here, or the occasions when my dad would come up here with me. Joy."

"That's what is was," I said, chuckling at the strangeness of it.

"Just pure happiness. It's a special feeling I only get up here. It works both ways. We can feel your feelings and you can feel ours. This was just a case when you felt mine. But like I said, it works better with you somehow. None of us could get a connection as strong. Penn and the girl calling you Equilibrium; I think it means something. I don't know what the heck it means or what powers you have, but I do agree that you're special."

"Yeah, well hopefully we get to find out what powers I have then."

"You actually think you have them?"

I shrugged my shoulders.

"I honestly don't know whether I agree with it or not. We'll see I guess."

"I guess."

We stayed there, sitting down. The beautiful sight that was in front us filled our vision and silenced us. I started to feel the same feeling of joy from Charlotte. We looked at each other and smiled.

I thought back at the events that have happened since the beginning of school. Meeting these people thinking that they were all groupies—thinking they were all snobs like the rest of the city. It just goes to show you the proof of what people say. Don't judge a book by its cover. No matter how much you study a person, you can never truly know them until you're around them—when you see them at their purest form. And the only time you get to see that is at time of stress and pressure. Little did I know that I'd soon get the chance to be in that exact circumstance.

We were going to all be tested. Changed. With these people I would get to know. Friends. Yes, these people were going to be the very thing I never had. Everything was going so perfectly. No more near death encounters. All it took was one week. One week for everything to collide and force an insurmountable wrath upon us. The week of Oblivion.

# Chapter 5

When I say it was a bad week, I mean it was a bad week. Sure, I whine about every other thing, but this was different. For one, it was spring break. It had to be on the long awaited week after winter break. It was when the parties and gatherings started back up because of the weather returning to its warm state. Not to mention all the other things people could come up with doing who actually had a creative mind unlike the five of us. It was pitiful when someone found out the routine things we did day after day but I wasn't complaining. Overall, everyone liked the break. For me personally, it meant time with the people I liked the most.

It'd been almost seven months since I first step foot on Springfield High's grounds and got shoved into the mess of superhumans. I was lucky, I guess, to not be in another tense encounter with BloodLip. Well, let me rephrase that. I hadn't been in another *fight* with them.

There were always tense moments with them. Every time we'd walk by them in school, we'd get different facial expressions from the four of them. Penn and Brittany would have jaunting smiles on their face like they always did. Eli and Sarah, being the exact opposite from the other two, stared us down, probably hoping to see us fall and break every bone in our body. I'd get special treatment from Eli. Any chance he'd get, he'd make sure to make my life even more of a pain than it already was. It was expected from the jerk.

I'd always walk to school with Penn. It was an everyday thing by now. After seeing what they were capable of and Monica bringing up the possibility of them being murderers, I felt uncomfortable with walking beside her. I'd need to hide every sign of my squirminess. After a while, I'd just try to remember what Charlotte had told us to do. I would make light conversation with her and that was pretty much it. There'd be the occasional time where we'd get into in depth conversations and I'd see her as a really genuine person. Of course, after having the conversation I had to remember that she was a deadly person. I had to convince myself that she was not like us. She was a monster who had the capability of murdering a human soul. She wasn't anybody I wanted to be spending time with.

But something else happened in that time span. It was gradual but I noticed every second of it. I loved what was forming and wanted it to continue.

*Swoosh*

"Good morning!"

The bright voice made me want to bash my head against the wall, not to mention she blew the curtains open with the wind of her teleport. It was way too early in the morning for her to be screaming in my ear. I pulled the covers back over my face to try and block out her presence.

"Don't tell me you're still sleeping!" she yelled. The disgusting hint of chirpiness breached my brain telling me I needed to take precautions before I died of annoyance.

The covers flew off of me in one sweep. I didn't bother to try and fight over them. I knew she'd have a better grip than I did, especially in the morning.

That brat. Those were my sacred covers. They brought me to a place no one else could take me. Slumber was a precious prize that could only be obtained with the right circumstances. Having bed sheets ruined by her hands meant they were forever cursed. It's all your fault.

"God! Wendy, do you really have to barge in here all by yourself?" I said, curling into the fetal position trying to give myself warmth before realizing how hot it actually was.

"Of course not! Do you really think I'd wanna come here by myself? In your room. Where you sleep. How gross do you think I am? Who knows how many "boy" germs are in here. If I'm to be infected with your filth, I might as well have them killed by it too."

I opened my eyes and saw the four of them standing in my room. Why was I even surprised that she'd do something like that? I knew her too well. If she'd have any common decency she'd call me before teleporting into my room I told her.

"Nah. That's boring. If you're going to enjoy your life, it's best to live it full of surprises."

"Ugh! I don't have time for your stupid lectures. And why are you guys here so early anyways?"

"Early?" Charlotte asked. "Mark, it's 10:45."

"What?!"

It made me jump up from my bed that was relentlessly destroyed by pigtails. Charlotte was right. The big red letters on my clock didn't lie.

"Mmm, it gives you around fifteen minutes," Will said, not even giving me a look in my eye knowing he'd get irritated at the sight of me, especially in the morning. He was too busy on his phone checking whatever the heck someone as "cool" as him does. "I say you better get ready unless you wanna get caught in rush hour. You better not make us late again."

We had planned that day to head out into downtown like we did so many other weekends. It had become a routine thing. Go eat somewhere. Go to the mall. Amusement park. Whatever. All that mattered is that we had fun, as Charlotte would put it. What was different was that this time it was the first day of our spring break. Everyone else in school was going to be downtown too along with the rest of the city, hence the reason why Will was antsy to get there before every street would be bumper to bumper for as far as the eye could see.

The next day was gonna be a party that Emily planned, the one who I saved from Sarah's fist. Despite all her humility and humbleness, she was actually from a rich family. Who knew. She lived in a mansion that was at the top of the mountain. Everyone from school was invited, even Sarah and Eli. Ew. I know right. She was a little too humble in my opinion.

I stood and gave a good stretch. Charlotte gave me her usual lovely smile that I enjoyed seeing so much, making me look like an absolute freak as I raised my hands to the ceiling and my face smeared with the bed creases. Monica hadn't said a word yet, as expected. She was facing my computer and had her hand placed on it.

The others followed my direction and watched as she was probably performing some task that we couldn't see.

She must've noticed the quietness and turned around.

"It's gone now."

"What's gone?" I asked.

"You told me your computer was being slow. I found some viruses and erased them," she said with a blank face.

"Oh. Thanks," I said, surprised at what she did. It wasn't something I expected her to do. I never even asked her to come over and fix it. To be honest, I don't even remember the conversation coming up.

I went over and gave her a pat on the back, refusing to pat her head and chance messing up the firm figure. The rare small smile appeared on her face only to disappear in an instant. I didn't care how long it was there. The fact that it was there was enough.

"Whatcha downloading, Mark? Hm?"

Wendy gave me her devious smile.

"What are you hinting at?"

"Oh, nothing," she said followed by a burst of laughter.

"Well, it's gonna be pretty hard to change with you guys in here. Can you give me a few and I'll be out?"

"Mkay," said Charlotte, holding her hands behind her back and lightly bouncing on her tiptoes for a brief second.

They all started to walk out of my room before I ran up and grabbed the arm reaching for the knob.

"What are you doing?! My mom's here."

"So?" Will said. He'd been to my house many times before. All of them have.

"How're you gonna explain coming out of my room without even coming in the front door?"

"Good point."

No one still knew about our powers. We'd been really good about making sure no other eyes saw the marvels that were trapped inside my friends. Sure, we had a couple close calls but no one knew a thing.

They were worrying about hiding theirs all the while I've been waiting on mine. There wasn't a point anymore. I completely lost hope of me having some a few months back. If they found out theirs at puberty I would've found out mine years back.

If I was this so called Equilibrium, what powers did I have? Penn always treated me as if I was special because of it. She'd sometimes mention how I was so great for having them. Yeah, well why the heck would I ever want to be known for being great because of something I had no clue about. It's as stupid as politics. People look up to these few thinking they have power when in reality they don't. And with the way she spoke, it almost sounded like she knew what they were supposed to be and she probably did too. I would've asked her but there's no point. It'd just give me false hope. I'd think about how great this ability would be only to burn out waiting for it.

They went ahead and teleported back out of my room to the sidewalk. I heard the doorbell followed by my mom's greeting and letting them into the living room where she's probably persist to give them some sort of food.

She was really happy that I made friends but it made her feel different. I felt that something *was* different. I'm sure my guess was right. Because I was hanging out with them so much now, I was sorta leaving her out when we spent so much time together before. We'd still do a lot of things with each other but just not as much. At least it gave her more incentive to go out and look for friends for herself.

But who am I to say something like that? I used to hate everyone. I'd look at them with disgust knowing that they *had* friends. It took me so long to realize why I felt like this. I envied them. I wanted what they had. Now that I had some, it makes me look at things so differently. To go and tell someone to find friends when you were in the same situation is great and all, but you have to look at it from their standpoint.

It's not entirely helping them. They don't want the change. They don't want the pain and rejection that comes with trying. Although they might be hurting and missing out, they'll gradually find that person they always desired.

I went ahead and put on some of my best clothes for downtown. If you're gonna go down there you had to look your best. New styles and trends were prevalent throughout the whole place. I didn't follow the trends that were worn but I still made sure I looked good.

I finished getting ready in no time and headed downstairs to meet up with the others. Upon getting down the stairs, I saw them all sitting down and watching the TV. I heard the stereotypical news reporter lady voice as she rambled about something. As I got closer, I noticed the attention grabbing **Breaking News** flowing at the bottom of the screen.

"What're you guys watching?" I asked, coming up behind the couch, trying to place my hand close to Charlotte's shoulder.

"I don't really know," Charlotte said, not looking back. "They're saying there was a failed attempt at assassinating the President yesterday."

I stood at the back of the couch and watched along with them. No matter how many times the news reporters went over the material, it seemed like they were keeping out some information.

Obviously.

They always have to retain some. The authorities aren't going to let all the information out to the public. It'll just cause more fear.

Apparently, it was a presentation of some new drugs and possible cures that were going to be made possible by this program. Different world leaders were there to show their support for it, but it clearly was a recipe for disaster with all of them there. The head of the program was assassinated as he gave his final speech. It sucked. He was supposed to make new discoveries for diseases and now he's dead.

We didn't bother to watch it all that much. To most of us, is was just news. Although, yes, it did involve the President, it didn't matter that much to us. Again, just another greedy and selfish human thinking. If it doesn't affect us immediately, it didn't matter. It was how a lot of people thought, especially here in this huge city which we were going to go out into and get sucked into once more.

We headed out on foot towards the bus stop. From there it would take us directly to the big buildings. It took no more than ten minutes in total depending on traffic.

I'd sit next to Charlotte like I always did. She'd make sure that she would sit extra close to me. Sitting in that seat meant comfort. I could feel her entire presence there next to me. The others sat along the remaining ones and Monica would always get the window seat.

Monica gave me a small look after taking a break from looking out the window. The black bow still held up after all the time that has passed. I've asked her before and she told me that the only time she takes it off is when she takes a shower. No one special had given it to her. She said that she only wears it because it's pretty. That's it. Do I believe that's true? Of course not. It's Monica.

"Hey Monica. What do you think we buy you a new bow?"

Her face stayed extra stiff. The surroundings of her eyes tightened almost as if they were flexing. I was afraid that she was gonna be upset at me for asking something like that. Instead, she slowly nodded her head.

I took it as a yes despite the look of uncertainty she had. Maybe I shouldn't have asked anyways. That specific bow seems really special to her. Either way, it was a gift. She could just keep it as a reminder of my courtesy or some stupid thing like that.

"How much do you think it costs to live up on the top floor?" Charlotte asked.

I followed the direction of her finger and looked out at the skyline of skyscrapers. I immediately knew which one she was talking about. It was the big penthouse that the most famous people lived in. Stacks and stacks of condos were layered on the cement block. Anywhere from actors to singers lived there.

"More than what I'll make in a lifetime I bet," I said.

Her smile peered over her right shoulder to meet my face. The playful roll of her eyes made it all the more better.

"Alright then, what if we combined our money? I'd say we'd have enough."

"Like this idiot would even make more than a buck," Wendy said, throwing her ugly face into the slap of an insult.

"Yeah, you say that now when no one's gonna give you a job because you're gonna scare all the customers away with that ugly face of yours," I replied.

"Ugly face? I think you should stop talking about yourself, Mark."

"Oh you'd know if I was talking about myself. I'd have you on your knees bowing down to me if I was."

Will gave me a look. His face said that he knew I jumped out of line with that comeback.

"Bowing down to you?" he scoffed. "Yeah, not even a desperate homeless man begging for money would do that."

He was right. It's not that I thought a lot of myself. It's just that any chance I get, I want to make Wendy feel inferior to me. Obviously, it never happened. She could always come up with something wittier to say with her smart mouth. Even if it was a bad comeback, she could make it sound like she thought about it overnight.

I guess that's what I liked about her. She could easily defend herself with words, not to mention she could do so physically. There've been occasions where she'd saved me with her mouth. I should've been grateful for it but the part I hated was having to thank her for it. It was another win for her, and they kept stacking up.

The bus stopped just where it was supposed to. It was the stop we got off every weekend. It was right in the middle of downtown. Once you got off the bus, it opened up to an area with benches and a fountain. A small little opening that was a common meetup place for people. Just in front of that was the mall. Surrounding that was restaurants along with the various shops that covered any other open spot.

This was it. It was the prime place for Springfield. It was the place where all the teens and groupies would come to hang out. It was the place where girls would come and stalk a boy they liked. A place where families started with proposals and marriages. The place where everything happened.

But apparently too much happened here. Way too much.

Right as we jumped off the bus Wendy raised her hand and bounced up and down like a child.

"I'm picking lunch! I called it so you all have to shut up and listen. Will, no complaining," she said while pointing at his chest. "I feel like eating at a diner. Maybe some sliders. Ooh that sounds good! Charlotte it's your turn to pay."

"What! Don't be stupid. I just paid last weekend."

"Well it sure ain't my turn."

Will put a hand on his forehead and let out a sigh.

"Why don't you just make Mark pay for it like you always do?"

"Hey! How's that supposed to solve anything?" I yelled.

Monica's voice poked out into the conversation so secretly.

"I'll pay."

After all the time we've been friends, I still couldn't get over the soft pleasant voice of hers. It comes out of nowhere when she finally decides to talk. She keeps her still image but the only thing that changes when she talks was her mouth.

She wore a black short sleeve T-shirt that stuck close to her body, showing just how much of a curve she had. To accompany the black, she wore more black with her pants. And of course, her usual bow.

I had to say, being close with three teenage girls was kind of nice. I don't know. Something about girls was unique. They were able to express another form of personality no guy could bring to the table. It was always the little things that made me appreciate them. The well cared nails or maybe the right amount of makeup. Whatever. I'll just stop now before you think I'm some perv obsessed with girls. But yes, even the brat was somewhat cute in the right light. Heck, I'll just come straight out and say it. If she wasn't so rude and annoying then she'd probably be way more attractive.

Charlotte, on the other hand, didn't need a change. She was so gosh darn pretty and the way she acted complimented that. She wore a plaid buttoned up shirt that she left unbuttoned, letting it be carelessly thrown about by the small breeze. Underneath was a white tank top and further, white shorts. Wendy's outfit looked a lot similar but she wore a yellow shirt that was actually buttoned.

Do I really need to explain what Will was wearing?

Obviously he was going to be wearing the best of his best clothes. Top of the line brands that made him look like a rich boy from England. He'd always get so many looks from girls. I would occasionally get jealous but I'd rather get those same looks from Charlotte over any other random girl. He was good looking and nothing was going to stop that, but he could enhance it with his dumb clothes.

I looked down at myself. Just a plain black hoodie with some jeans. Man, did I look out of place. To me, this was my best clothes. Do you know how expensive this dang sweater was? Apparently that didn't matter to people. It was how you wore it.

Jerks. I wore this for you and you don't bother to even look at me? How stupid was that thinking? I was wearing these "good" clothes to impress who? No one really but the city itself. Another point on our stupid thinking—or just mine.

"Well I don't want Monica to pay that much. I'll check for coupons," Wendy said.

I didn't even bother to complain to her. She didn't want her to pay that much, yet, she would have me pay for everything and not even give a simple thank you.

Wendy started to look on her phone for coupons as we started to head over to the diner we had in mind. In fact, it was the same exact one where we almost witnessed a murder. Behind it was the lot that we "talked" with BloodLip.

The closer we got to it, the more the sidewalks became crowded. It was hard to stay close to Charlotte at a time like this and I was forced to walk next to whoever was standing by my side. I bet by now all of them knew well that I liked walking next to her where she didn't seemed that concerned with it.

By now, I didn't question if she liked me or not. I was sure of it. One hundred percent positive. There was no need to doubt it. Yeah, there'd be days when she didn't really look at me in class and I'd get to thinking that she was over me. But next thing I know, the day after she can't stop peeking at me. I should expect that from her. I mean, she is a girl after all. One day you have a happy soul and the next you have one that could tear things to shreds.

At the time, I tried not to let it phase me and kept on trying not to bump into people. There were too many; way more than usual. Something must've been going on. Just when I started to think of what was happening, Wendy answered it.

"Oh my gosh! It's the grand reopening."

"Oh yeah," Charlotte said. "They were remodeling it, weren't they?"

"And it's fifty percent off today," she said, still looking at her phone. "No wonder. That's where all these people are going." Her eyes widened, causing me to brace for what was next. "Run! I don't wanna have to wait hours just to get some sliders."

She broke out into a sprint down the sidewalk, bobbing and weaving through all the people. The rest of us knew what we were expected to do. No, not just walk and we'll eventually catch up to her. We were supposed to run after her and make sure we tagged right behind her. This wasn't the first time this has happened either.

I started my run despite my utter hatred of doing it. People looked at me like I was some weirdo. No one ever ran on the sidewalks of downtown. The casual stroll was the norm for around here. To just go ahead and run down them was frowned upon. As it should be.

The four of us tried our best to catch up to her but just watched as she disappeared in the crowd. Next to me I heard Will mumbling something to himself. His entire face scrunched up with a bitterness far worse than alcohol.

"No need to keep it to yourself," I told him, knowing how much he wanted to let it out.

"Oh yeah?"

He went ahead and started to curse as loud as he could, throwing every insult at Wendy. She wouldn't be able to hear it but I enjoyed every second of hearing what she deserved. A wide smile occupied Will's face. He kept on going and didn't stop. That is until his voice abruptly halted and got yanked down from behind.

"What'd you call me?!"

Wendy was now behind me on top of Will. He couldn't hold in his laugh, making her more frustrated.

"Did you just teleport?" I asked.

Her face quickly whipped up and glared at me.

"How else do you think I got behind you?"

"Wendy!"

She knew very well the rules we'd set. No one was to see us use powers. That meant not using them in public. My enforcement of the rules meant nothing to her as she punched the life out of Will.

I turned back around to head over with Charlotte and Monica but hit something. I again found myself falling to the floor. I was expecting the hard concrete but landed on something soft. When I started to gather my bearings from the surprise of the fall, I realized that I was on top of someone. My face was practically buried in the crevice of her chest.

The body started to shake from laughing and the vibrations of her voice pushed itself through my head.

"Well isn't this a sight. Two people on the floor with someone on top of them in the middle of the sidewalk. I gotta say, it's not that often you see this happen."

I quickly got up from the floor and tried to act like nothing happened. The girl on the floor stood up and gave me her usual crooked smile. I knew this girl.

Eris.

She wore her same gothic clothes that she wore on the first day of school. It seemed like she never changed her outfit. Whether it was that I couldn't see a difference in dark clothes or that she actually never changed them, I don't know.

On the floor next to her was an ice-cream cone smeared into the gray floor. Dirt and stray pebbles mixing into the cream and all.

"Oh! I'm so sorry," I said, knowing that I ruined someone's day.

She looked down at the melting cone.

"Nah. It's fine. I'll just get another one."

I couldn't let her do that. To trip over her was one thing, but making her drop her food was another. I insisted I would buy her another.

"Where'd you buy it?"

"The shop over on seventh. You need to try it. It's my favorite one. They have so many flavors. They have Peppermint, Vanilla, Chocolate, Strawberry, Cherry, Brownie Bits, Bananas and Cream..." She continued to list off various flavors I've never heard of before that I eventually had to cut her off.

From the little that I spoke to her right now, I came to think that she was always like this. With Wendy starting to already tell me that we needed to get going, I couldn't go down three blocks to buy an ice-cream, especially with someone like this.

"Tell you what. How 'bout I owe you one?"

The thick black of her eyes stayed half-shut in a creepy way. It somehow made her seem more alive even with the dead look.

"Sure. That works. Just know that I'll hold you to it though. I need my ice-cream."

"And you'll get it. I promise."

Out of nowhere, she jumped on me and gave me a hug.

"Have a fun one, Mark!"

*        *        *

"Hi Mark."

How many times did I have to run into people? Violet and Penn were in line to the diner standing next to the others.

"Uh, hey," I said, flustered at the meeting of other people.

Violet raised an eyebrow and let a hip drop.

"What? Nervous seeing your teacher outside of school? I have a life too you know."

"No it's not that. It's just I didn't expect seeing people I know here."

"That's kind of stupid if you ask me." Her choice of words took me aback. She was clearly insulting my stupidity. "You know everyone goes downtown. You're bound to see someone. And I personally think it's kinda rude you aren't happy to see me or Penn at least."

She was right. I shouldn't be surprised if I walked in the diner and saw my whole class in there.

"That's not it! I swear," I said, trying to not sound like a jerk.

Penn stood next to her mom with bright cheeks. Her arms were pushed in close together to provide some sort of haven. When I looked at them as a whole, they didn't really fit all that much. They weren't related after all.

One day when I was walking to school with Penn she explained and answered some of the questions I had. She was adopted when she was a tiny baby. I did the math and that would've meant that Violet was eighteen when she adopted Penn.

I'm no one to judge people on their choices in life, but if you ask me, that's a little too young to be wanting a child. Penn had no knowledge of her real parents and neither did the adoption house that she came from.

"H—hey, Mark, was that Eris?" Penn asked, twirling her hair around with a single finger, making a curl at the end.

"Yeah. We bumped into each other."

"Quite literally I see," Violet said.

"She's kinda weird, isn't she?" Wendy said, fixing the collar of her shirt.

"She's a nice girl. She actually has some of the highest grades in the class. And you should've seen her scores for the state test. Last year she got every single answer right. But if you're talking weird, yeah, I guess."

"That just her style," Charlotte said. "It fits on her. Kinda like Monica, but creepier."

"No." The small voice randomly appeared again. "I know where she's coming from. Dark makes you different *and* fit in. It's the choice that one makes to decide which they'll do."

"Then what choice did you make?" Will asked.

"The one that makes everyone shut up and ignore me."

The laughter eased everything up. I wasn't planning on spending the day with Violet and Penn, but if I was, I wanted it to be tense free. I chose that day to see her as normally as I could and ignore the constant harassment from my conscience.

Another thing I didn't expect was seeing Violet out of her work environment. She wore extremely young clothes. She made everything work so well together. Her denim pants and T-shirt along with the curly hair disguised herself as one of us.

Penn gave me her usual quick looks like Charlotte did. I tried my best not to entertain her with looking back. It would feed her and give her the wrong message.

We all conversed smoothly while we waited for the line outside the diner to slowly roll on in. Once we finally made our way in, I was able to notice the changes that were made to it in full. Everything from the rearranging of the seating and to the kitchen were changed. From what I remembered about it, it felt like a new diner. Already, every seat was practically taken, adding warmth and sweat to the fresh new cushions on the booths. We were quite fortunate to be somewhat close to the front of the line so we got in at a reasonable time.

"Right this way please."

They directed us to one of the few open tables. Violet and Penn went on ahead and sat with us. As selfish as it sounds, I was glad that they did. Violet would most likely offer to pay for the bill.

People started to sit down not really caring what seat they were choosing but I couldn't help but feel appalled at the fact. Well, I guess to them it shouldn't. As I've said, Charlotte doesn't seem to care about sitting next to someone she likes all that much. But that doesn't mean you take me out of the question. I mean, c'mon Will. You're supposed to be my wingman. Cut me some room bro. Make the plays to help me be closer to her.

I was eventually forced to sit completely on the other side of her with a view of Violet. Charlotte was sitting in front of Penn and was already chatting it up girly style. I guess you could say that was one thing I disliked about Charlotte. She was too quick to forget about people. I'm not saying she's inconsiderate, but she can easily switch over to focusing on someone else. Or I might be a little selfish here but I think I hold some credibility here when I say I feel abandoned by her sometimes.

I was all too busy on trying to get a better view of Charlotte and find the perfect position in my chair in case I wanted a quick look of her that I didn't hear Violet's voice at first.

"Mark? Did you hear me?" she asked.

"Huh?" I said, whipping my head back to her direction.

"I said that I haven't gotten a chance to talk to you about something not involving school work." she said, sipping from her straw. "Penn talks a lot about you know. All good things. Nothing bad, believe me. So, what's so good about Mark? I don't really know who you are."

"Nothing. I'm not special in any way."

"Oh shut up. Yeah you are. There's something special about everyone. Alright, let's see. What do you like to do for fun?"

The rest of them were already chatting it up. It was just the two of us in this conversation. It meant I could actually find out more about her. It'd help out in giving me my advantage that I liked having over people.

"A lot of stuff."

She rolled her eyes.

"Don't be so boring. I'm talking specifics."

"Okay, let's see. It might sound weird, but I like to study people. Not in any creepy way but just to know and understand how society works."

Her face kept looking right on at mine. Her smile was precious in a way that didn't seem like it belonged to her. I didn't know why but the more she looked, the more I wanted to hide my head under the table.

"Uh…," I said, not really knowing what to do with her long pause.

"Really? Sounds kinda strange. I guess I kinda know what you mean. But I don't see a need to do that if you talk to different types of personalities every day."

Yeah, but the thing was that I hated society's personality. I hated the arrogance, the sloppiness, the carelessness. She sounded like she thought I enjoyed it. I do it to make fun of people and point out their flaws.

"What about you?" I asked, trying to reverse things to her direction.

"Spending time with Penn and riding my bike."

Violet's popularity at school was stacked with the fact that she rode a street bike to school. Her matching black and violet colored helmet and bike looked pretty good on her. Not to mention there were occasions where she'd wear the tights with it that never failed to woo the guys taking in an eyeful behind her as she walked in school.

"You have to give me a ride one day." I smiled, trying to get her to loosen up and copy it as well.

The corner of her mouth pulled in a smirk making my mirror successful.

"Maybe one day." There wasn't any assurance in her voice. It was simply there to give me false hope that maybe she'd fulfill my wishes.

I noticed the dark eyes of Monica peeking over. She'd been listening for sure. She was exceptionally well at eavesdropping on people. Since she had a great memory, it helped her out a lot I bet. Storing something for later, ready to bring it up and destroy someone's day. Now that was something. So quiet. So devious. Her soft but firm state was something I admired.

I looked back at Violet. Her face was still focused on me. She was searching for something in me. It felt painfully awkward and uncomfortable to feel her eyes pressing in like they were. Her smile never wavered. I decided to go ahead and ignore it, focusing on whatever Penn and Charlotte were talking about.

Even when I joined in on the conversation, it still bothered me. The more I thought about it, the more I realized that I've never met someone who could do this so well. Monica did something similar with her death stare but Violet's was different. I couldn't help but feel inferior next to her. Despite her childlike attitude and playful demeanor, she was highly overpowering. She displayed a control like no other.

Dare I look back at her?

The corner of my eyes were enough to notice her still looking. She would occasionally sip from her drink but it was the same nonetheless. What do you do in a situation like that? Do you confront a person that's staring you down for no reason at all? Do you continue to ignore it and hope they give up?

I thought the best way to handle it was with striking up a question. It was never in my intentions to make it a weird one.

"Do you have any friends?" I blurted out, hating the randomness of it.

Her face was still facing me but took on a confused look. No words. Just her face was all.

"You're funny, you know that."

"Me?"

"Well who else?" she said chuckling.

"Why?"

Violet shrugged her shoulders and immediately forgot our conversation, moving into theirs. This woman claimed I was the funny one. Has she looked in a mirror recently? You don't just stare someone down and tell them they're funny only to just shrug off your claim.

It was here that Violet started to scare me. Her domination was something I've never experienced. She made me realize that I wasn't important. I was just another person in this mess of the world. Nothing about me was special. With one look, she could put me in my place. I'd sooner take a bullet to the face then get a look from her.

I started regretting sitting with them. My view of Violet changed and I didn't like one second of it. She was part of the fun in school and now that was over. I saw her at her purest form and wished it would've been covered up. But would you rather know someone for who they are and judge them on that rather than a mask they wear?

Gosh dang it Violet!

*       *       *

I hated food now. Absolutely hated it. Who could eat such an abhorred thing? I mean, it just goes into your stomach for what, just to get full and curse at yourself for eating too much?

"Why?!" Wendy yelled out to the world, not caring about letting the obnoxiousness getting into the ears of passersby. "Too much!"

"Did you really have to order three plates full of sliders?" Charlotte asked, sharing the same pain.

"Hey! I was hungry."

"Trust me," Will said, "she needs the calories."

Wendy looked down towards her chest and crossed her arms over it, knowing well what he was referring to.

"You're lucky I'm full," she said, glaring him down with her forceful eyes.

"Yeah? Or what, you would've jumped on me again? Ooh I'm so scared. All seventy pounds of nothingness would hurt so much."

"I'm not that flat you jerk. I weigh more than a hundred, I can tell you that. And I'm not that small either."

"Be happy Wendy." Violet said. "When you're my age, you'll wish you're that skinny."

Wendy looked Violet up and down.

"But you look perfect."

"It's not that easy keeping this figure," she said, striking a pose.

She threw me a wink and asked me how she looked. I might as well jump on the train of screwing over Wendy.

"Better than she'll ever look."

Everyone started to laugh. I joined along too but never bothered to look at Wendy's face. Usually there would be a sneer on it or she would've said another comeback already. Rather, her head was tilted towards the ground. Her eyes scanned the streets for a salvation.

I guess we hit a touchy subject. It was good to know. No, not to mess with her later. Well, maybe a little bit but that wasn't what I was trying to say. I never thought much of girls bothering to care what they looked like physically. Not facially but the features they develop over time. It clearly bothered her to a certain extent.

Monica, seeming unamused by all of this, stood there amongst us with stiff arms.

"Oh yeah, Monica. I still need to get your new bow."

"Mhm," she silently mumbled.

"You can find a bow somewhere on first, right?" Wendy asked.

"Yeah. Why?"

"There's a Victoria's Secret there," she said quietly.

Everyone stayed silent until Charlotte broke it.

"Oh! You want to by a push-up bra don't you?"

Wendy smacked her hand over Charlotte's mouth, preventing her from saying anything else.

"Shut up! God!"

She rushed Charlotte over with her, hurrying towards the shop. The other girls and Will decided to head on in the store with them. Monica and I went looking for a little stand or shop that sold some bows.

There were plenty of things you could find downtown. It didn't take long at all for us to find one that had a wide variety of them.

Monica didn't hesitate and jumped on in. Her eyes scanned over them individually just the same way I saw her do in the computer lab. It was something that was only present when she had a passion for it.

"Pick whichever one you want."

Her dark eyes appeared puppy-eyed as she looked up at me. I gave a nod, reassuring my statement. My first instinct was to pet her. She acted so child-like it surprised me. I was used to the quiet emotionless Monica that hardly spoke.

It was no surprise to me that she chose a black one. I pulled out the dull one from her hair, obviously asking before, and placed the new one in. I was careful not to touch a single strand of her thick black blanket, being afraid that I'd be cursed in some way if I did. Once I placed it in, I stood back and admired it. It exposed itself way more than her old one did.

"Thank you."

"No need to thank me. It seemed like you wanted a new one anyways."

Monica looked in the mirror of the little stand admiring her new bow. She caught my eyes in the mirror and the top of her pale white cheeks started to be replaced with red.

Wait. Was she blushing?

She suddenly turned around and hesitantly reached her arms out towards me. I couldn't tell if she was trying to give me a hug or was in unbearable pain. Her face contorted standing there trying to decide.

This wasn't Monica. Blushing and trying to give me a hug? It couldn't be. Could it?

My questions were never answered. They were put to a halt because it started. What made that week horrible rammed into our day, begging for attention. Begging for our participation in its game of chaos.

A noise booming louder than anything I've ever heard pounded directly above us followed with intense heat. The back of my neck singed with an unbearable amount of pain. The two of us dropped to the ground instantly as our hands instinctively went up to the back of our heads. Screams filled the streets as everyone started to panic and chaos ensued.

What was going on?

Staying planted to the floor, I looked up towards where the sound came from. What I saw was horrifying. No matter how many times I blinked or refocused my sight, it was still there. It forced me to fear. It forced me to realize the situation at hand. It was then that I felt smaller than I ever had, completely forgetting anything that happened that day.

A massive ball of fire spewed out of one of the skyscrapers. One of the top floors was directly hit with the explosion. After regaining my bearings, I realized we were on First Street. That meant this was the building Charlotte and I were talking about on the bus. This was the one full of the faces of Springfield. The most known building in downtown Springfield was now on fire.

Seconds after the explosion, debris hit the streets below, toppling cars and people. The sound of crushing proceeded to take up and replace the screams as I watched humans get thrown all the way across the floor.

"What's going on?" I asked, trying to raise my voice over the commotion.

Monica looked me dead in the eye, forced out of her previous state.

"The others. Now."

She ran into a sprint towards the Victoria Secret across the street. I had no choice but to follow her closely. As I ran, I looked up to see the fire still blazing. Black smoke was already starting to fill the air and taint the sky with the harmful ash.

With the different directions people were running, it was impossible for people to clear the streets. Monica didn't bother to carefully move through the horde of people trying to flee. She would run straight and didn't stagger. People would be knocked down to the floor, scrambling to get up and keep running.

Panic started its course through my body. My legs shook with despair and I didn't have that good enough grip on the ground.

Shoulders bumped me and knocked me all over the place. Hands and elbows found their way to my face causing immense pain. I was already starting to sweat because of the heat from the fire despite it being hundreds of feet in the air.

The doors of Victoria's Secret kept getting thrown open from people rushing out the store. When we got in, racks of clothes were on the floor and things were broken from the panic. All it took was one explosion for all this chaos.

"Charlotte!" Monica screamed. "Will!"

"Wendy!" I joined in.

As we ventured further in the store in search of them, we noticed that a car was inside the store, crashed through a window. The others were there, surrounding something near the window.

"Mark! Monica!" Penn called us over. Her face told of the amount of anxiety she was in. "She got stuck when that car crashed in here," she said.

Charlotte was behind a wall of wood mixed with other material that was from a cheap wall that must've knocked down.

"I'm fine! Don't worry about me," Charlotte shouted to us. "What was that noise?"

"It was an explosion," Monica said. "The penthouse is on fire."

"An explosion?" Violet asked, her eyes widening.

Monica gave a fast nod.

Violet didn't hesitate at all and hurried in every way she could.

"We need to go. Mark get over here and make yourself useful. Lift that end and I'll lift this one," she said.

I got to where she wanted me as fast as I could. It'd be no point though. When I was scared and afraid, it affected me physically. For one, my whole body would shake like I was cold. My voice would crack and become shaky. I would turn into a total wreck and to lift a wall when I'm like this would result in nothing but more stress.

I tried my best to lift when she counted to three but I couldn't. I gave Will a look who was to the side of me. He knew I wanted his help. Without revealing what he was doing, he lifted his hand and helped us raise it.

Once the wall was removed, I reached out and grabbed Charlotte's hand, helping her up and out of her dark corner.

"Go go go!" Violet said, pushing us out of the building.

She was really bent on getting out of here. I was too so I had no objection to her direction. Right when we all got out of the store and back out into the street, a second explosion hit. This time it was closer to the middle of the building. The impact of it knocked us over, throwing us about like ragdolls.

I was flung into a car that was abandoned in the middle of the street. My backside rammed into the side mirror of it, making it almost impossible to stand now. I thought it would be best to just lay there and wait for the firemen or whoever to figure out what was happening in that building.

But then I remembered, this wasn't occupied by random people. These people made a name known for themselves. Obviously, there'd be no malfunctions in anything inside the building. Maintenance would be a high priority for the living conditions of these famous people. And with the power of the explosions, I was sure that this was no accident. It was an attack.

I looked around for the others and saw them struggling to get up as well. I wanted to try getting up again so I grabbed onto the car to try and pull myself up. My feet were almost back to standing but then I heard something. A cracking.

I looked back up at the building and saw that near the area of the second explosion, the thick foundation was giving way.

"Oh no. Oh no. Oh no." I quickly said to myself.

It was the encouragement I needed to stand back up.

I knew without a doubt this building was going to fall. So did the other bystanders that weren't as smart as the rest and stuck around to watch. The last flow of people pushed to make their way out of the clearing and we were among them. While we were running, there was another explosion on the opposite side of the cracking. With the way of the placing of the explosions, it meant only one thing. It'd be toppling over to one side, and that side was ours.

Trying to keep an eye out for where I was going and trying to watch when it was going to fall was difficult. The black of the street started to darken even more with the shadow of the building. It was now leaning and going to be starting its descent.

People were jumping out of windows hoping somehow they'd survive the fall. I couldn't bear to watch the result of their fall and kept running.

The seven of us ran with speeds that was spurred with the sheer impulse of living. There was one person out of all of us that outran us and constantly stayed a few feet ahead of us. Violet positioned herself at the front and pumped her arms so fast that they were a blur. She never wavered in her form. It was precisely like an athletic runner. Without a doubt, she must've had some practice running.

Glass started to shatter at the force in the shift of their usual vertical direction. The upper half of the building was hurdling its way downwards on top of us. This enormous structure appeared completely different when it was up close. Massive amounts of materials used to make this well-known building. Time, detail, and planning went into this and it was now going to be the death of me.

I tried my best to measure out and weigh if we were going to be able to get out in time. With how fast it was falling, we probably had a fifty-fifty chance at making it. We'd all be cutting it close. But what about them? What about the ones that were lagging behind; all those innocent people who happened to be on this street today?

It must've be instincts or something, but I naturally started to look for the top priority and that was women and children. So many people were behind us and I still wasn't sure *we* were going to make it. Surely they were doomed to the crushing weight of the building. But I saw someone. It was a lady. She was crying and struggling to run as fast as she could. In front of her was a stroller containing a baby with a blanket carefully placed over it.

My heart dropped at the thought that she wasn't going to make it. She was left for dead like the others right next to her. Why was I worth making it out and not her and her child? I looked among the superhumans running in front of me. Would it be worth showing what they can do to save two people; a mother and her child?

"Wendy!"

I only hoped she'd hear me above the screams. I tried inhaling as much as I could for my next shout, starting to get furious at the fact that I could hear her loud mouth at any time of the day and now she couldn't even listen for one dang second to save someone's life.

"Wendy!"

It was pointless. She was way too far ahead and concentrated on fleeing.

Mark, you selfish idiot. Why couldn't you help? So what you don't have any powers. What difference does it make? Someone's life is still in danger and you hoping to get their attention is not gonna help anything. Asking whether people seeing their powers is worth it is one of the stupidest things I could've asked. That wasn't the question at all. Was *my* life worth theirs?

Seeing Violet run as she did reminded me of who I was. She was the one who made me realize that I was just like the rest of the people in this world—the one that made me feel insignificant. I was no more important than anyone else.

My legs shifted directions as I started to head over towards her. Just as I was confident I wasn't going to be making it, Will came running from behind me towards her. His sprint was far exceeding mine. Using the momentum from his running, he threw his hand forward. She and the stroller were thrown out of the falling shadow only to be hit by a speeding car.

The shock made me slow down, forgetting about my demise above me. Her body lay there looking dead, blood already splattered across the windshield. The stroller had been launched into a glass bus stop, completely shattering it.

Both of us now stopped and stood next to each other, letting the rest of the people run by, not giving a care about us. I knew the building would make contact any second now. It was no use. We weren't going to make it.

Will's face watched in horror at his attempt to save someone. His hands lingered over his mouth. I was taken aback at the sight of him. His eyes watered with tears. The onslaught of emotion that he threw out terrorized me, showing me a side of him that was forbidden to any eyes other than his own.

*Swoosh*

"Come on!"

*Swoosh*

My hand was yanked on and I was suddenly where I was previously looking, just barely behind the line of sunlight. It took me a couple seconds to find out what actually happened. Realizing Wendy saved us, I kept on running. Will's eyes showed that he wasn't focused on the whether he'd be clearing the fall of the penthouse but rather on the lady on the floor, determined to make his way towards her.

The crumpling occurred right where I was a second ago, throwing up any debris on the floor into the air. My eyes and lungs filled with dust and forced out wheezy coughs.

I'd just barely made it. I cheated what was supposed to be the end of me. A part of me ticked. Yes, I should've been happy that Wendy helped us and made sure that we weren't underneath the penthouse, but yet, she doesn't even have the decency to care for others? Were we really all she cared about? I didn't feel relieved in the slightest. There were people who were laying under the building, completely flattened and I was here able to witness terror.

Will ran over towards the woman and Charlotte, seeing the stroller thrown, made her way towards the baby. Surprisingly, the child was okay. The mother on the other hand was another story.

"My baby!" she screamed from the floor, ignoring whatever pain she was in. Will had already propped her up against the door of the car and tried his best to comfort her. "Where's my baby?!" she continued to shout.

"He's over there. You see the girl with the short hair? Her name's Charlotte. She's holding your baby right now. He's okay. Now you need to tell me if you're hurt."

I'd never seen Will like this before. Usually he's just being a snob about everything and not giving a single care to anything but himself. He acts like he's better than everyone and this was exceeding all boundaries he'd set.

Once he'd made it to her, his eyes seemed to clear up and his face was as calm as could be, if it ever was calm.

"My leg," she whimpered, starting to realize the intensity of it.

Just then I noticed her leg wasn't in the right position. It must've torn ligaments and cracked bone, exposing the shredded muscle.

"We'll make sure that's dealt with, okay?" He turned around to get Charlotte's attention. "Bring the baby please."

The sight of her baby was all it took to fulfill her need of medicine. No amount of morphine could match what her child did.

"I don't think it'd be best if you hold him right now. You're in a lot of pain and it's not going to help."

"Will."

Violet stood next to him. He didn't bother to answer her. He was too focused on treating the woman as best as he could.

"Will," she said more stern. "We have to go. All of us."

"Yeah, and leave her here? I don't think so."

Violet drove her hand in his underarm to pull him to his feet, exerting an incredible force to her appearance.

"Charlotte, give her the baby. We need to leave. Now." Charlotte slowly started to hand over the baby, clearly not sure if what she was doing was the right thing. "Who's to say there isn't going to be another attack."

Charlotte, just handing the baby over, stood firmly. Her face contorted in frustration.

"You wanna leave when there's tons of people here who are hurt? How could you just leave them to die?!"

Violet looked Charlotte right in the eye, taking on her defiance.

"You don't think I care about these people? Of course I do. But it's my job to make sure you guys get out safely and back home to your parents."

Despite Violet not having any powers, she seemed to oppose us as did BloodLip. She was on Penn's side and she didn't have any objections towards her mother's commands.

Fortunately, the lady on the floor broke the tension.

"Hey guys. Go with her. Get out of the city. Please. It's the least you can do after helping me."

With the blood on her face and the broken leg; I couldn't stand to think that she'd just sit here and wait until someone would come and help her as we did. There were going to be so many other people needing medical assistance and who's to say that she'd get any help at all.

The corner of my mouth twitched.

"I'm not gonna leave you here."

"Yes you are." She looked up at Violet. "Your name?"

"Violet."

"Go with Violet. You've done enough."

How could one say no to her kind face despite all the pain in it? And if I were to oppose Violet, then what?

Violet, already leaving the scene, meant to leave in a hurry. She started off in a jog and headed off towards the suburban homes on the upward slope.

"I don't like this," Monica said.

"That makes two of us," I said, holding my frown.

"Five."

I turned towards Charlotte who had a face nastier than my own. Oh how she was right, I thought, as we stood back and watched Penn and Violet retreat not showing any compassion. You have no idea how much I wanted them to turn around and get smacked in the face with our opposition—our glares of disgust.

Our first few steps were met with hesitation to walk beside them, leaving behind the woman who was kinder than they ever would be. The woman who I'd meet once again and return the kindness.

\*      \*      \*

The more we ran through downtown, the more I realized what this had already done to people. Police cars, fireman, and paramedics. They were all there. They surrounded the extent of the building and started to search for any possible survivors in the wreckage. When I'd look back where I had bought Monica her bow, it was replaced with the extensive mass. It reminded me of the horrendous pictures and footage that we'd see in school of 9-11.

People stood on the sidewalks and cried. People would stand and take pictures. People would stand and watch. People were being people. I watched in awe all the different reactions to this. I was so engrossed in it that I didn't even have time to evaluate my own feelings on it. Heck, I was standing underneath it and if it weren't for Wendy I'd be dead.

I focused back on what was ahead of me as we trudged through. Violet would keep looking at her watch like she was waiting for something. Her head also didn't stop scanning the whole place. Every little detail would seep into her eyes and determine if it was lethal or not.

It was right when we were passing by the overpasses that overlapped each other. They snaked through the whole city connecting every little place with the overly used freeways. It was here that I noticed something. I was expecting the freeways to be packed by now because of the commotion. Instead, traffic was flowing just fine. That wasn't the thing though. There was a person standing in the middle of it allowing cars zip by this person. From what I could make out, it looked like a girl. Smaller stature so maybe a teenager? But a fixed position as hers meant opposition towards something. The others realized that I was staring at something and followed my vision.

Out of nowhere, the roar of two engines came into reach and filled our ears, replacing all other sounds with their own. I couldn't make out the models of the cars but they were no doubt high powered sports cars. They were racing towards this person that was standing there. They didn't budge one bit and but pressed on.

I was expecting a head on collision and the collapsing or even splattering of a body. Instead, the person lifted up their hand and pressed something. The ground in front of the person caved in and fell to the streets beneath the raised elevation. It was a second later that we heard the boom. The amount of smoke and debris from the explosion was consuming everything so I couldn't tell what happened to the cars or the girl.

The whole thing added to the confusion. No doubt the person on the bridge was related to the explosion and collapsing of the penthouse. But why? Why were they just standing there and who was in the cars? Were they chasing this person, hoping to run them over? Something about looking at the person standing there gave me a great sense of fear. You could see their outline drawn out by the shaded side of the sun. The more real this person became, the more I realized that human souls were involved in it, slapping me back to reality. There were people like this. Complete murderers with nothing more in their heartless pits of the joy of fear.

My eyes still focused on the overpass, encased in smoke. I didn't realize that Violet had pulled on my arm, forcing me over towards their direction. My ears were ringing because of constant barrage of explosion that I couldn't hear what she was telling me.

The whole experience was surreal. I didn't know what was going on the whole time. From what Penn told me, being confident involved knowing what was going to happen. What happened here was the complete opposite of that. There was no room for confidence. Only fear and confusion.

It was just what these terrorists wanted, a reaction, and I was giving it to them. The very feeling inside is what drove them. It's what made them happy. To entertain a thought like that was brutal.

All my life I thought I was safe. Even when I did encounter BloodLip, I didn't feel as threatened as I did now. These people were taking something from us and I didn't know why. No one did.

*     *     *

The walk home was quiet and morbid. Everyone's face was staring down to the floor. Each step being heavy, just lifting it up was a feat on its own. I could hear the soles of feet dragging along the sidewalk, slowly eroding their shoes.

Violet looked over at us and tried to say something but nothing came out of her mouth. She was most likely going to try and say something to cheer us up but it probably wouldn't have worked anyways. How could someone start a conversation after this?

"Hey Mark," Penn whispered.

Well, I guess the only person would be her.

She was walking besides me the whole time. When I looked up to face her, I noticed there were a few marks on her face, some showing blood.

"I need to talk to you."

"About what?"

We were on our street when Penn stopped in the middle of the sidewalk. Her quick stop made everyone else look back. She eyed her mom and bobbed her head towards the end of the street, signaling her to keep going. I didn't know why she wanted to talk to me but it was clearly something related to her abilities I supposed.

Charlotte and the others looked at me to see if they were supposed to go as well. I gave a nod assuring them that it was okay for them to go. Leaving me with Penn was something they knew I didn't particularly enjoy, but giving her the privacy she wanted was important.

After waiting a couple seconds for there to be some distance between us, she started to speak.

She started off with a huge sigh.

"I know it's kinda out of the blue, but it's something I need to ask you. Well, I've been wanting to ask you this since the day we met."

I had no idea what she was leading towards.

"Do you want to join BloodLip?"

"What?"

"Look. I know. We started off kinda rough with each other but it was needed."

"Why would I ditch my friends and join you guys?"

"I'm not saying you can't be friends with them. I'm just asking that you join us."

"Yeah? And what exactly are you? Because to me, you're all a bunch of murderers who think they're higher than everyone else."

I didn't hold back from what I knew. It was too long that I knew what she did. It bothered me to the point of not wanting to look in her eyes. And with the way she was asking me to just join them was starting to infuriate me.

She skipped a breath and her eyes widened. letting the smoke stenched air sting her eyes. She'd been found out. The surprised looked was soon replaced with an angered face that matched the one I saw in the shed a few months back.

"How'd you know about that?" she muttered hastily.

"You didn't think we'd find out about you guys? I mean, how more obvious could you get?! You were practically giving yourselves away!"

"You think I had a choice?! Do you think that I wasn't scared out of my mind when I had to pull the trigger, looking into the eyes of the very man that'd be killed by *my* hands? Do you think that I had a say in any of this?!"

The raising of her voice started to take me aback. She began to set her dominance and I didn't like it. The way her eyes peered into mine and claimed everything I owned. She started to strain with every word and made me feel inferior. But I wouldn't let her do it. She wouldn't take control of me. Not this time.

"But you still had a choice whether to pull the trigger or not."

"You don't know what's really going on, Mark. There's so much that you don't know. That's why. That's why I need you with us. I want to tell you so much but I'm not allowed to unless you're a part of us."

"So there's more of you then."

"Yeah."

Monica honed everything down pretty well. It seems like she hit it right on the dot.

"And you want me because I'm the Equilibrium?"

"Not entirely. That's a part of why we want you, but, that's not all. I need you."

Tears started to well up in her eyes as her voice broke up. She leaned in for a hug and I didn't know what to do. It was unexpected. She was just yelling at me a second ago and now this. I allowed the hug but didn't do the same to her.

"If you don't say yes they'll give me orders that I can't carry out," she whispered in my ear. "I have to protect you. Please, Mark. Just at least think about it. Promise me that."

Fear wasn't a factor in this. I'd known this feeling when I got the call at school. The heads of this group wanted me dead if I wasn't on their side. But why'd they want me so badly? It just goes back around and makes a full circle coming back to the question: what the heck am I?

As much as I'd regret doing so, it'd probably save the others from trouble. Would it be worth it though? I didn't want to think about it right then and there.

"I promise."

She stood back and unlatched from her hug. Her eyes examined my face and smiled. I saw the tears that had fallen from her eyes and smeared all over her cheeks and probably my sweater.

"You going to the party tomorrow?" she asked.

"If it's even still going on."

"I'll ask Emily and see."

"If it is, then yeah, I'll be there."

"You think you could have an answer for me then?"

"Sure."

Penn took in a ragged breath. Now that that was over, I could see her a little differently. She was trying to protect me. That was all. Was I so selfish to think that she was cruel—a ruthless person?

The pain in her face was evident. It probably wasn't easy being in BloodLip. Although I didn't know a thing about it, I could see it had a big effect on her.

Tears rolled down her face again as she gave me a desperate look. Her small hand came up and gave a tiny wave before turning around and heading back home.

I was left there to my thoughts. Who knew who these people were, what they wanted, or why they wanted it. If I wasn't to be joining Penn, I'd be killed like the man in the 911 call just because they wanted my dumb powers that I didn't know what they were. Why was I the special one? Why am I the one they wanted?

If it means the protection of Charlotte, Will, Monica, and Wendy I might do it. She said I could still be friends with them. I'd just have to do what they do, whatever that is.

I still had time to think it over so I tried my best to save it for later that night when I'd be alone by myself in my room.

Before I started to head home, I turned around. The upwards street that continued straight towards the school was tilted because of the inclined slope of the mountain. Anyone following the road towards downtown would have a perfect view of it. Usually when I looked at it, it'd be just as huge as it always was. When I looked at it now, it looked like a complete mess. Smoke still billowed up from the streets and the penthouse that stuck out of the ground was now nowhere to be found.

I didn't know how to really feel about it. About everything. Once again, I was thrown into something I never asked for. Hopefully the party tomorrow would make me feel better.

After all, it was just a party.

# Chapter 6

There was a soft cool breeze that comforted me. The sun was now starting to set and painted the sky with a beautiful masterpiece. The way the colors mixed and blended into the clouds made me think of how far the sky was. It had its own realm and was secluded from everybody. The clouds were beings so grand and marvelous that no one could touch them. No matter what someone wanted to do to them, they couldn't contain it. They silently floated, not giving a care to a single problem, to anyone or anything.

Why couldn't we be like them?

The collar of my shirt irritated my neck. I hardly ever wore dress clothes. Penn texted Emily and found out that the party was still going on despite what happened. She said that if anything, it'd help take it off the minds of people. I hoped it'd do the same for me.

The party was to be a formal one she explained on the last day of school before break. Everyone was to dress formally in suits and dresses. There'd be some formal dancing for the beginning of it but after that they'd shift into the regular pop music for parties. All this would be held at her mansion. She told me that her parents are both big corporate people that own companies around the world. They had some things to do with it this week and needed to travel. They told her she could have a party or whatever she wanted. It's funny because it's usually the opposite. Parents tend to not trust their children as much and think they'll do the worst possible thing they can think of if they leave them alone. But with Emily, she was the most well-mannered person I knew, not lashing out to any sort of opposition she came into contact with at school, or anywhere else for that matter.

Her mansion was located at the top of the mountain, somewhat following the same path that Charlotte and I took to get to the spot she liked.

I texted everyone to see if they wanted to walk together. Of course, three of them being girls and one of them being Will, it'd take longer for them to get ready.

You have to be reasonable when you're in this type of situation. I wasn't a girl. I had no idea how they worked. Not mentally nor anything when it came to their style. To me, all it involved was putting the dang clothes on and not taking an hour looking in the mirror to see if it compliments you or not. You know, I said I have to be reasonable with them, doesn't mean I was though and found myself frustrated that they couldn't just put on the dang dress.

I was told to go on by myself and they'd meet me there. I would've overall not really cared but I wanted to see Charlotte in her dress before anyone else could. I wanted the sweet air between us to clasp together as we talked and made our way up to her mansion. I wanted that moment that'd add to the rest of the recollected memories I'd never forget with her. Instead, I just had to let out a sigh and deal with it, convincing myself I shouldn't be stingy.

Charlotte did, though, tell me she was almost done even though she really wasn't. I could hear her dropping stuff in her bathroom when she was talking to me as she tried hurrying up, carelessly putting hairspray on and not giving thought to getting her phone all sticky. Wendy being in the same bathroom as her was quick to tell her to just stay with her. And, me being good old me, told her to go ahead and do as she said. As bad as it sounds, I loved the sadness in Charlotte's voice as she gave a solemn okay, knowing she wanted to do the same as I did. I used that and reminisced over it as I trudged up the hill.

When I was walking up the long street, I looked at the entrance to the housing track that Penn and Violet lived in. She was no doubt getting ready as well, awaiting my answer. I gave it a good long think over last night. I got to the conclusion that if it meant saving the others, I'd join them. At least I could find out what I really was and how we got these powers.

When I drew nearer to the top of the mountain, I realized that I'd never been to a party like this. I'd been to some graduation parties for relatives but this was different. I'd be accompanied with friends that I never had. I would actually enjoy myself and experience what everyone has been feeling from the beginning of time. I'd been left out too long and I wanted to make up the time I'd lost.

Just let me fill the pains of sorrow.

\*       \*       \*

The place was huge! I never knew there were houses this big.

Everyone was walking in through the gated entrance that welcomed you to the grand estate. A lawn longer than any park complimented the home. Of course, there were fountains and luxuries that occupied it.

As I made my way through the entrance, I saw many faces that were familiar and said hi to the occasional person who took the initiative. When you invite the whole school to your party, you start to actually realize how dangerous this actually was. Hundreds of teenagers were going to be in the same place for a whole night and there'd be no parent supervision.

Like it'd matter all that much anyways.

A crowd of people were standing around outside near the side of the house. There was a patio, porch, deck, pool, tables, and a DJ. A perfect place for a party. On the opposite side of the house was another building that connected with it, making a perfect little cocoon. It made easy setup for the place. Without a doubt, Emily had a pleasant time putting this together.

"Hi Mark."

Emily walked up to me and greeted me personally. She was wearing a simple and plain dress with a light amount of makeup allowing the small touch ups to bring out the beauty of her naturalness, something a lot of girls had trouble doing.

"Hey, um, listen," she said, trying to find the right words to say. There probably wasn't a moment when she was talking to me that she looked me in the eye. "Penn told me you were there yesterday. I was watching everything on the news and to think you were among the people who I saw running away from the penthouse is pretty scary. Are you okay?"

I loved her sincerity and I followed it with an involuntary chuckle. Not being used to it and all made it hard not to.

"Yeah, I'm doing okay. Thanks."

"Good," she said, her face lighting up and dipping like a child pleading for something with their hands clapped together. "Thanks for coming. I really didn't think you'd come but you're here now right? I guess that shows not to think you know someone cause you really never know. You could be hiding something for all I know," she said with a giggle.

"Uh…yeah. Hehe."

I rubbed the back of my neck, doing the complete opposite of not looking nervous.

"Anyways, I don't expect you to stay here long since you could still be caught up in what happened yesterday but do me a favor and just try to have fun, okay?"

"Sure thing."

She gave a small bow and ran off to greet the other guests with a wide smile as I made my way towards the crowd ready to hide myself in their carelessness.

Lights hung from the patio and all over the elegant fences that encased the area. The tables that surrounded the dance floor served all kinds of snacks and appetizers. I didn't feel that comfortable because some of the people here were people that I just saw. I never really talked to them all that much. So instead of standing there waiting for Charlotte, I occupied my time with slowly stuffing my face with the food. And of course, taking drinks from the classic punch bowl.

Next to the punch bowl was a bench. On that bench were the two siblings that wanted me in pain for some reason that I still didn't know. I made eye contact with the one who hurt the daughter of the very owner of this house, wishing I never looked in this direction.

"Well howdy!" Sarah shouted, giving an overly dramatic wave of her hand.

"Uh...hey."

I grabbed a cup of punch and sat in the bench next to theirs, forced to interact with them more. If I were to just leave after saying hi, I'd look like a complete jerk.

I was surprised that Eli actually had a smile on his face for once. His suit jacket that was almost just as tight as his regular tees was on the verge of snapping the useless button that held it together.

"So where's your pretty faced girl. You're dressed up in a suit and she's not even here?" She scoffed. "You're pathetic."

"You mean Charlotte?"

"Well who else you dunce?" Eli said.

"We're not dating."

"I never said you were. Everyone knows you guys like each other so stop acting like you don't when someone comes out and says it." I didn't have anything to say in response so I sipped from my cup. "Ugh! You're an idiot you know. Where's the others?"

"They're still getting ready."

"Even that Gucci little jerk?"

I nodded my head, not needing to think twice of who she was talking about.

"What about Brittany?" I asked. "Is she coming?"

"She's here already," Eli said. He nodded his head in the direction she was standing. She was chatting it up with one of the girls from one of my classes.

"I hope you decided," Sarah said, coming out of nowhere with it, still looking in the direction of Brittany.

"Yeah," I said, almost with a sigh. The fact that she knew what decision I had to make meant that Penn told them. How much did they really know? What was the grounds for communication in this group? They all must've known that Penn wanted me for a while now.

"What do you mean yeah? Did you or not?" said Sarah. She was quick to return to raising her voice at me just as she did at school.

"Why would I leave something like that just floating in my mind and not answer it?"

"I don't know. Maybe because you're stupid."

"You think that's supposed to help in persuading me into joining you guys?"

They both looked me directly in the eye with malice.

"We don't want you in BloodLip."

"Penn surely does."

"Well that's Penn," Eli said. "We want to help her and make her happy, even if that means bringing you in. You should consider yourself lucky that she wants to help protect you."

"I'd surely be grateful," Brittany said in a cheery voice, coming out of nowhere. She sat next to me on the bench and wrapped an arm around to touch my other shoulder for a quick side hug.

"When's she coming?" I asked.

"She should be here any minute now."

For a few minutes, we sat in silence. I begged that one of them would walk through that gate and save me from this torment.

The amount of perfume that Brittany was wearing was overwhelming and distracted me from the awkwardness of the situation for a few moments. It didn't get to the point where you'd start to die of coughing too much, so it was somewhat enjoyable to smell.

She wore a white dress that acted as a cloth that wrapped around her body, pulling at the waist. When she lifted a hand to pull back her hair a bit, I could see inside her dress. In there I saw the same brown tank top that she wore when we first fought on the second day of school. Her eyes just barely caught me peeking and spoke of all revulsion.

She quickly pulled her arm down to stop me from looking in.

"Aren't you naughty."

"No, it's not like that! I just noticed your tank top."

"Well you still had to look to see that. What if I didn't have it on, huh?"

"It's not my fault you wore a loose dress." She rolled her eyes and secretly tugged at the back of her dress to bring it in closer to her body. "Is that the same tank top from when you fought us?"

"Yeah. I always wear it in case I need to use my powers. It's fireproof. I like my body, but not enough to go around fighting without a shirt on."

"And where do you find that sort of thing? Black Market?"

"Sure, because I'm all over that market," she said sarcastically. "I had someone make it for me."

"Who?"

She wrapped an arm around my neck to lean on me as couples would do. Her hand gradually started to heat up and burn as she rested it on my neck.

"Well, I could tell you that once you join us. Actually, I wouldn't need to. You'll just meet her in the first place."

My neck was stinging with pain, silently begging her to stop her weird seductive approach.

Her face changed in an instant and, as letting a curtain dropped, revealed a classic BloodLip face full of anger and annoyance. She spoke in a firm voice toying with my reality.

"Don't disappoint, Mark."

Brittany let her hand go and helped me stand up. She then scooted in towards Eli and Sarah where I was previously sitting. I stood wondering why she made me get up but as I awkwardly took up space in front of them and they started a conversation of their own, I realized they didn't want me there anymore.

My eyes scanned and searched for something to recover from my awkward position. At the start of the tables, I saw the others. They were all wearing formal dress clothes as they were told. It looked strange to see them like that, almost like I wasn't supposed to for some reason.

Wendy walked towards me as the rest lagged behind and started to chat with a few people. She wore a modern and outgoing dress; if you could even call it that. It was in two pieces. She wore a sleeveless top that exposed some of her slim stomach. For the second piece, it was a grey tight fitting skirt that came down to around her knees. It was accompanied by some black heels and white cuffs that seemed like they were detached from another article of clothing. They stood on their own on her bare arms marking themselves as accessories.

What surprised me the most was that her trademark was gone, nowhere to be seen. Those fat gold pigtails that slapped me in the face so many times were rolled up into Leia-like buns on the side of her head. Looking at her as a whole, she looked really good.

I decided I might as well go ahead and tell her since she did saved my life yesterday.

"Wow Wendy."

"Shut up," she said, quickly looking away.

"No, you look really nice."

"I said shut up!" Her face started to blush. The brown eyes of hers would meet mine and immediately give up and retreat, falling back at the ground. "I'm not the one you should be complimenting."

She jerked her thumb back towards where Charlotte was standing. Charlotte, chatting away with some other girls, caught me looking at her. A beautiful smile that was worth more than anything greeted me. She ended her conversation and walked up to me.

"Hey," I said.

"Hi."

My insides started to bubble up. She looked wonderful in her dress. It was just as I imagined it'd be; modest in every form. It was a black and pink dress with a belt that wrapped around her waist. A bright pink shawl was draped over her shoulders.

For once, I was lost for words. I had no idea what to say. I finally understood the meaning of when a girl makes you speechless. I could've been stupid and said something completely random or maybe do the right thing and compliment her, but I did neither. I somehow felt that I already complimented her. Doing so would only sound pointless.

We stood there for a while and enjoyed the awkwardness. I didn't mind this kind. It was enjoyable for my stomach to go on this rollercoaster of joy.

"You look good," she said, finally breaking the barrier of speechlessness.

"It's only because of the suit," I said.

"No you always look good but..." She caught herself again. Her word choice was always something I enjoyed when she was nervous. No matter how upset I'd be, it would always lift me up.

"Well don't you look fancy," Will said, approaching us and helping Charlotte recover from her unfinished sentence.

He wore a suit that was as stylish as can be. The slim and pressed dress pants that he wore with it made him look even taller than he already was.

"It's not like it matters. You out dress me every time."

"Oh give yourself some credit. When was the last time you wore a suit? Never, I presume. These things aren't that cheap you know, and buying one meant you wanted to look good. Right?"

"It was my dad's."

"Either way, you put an effort."

"And since when has that meant anything to you?"

He gave a small chuckle.

"I sometimes like to think I'm a good human being. This just happens to be a day when I do."

"Yeah, but that doesn't necessarily mean that you mean it."

"Well that's up to you to decide."

I gave a scoff. Of course he wasn't being sincere. This idiot was as heartless as Wendy.

He passed me and gave a pat on my shoulder.

"Nice try with the suit," he said as his voice faded away.

Charlotte seemed to return to her normal self.

"Don't listen to him."

"You don't think I know how to deal with him already?"

"I sometimes forget myself. His words can sting."

"Just rely on Wendy to sting him right back but even harder."

While we laughed, I realized that Monica was standing there the whole time. She wore her blank expression along with her new bow that I bought her. Seeing Monica wear a dress was something I never pictured. Of course, she chose the darkest dress someone could possibly wear. Her one piece dress reminded me of the ones that people on the red carpet wear. It was so plain that it matched her expression.

Seeing all of them dressed like that made me feel somewhat special. Although there were people that wore these kinds of clothes all the time, we didn't. It felt like there was some unwritten rule that you needed to be someone of importance to see them like this. Whether or not I was the only one that felt like that was something that I couldn't answer.

The area dedicated towards the party was now starting to overflow. It had already started to feel like a party with the soft play of music in the background and the ambiance of the chattering.

People started occupying the dance floor. Couples were draped over each other as they glided around. I wasn't much of a fan for the kind of music they were playing. I guess some of the reason that was the case was because I didn't know how to slow dance. It looked way too complex and too hard to bother even trying.

I continued to spend most of my time with the others at the snack tables. There were types of foods that probably cost hundreds of dollars. I kinda felt bad to be eating them. This food was reserved for the people that could actually afford it.

My jaw froze mid-chew when I felt a tap on my shoulder.

I turned to see Penn standing right in front of me, dressed to perfection with a red one piece dress that split at her thighs and back.

My immediate reaction was fear. In my mind she was associated with the fate of my life. Despite all that, I was ready to give her my answer. The recited couple sentences that I was planning on telling her were ready to be told.

She put up a hand and paused me before I could even say anything.

"Don't tell me yet. I don't want to think about it that much today. Yes, I'm going to need your answer but just tell me after the party. I'd rather have fun today. Agreed?"

"All right." I said, hating the fact that I'd have to wait. I wanted to get the dang thing over with. I wanted the stress of the matter to be gone. Done.

"Great." She extended her hand and reached it out to be grabbed. Oh boy. I wasn't ready for this. She just gets to the party and she already wanted to dance? I wouldn't really care all that much if it wasn't this type of music. "Would you like to dance?"

I knew I had to. There was no way around it. Even if I didn't accept, she'd find a way to convince me with her dominance. Better to just get it over with now when there were people still getting here.

I reached out to grab her hand. I was expecting a soft grip, but was, instead, met with a tug from my hand, pulling me away from Penn.

"I'd love a dance!"

Penn's face turned and followed me while I was pulled from her. The voice of the girl was distinct. It was one that had a creepy tone to it. One that could entice and lure in anyone with the seductive vocals and this Siren had just snatched me.

I remember red's mouth dropping open in utter shock that someone had just stolen her dance without even acknowledging her.

The hand that grabbed mine spun me around to make me face her. My assumption was correct. I'd be more upset if someone else did that sort of thing, but I did kind of owe her.

Eris eyed me down with her deceitful eyes. Somehow they appeared darker than Monica's. That combined with her pale white skin made her look like a member of the living dead. She wore a dress very similar to the one that she normally wears. Black laces that mimicked spider webs filled the holes in her ruffled skirt.

For a few seconds, we danced, if you could even call it that. We were practically throwing our limbs around in random patterns. We weren't even following the flow of the song that was playing.

She showed her white teeth when she started to laugh.

"Let me guess. You don't know how to dance."

"It's not something you'd need to guess."

She looked up and kept her gaze with my eyes.

"Okay. Follow my lead. By the end of the night you'll be able to dance with Charlotte." Her creepy smile was amplified to an extent I never thought was possible. "I promise."

Her hand grabbed mine and she placed it so I was holding her hip. Her other hand laced around my own hand and her fingers fell through the webbing. Our hands were now interlocked. To top it off, Eris put her hand behind my back and laid it out flat.

"Alright. So this is how you're gonna do it. When you place your hand on her hip, you'll surely surprise her. When she's caught off guard, grab her other hand and hold it like we are right now. Just make sure that when your fingers fall through hers, that they fall slowly. If she doesn't know where to put her hands then go ahead and help her."

"Eris. I need help dancing, not help in trying to seduce one of my friends."

She gave a giggle.

"It can work both ways if you want. Just make sure you keep eye contact."

Despite her telling me to keep a locked gaze, I still looked down at where my feet were going. I was careful to make sure I didn't step on her black high heels. She must've had it way harder than I did, and yet, she still managed to pull off dancing with an idiot that had no idea how to move to a rhythm. Her swift body movements and the way she moved her hips in circular motions made her look quite enticing.

Both of us turned our heads when we saw Emily walk out of her mansion and out towards the tables. She called Wendy and Penn over inside the house. Wendy left the group that Charlotte and Monica were in and followed Emily and Penn in.

I gave Charlotte a look to see if she was watching us. She was watching intently while she sipped her cup of punch. It took her a while to realize that I was looking back at her. She gave a nervous smile and looked away in embarrassment.

"What do you think Charlotte's thinking? You know, we're dancing and all. You with another girl. Hmmm?" Eris asked.

"Uh...I don't—"

She leaned in close to my ear to the point where her lips were practically touching them.

"What if I gave you a kiss? What about then?"

I could feel the muscles in my face contort. The way Eris talked was so random. One second she could be behaving modestly and the next trying to manipulate someone.

The picture of her lips being on mine made me quiver. It's not that she wasn't pretty. Heck, if I was into the gothic look, I'd be completely into her. It was just that

Charlotte was looking, and for someone to kiss me when I liked her would go against all my desires.

She was quick to read my face and shot down her own suggestion.

"Geez! I was only kidding."

"You're going to confuse someone if you keep doing that."

"Yeah. I forget how hormonal you teenage boys are."

"Like teenage girls aren't."

"We can hide our emotions a little easier."

"And you say that why?"

Her smile broke through the music and the chatter.

"Because it's the truth."

After dancing for a few minutes, I started to get the hang of how I was supposed to dance. I would place my foot forward as she slid hers back. I would also use the leverage of me holding her hip to direct us through the dance floor. While I held her hip, my heart would randomly jump. Something about the way her hip felt, the firmness of the bone and the slight amount of fat that expressed it to some extent had such an amazing impact on me. I didn't realize that being this close to a girl really had that much of an effect on me. I guess Eris was right. It's hard for us to hide our emotions. If I can't be fine while holding a girls hip, how would I get if a girl kissed me?

I thought again of the sensation I'd never experienced. The feeling of another person's lips against your own. It was so common but when you broke it down, it seemed kind of weird. Even though I'd never kissed a girl, it was always something that was praised. If you hadn't kissed a girl yet, you were looked at as weird. I'm just glad the conversation hadn't come up yet.

It made me wonder. Had Charlotte ever kissed someone?

I directed us so we were slowly turning and I wouldn't make it obvious that I was looking at her. Eris seemed to catch on to what I was doing. She let a puff out of her nostrils in a silent chuckle and disregarded my secrecy, looking at where Monica and Charlotte were standing.

After looking for a while and me hoping she'd stop, she started to shake her head.

"Monica's funny you know," she said.

"Why's that?"

"She thinks she's doing it right."

I darted my eyes over to the right to see what she was doing. Monica stood with her normal face and quietly talked to Charlotte. She wasn't doing anything wrong.

"Doing what?" I asked.

"Funny enough, Monica and I are alike in many ways. We don't want people to know about us. We rely on the advantage we have." She put a hand in front of her face and slowly slid it upwards, waving and wiggling her fingers around. "The mystery."

"And how's she doing that wrong?"

"She does it by not giving any information at all. She tries her best not to budge when someone persists to find out about her. The face she uses; it's not the best. If that's always displayed, people look at you even though you want the exact opposite."

"But if they see her face, they realize what kind of person she is and leave her alone," I said, trying to defend Monica's uniqueness.

She returned her hand to my back and lightly scratched it. Chills built its way up towards my neck.

"Wouldn't you think it would be better if you deceived someone? If you were arrested for murder and the investigators are questioning you, would you rather not say anything and hopefully they'll leave you alone, or would it be better to mislead them and tell them someone else did it? That way they leave you alone and arrest someone else and they think they caught the right person."

She was starting to scare me because of how true her words were.

"This face," she said, pointing at it, "is the one that she should be using."

It was her usual haunting grin. It spread from cheek to cheek and never wavered. I'd never seen her without it. Every day when she walked through the door for homeroom, I saw her with that smile. Without it, she wouldn't be the Eris I knew.

"I use it to make sure people don't know me. They see a smile they don't like and they leave me alone. It also helps me hide my feelings. When I get upset, I make sure it grows. I want to keep people in the dark with every chance I get. With Monica, people aren't that intimidated. I'm not saying hers doesn't work. I'm just saying it's not that effective."

I looked at the ground as I thought about what she had said. Monica with a smile like Eris's? Yeah, that's not gonna work. Monica was fine just the way she was. I loved her blank face. It made me feel safe and reassured me that everything was okay. For that to be broken would seem like a crime on some of the highest levels.

Eris's hand left my back and was waving around in front of me. I focused on what she was doing and realized that she was signaling to the DJs. There were two people behind the turntables. There was a girl with dark hair that seemed to have a purple tint to it. There was also a guy with scruffy hair that blew around with the slight breeze. The black dye in it was incredibly overbearing, not trying to keep the natural look at all.

"You know them?" I asked.

"Mhm," she said as she gave a nod.

"Oh, I didn't know you had friends."

The grip that we had in our interlocked hands intensified. I could feel the straining of her hand as she squeezed with all her might. The fingers that wrapped over my hand started to press into the top of my hand where all the tendons to my fingers laid.

I quickly checked her face for anger but I saw nothing but the usual smile. The only difference I noticed was that it was larger.

"Friends?" she said in a calm voice.

She unlatched from me and looked me in the eye.

"Thanks for the dance. Remember. Hips, hands, and eye contact."

Still confused from her sudden fit of anger that she hid, I gave a small nod. Eris gave a wink and blew me a kiss before entering the mansion with hips swaying in her seductive manner, making heads turn.

I wanted to get off of the dance floor as quickly as I could. Without a dance partner, I'd be out of place.

Instinctively, my feet directed me towards where Charlotte and Monica stood. Will and Wendy had already seemed to join them.

"What'd Emily want?" I asked Wendy.

"She needed help moving boxes." She put her hands on her hips and I readied myself for a rant. "Out of all the people here, she had to choose me. I mean, why the heck didn't she ask you to help? I got dressed for a reason and it's not to lift dang boxes."

Will caught my attention with a mischievous smirk.

"So how'd your dance go?"

"Alright, I guess."

"What was Eris saying?"

"Just a bunch of random stuff."

"You mean about how she thinks *she's* doing it right?" Monica said, looking away that made it seem like a silent scoff. "She thinks she knows how to do it."

"Wait. You heard what we were talking about?"

I felt a buzz from the phone in my pocket. I pulled it out and saw that I got a text message from Monica.

*Yes*

"I'm hooked up to all your phones. I can access all your information if I wanted to. Don't worry, I don't look up what you're doing. I mainly use it for safety purposes. But just now I used your microphone and listened to your conversation." Good thing I didn't say anything bad about any of them. "Including the conversation you had yesterday with Penn."

My intestines felt like they gave way to an extreme amount of gravity and fell to the deepest part of me. I knew I screwed up.

All of them were looking at me, waiting for my reaction to this. I held my head in one place. To turn it meant looking into the eyes of the person I loved most. Seeing Charlotte's face would make me kill myself.

"Why didn't you tell us?" Monica asked. "You didn't think you could trust us?"

Wendy went ahead and threw in her two cents.

"You better not be joining them."

"Are you?" Charlotte asked with a voice that I'd never heard before. It was one of deep concern and one that I never wanted to occupy the space in my ears anymore.

They were all right, though. I should've trusted them. What am I even saying? I did trust them. They would've helped me regardless. It was just that I didn't trust myself all that much. I felt that this was my problem. That was just selfish of me to think that I should be the one to decide. It involved them greatly. BloodLip had once attacked us before and another one was imminent, and this time, they wouldn't hold back.

"Are you that desperate to save your own skin?"

Her voice made me finally look up and into her eyes. Monica was never one to speak like that. I could clearly see that she was upset. It was something only someone who'd been around her for a long time could see.

"Of course not! You know that. If I joined them, that'd mean I could get some information for you guys on what exactly we are. I didn't want to save myself, Monica. I wanted to save all of us. They'd find me and you're aware that they won't hold back on you guys either."

"It was pretty stupid of you to not talk to us about it," Will said. "It's our problem too."

"Yeah I know. I screwed up, okay? Now we have the chance to talk about it."

"You had your chance," Monica said. "Now you make your own decision."

To hear that from the person that I knew the best felt like a bullet through my heart. We had so much in common and she not once had gotten upset at me. It made me remember how she was back when I first met her. Had she slipped back into her old self? No. She was the same exact person I met. She just adjusted around us. She tolerated things that would've ticked her off previously. She was able to express herself more freely and in ways she had never done before such as the attempt at the hug she tried giving me yesterday.

I couldn't help but agree with Eris once again. As much as I wanted to side with Monica, Eris had some degree of logic to her claim. Monica, although very quiet, was able to express her emotions easily this way. When I thought about it, I didn't know what kind of person Eris really was. And if she wanted to her keep her true self a secret, then why'd she let me know what she does to hide it?

Monica sat down in one of the benches next to me and sipped from her cup. I desperately wanted to say something to her or apologize but for some reason, I couldn't. My mind was empty. It was all my fault and I couldn't even do the least of things and say I was sorry. What kind of friend was I?

Just as I was finally about to tell her something, she stood up.

"Where you going?" Charlotte asked.

"To the bathroom. Where are they?"

"Oh! I know where they are," Wendy said.

All of them, including Will, followed Wendy inside the mansion to the bathrooms. I thought I might as well follow them even though I wanted to just stay away from them since I felt like I didn't fit in and sat as far back as possible.

Wendy explained that the bathrooms were like ones at a restaurant or the mall containing multiple stalls and sinks. I was pretty much lost in thought the whole time to even look around at the decedent decorations on the walls.

Once you walked through the doors of the mansion, the hallway was blocked off with a wall that forced you to either go left or right. The girls was on the left and the mens on the right. We split and went our separate ways and that was when I walked through the bathroom door.

*    *    *

My hands had already started to dry up due to the quick exposure to the air after being submerged in the faucet's water. I'd splashed some water on my face to try and help me wash away my previous conversation. Hearing Monica's voice like that was horrible. Feelings of regret weighed heavy inside me. I still needed to apologize and I still wanted to. But I wasn't sure if I had the capability to do it. If I joined BloodLip, that'd just go to put her down even more, making me look a complete idiot for not doing what I should've. I shook my head to get the thoughts out of my head. Penn was waiting for the end of the day and that meant so was I.

The paintings on the wall called me over to draw my attention away from my stress. Delicate and precise works of paint filled in the canvas where white used to occupy it. Every stroke seemed like it needed a series of math calculations to pinpoint where that brush would be making contact. It was so far from me that someone would have the patience and ability to do this.

I looked for an artist's signature. Down at the bottom left hand side was black scribbling so small I could barely keep its place after I blinked. It amazed me to think this person left behind something so beautiful. The painting consisted of a stormy night and a ship was right in the middle of it, helpless to the waves of the sea. Maybe the painter and I had something in common. We both were thrown into something we never asked for. It was something that happened every day, but to be controlled and manipulated and all you can do is stand there was a cruel form of torture.

The more I looked at it, the more I appreciated it. Art never really intrigued me, but now I saw a reason as to why it did for some people. You could find a connection to your own life and problems and sympathize with the artist. I had no idea who the person that painted this was and even if I could read who it was, I still wouldn't know. But whoever it was, I hope that whatever storm he was in, whatever trials befell him, that he was able to make it out. Another part of me started thinking and thought maybe he didn't. Maybe he was destroyed by it in the process. Would I be like him?

Would I be able to look back at this mess I was in now and remember how desperate I was?

I heard a door open on the other side of the hallway. The triangle with an image of a girl with a skirt standing in it was displayed in the light. Charlotte had walked out of the bathroom with a smile on her face so wide I was convinced someone was pulling on it. I stood there, confused as to why she'd be smiling after finding out that there'd be a chance I was to join BloodLip. Maybe she was trying to make me feel better. After all, she was probably the only one who could do that very thing. With a smile that contagious, it'd surely pick me up. I turned to face her as she walked down the hallway towards me. My mouth had already started to be lifted at the sight of her, but this time it was trying to match the extent of her grin. Once I realized how wide her smile actually was, I reevaluated the reason for it.

A hand traveled behind her. It was left there a second before coming back out, revealing a pistol.

My smile fell at the sight of the gun. The last time I saw her with a gun was when we first fought BloodLip. The girl on the phone left a duffle bag in the supply closet for our use. Seeing the gun meant the next couple of minutes weren't going to be good. There must be another fight that was supposed to happen and the girl contacted one of them again.

The two other girls walked out of the bathroom and joined Charlotte. Wendy looked as happy as can be as she hopped her way down the hallway. Monica's face was somehow different. It wasn't that she was upset form our talk, but rather, she was confident. Her walk was casual, but yet, she was able to pull off her firm look. Something was different and I could tell.

I looked back at Charlotte and noticed as she drew closer, that she was holding the gun in her hand with the nozzle looking up at the ceiling as if she were holding back from shooting something. The gun then came down and was pointed at the ground as she pulled the top, letting it fly back and make a sound only meaning imminent death.

For her to load the gun meant someone was right behind me. I turned my head and looked only to see the thing I feared the most. What was happening? Why was the gun cocked? Why were they all coming towards me? All these questions started to pour in while my eyes stared back at the wall that was behind me.

"Charlotte?" I asked, realizing my voice was already starting to crack.

"Yeah?" she said nonchalantly.

"What are you doing?"

All of them started to laugh. Please. Please let me in on the joke. What was it that I was missing? My feet backed up automatically. Was I really afraid of them? It must be some kind of prank they were pulling. They knew better than to walk around here with a gun open for anyone to see if they walked through those double doors.

The worst started looking like it was the only reason for what was happening. As much as I didn't want to believe it, I had to accept the truth. I had to accept what was right in front of me. And that truth was that they wanted to hurt me.

I turned around and ran the other way. The soles of my dress shoes dug into the expensive carpet, pulling me forward. The second I started running, I questioned what I was doing. I'd known these people for so long and knew them better than anyone else. There'd be no reason for them to hurt me.

A pain sharper than anything I'd ever felt stabbed me through my back. It sent me tumbling to the ground, crippling in pain. I thought it was for sure a knife, but then the feeling started to course through my body. It burned every place possible, throwing me deeper and deeper into torment.

"It surprises me to this day how amazing Monica's powers are," Charlotte said. I heard scuffling on the carpet. They were all no doubt looming over me, watching me squirm. "As you know, she can control where her electricity travels after it leaves her body, such as in a computer, but to learn that she can control it in a human being is marvelous."

There was a tone to her voice that made me fear her every second I heard it. This nightmare was starting to feel way too real.

"Hmm, how about we try sending it all to his head."

Before I could realize what she said, the buzzing made its way there. The pain was worse than any headache I'd ever felt. My hands immediately went to my head to try and relieve the pain. No matter how hard I clenched my skull, I couldn't take the agony away. I tried opening my eyes but I saw nothing. My vision was so dark I could barely make out the red carpet next to my face.

By this point, my whole body was jittering. I had no control whatsoever. I was in subjection to their will. They had complete dominance over me and they were making sure they kept it that way.

"Okay Monica. That's enough," Charlotte said.

And just like that, the pain had left my head, almost as if she had flipped a switch. I was still left on the floor with an ache, completely exposed.

"Wow! Isn't that something, huh Monica?" Wendy said.

There was a short pause before she responded.

"Indeed."

Still, with no idea what was going on, my objective was to get out of there. I used my hands to push myself off the floor. Using the little strength I had left, I ran towards the end of the hallway, deeper into the unknown mansion.

I already knew I wouldn't get that far. Right as I was about to take a left turn down another hallway, my body froze. Control was a thing now unknown. With the kind of powers these people had, there was no doubt there'd be anything I could do. Combined, they had the ability to hold someone in place, quite literally actually, and make sure they stayed there.

My feet were slowly escalated off of the ground. I was now raised up in the air, completely ignoring the laws of gravity. Who'd Will think he was that he had the authority to just overlook natural rules like that?

The hallway started to turn when he rotated me to face them. When I saw Will's face, I could see disgust, making me have an incredible urge to punch him and ruin his pretty boy face. He threw his hand forwards, sending me back towards the wall. I then heard a *swoosh*, followed by the ignorant face of Wendy. She jammed the side of her arm into my neck, forcing me back to the wall. The wall against the back of my head along with the previous massacre of electricity in it must've made me lose so many brain cells.

She lifted her skirt and revealed a black strap wrapped around her thigh. In it was a knife with a blade twice the size of any kitchen knife. Without even breaking eye contact, she reached down for it and threw it in my left side.

This smile. This smile that I saw so many times revealed its true nature. It always looked like she had the ability of severely hurting someone and I now found out that she could.

No. It wasn't just her regular devilish smile. It was mad. Wendy showed her teeth and was almost snarling like a dog with rabies. She left her hand there even after the initial piercing of the knife through my skin.

I screamed out in pain. The feeling of this thick piece of metal inside me was more than anything I could bear. The cold feeling of the tearing muscle was far too much for me to handle. I wanted relief in any way possible. My body's natural reflex to it was to kneel down and fall to the floor but Wendy wouldn't allow it. She wanted me in misery and held me up to the wall with her arm, making it hard to breath.

After letting me rot, Wendy yanked out the knife without warning. She grabbed the collar of my suit jacket and dragged me over back to where Charlotte stood in the middle of the hallway. Wendy threw me down like I was a piece of steak for a dog that had just hunted down a coon for a hunter. There I laid in my own puddle of blood that stunk of metal.

I couldn't take it anymore. The pain was tearing at my sanity. It brought out voices I never thought were possible to leave my throat. I felt humiliated and beaten by the ones I loved. By the people that I trusted.

I rolled on my back to try and alleviate the pain. No matter what position I assumed, it felt the same.

"What—what are you guys doing?" I asked. After hearing the first word I said, I realized I was crying. I was in complete turmoil and didn't know how to respond to it other than return to my old roots of feeling pain. The tears blurred my vision of them, but I could still see the monsters. The smile on Charlotte's face was immensely beautiful and violent. It was just like a sweet and salty food, combining two things that didn't go together but somehow found a way into this universe.

"It still amazes me how little you know," Charlotte said. "You really don't know anything do you? Not a clue as to what's happening?"

"How should I?!" I yelled with tears still streaming down my face.

She put a hand on her chin and thought for a second.

"I guess if I was in your position I wouldn't know all that much either. But still, Mark. For an Equilibrium to not know what he is? Seems kinda pathetic to me."

I still had no idea what she was talking about. The more she opened her mouth, the more my head hurt.

"I trusted you guys. All of you!"

"Trust means nothing," Will said in disgust. "If you trusted us, you're going to have a real hard time with everything else."

Charlotte brought attention to the gun and examined it as she spoke.

"Consider it a favor you won't have to deal with that. We've been honored with the task of killing you," she said with a smile.

The pain seemed to subside at what she said. Tears stopped for a split second and allowed everything to freeze. The gun was illuminated by the light, mocking my life with the bullet that had my name on it. Charlotte's hand gripped it firmly, resting one finger on the trigger.

I was about to be killed by my friends.

"Aww, look at his face," Wendy cooed. "Don't be like that, Mark. It ruins your handsome getup with your suit."

"I believe he is confused," Monica said. Emptiness filled her voice, consuming anything around it. Her voice sounded completely different. It was monotone and she spoke as if she were an actual computer.

"Do you know how many people want you dead?" Charlotte asked. "You possess something wonderful, and yet, you don't even know what it is. You can change everything. Make something beautiful. Something ugly. The choice is up to you, but heck, we can't help but feel frustrated for you not knowing."

I've heard that same kind of thing from Penn. She was the one that always said my powers were amazing. When we did talk about them, she treated me almost like I was a god. To think that Charlotte and the others had knowledge of what I was all along and Monica was even the one to suggest that there were more to BloodLip.

"You're part of them," I said.

"BloodLip?" They all looked at each other and smiled. She gave a small menacing chuckle before continuing. "We're something far worse."

She leaned down next to me and sat on her knees.

"I thought you liked me," I said, trying to say anything to get them to realize what they were doing. Despite Monica being a different person than I thought she was, her claim was true. I do just care about myself.

"No. I loved you and I still do. That's why it's a pleasure that I was asked to be the one to end your life."

What happened to you Charlotte? This wasn't the girl I liked. She wasn't the one that I thought of before going to bed. She wasn't the one I met in the hallway of school, giggling at me falling down. This wasn't her at all.

I looked into her eyes and saw the brown that I loved. Looking back was me on the floor. Seeing that made me realize how low I'd gotten. They brought me to a point I'd never been.

Charlotte scooted up towards me and stared me down with her deadly smile that she must've adopted from Wendy. Nothing about it actually changed. It was still the same one I was used to. Just the sheer fact that her pleasant stature was changed with her word choice was enough to make me cower down into the state I was.

I needed to get out. My heart started its course again and tried to save itself by jumping out of my chest. There was no savior in sight. I was left to fend for myself with this last chance to save my life. Calling for someone appeared to be the only option and there was only one person who I'd trust at this point.

"Penn!"

Charlotte let out what almost sounded like a sigh.

"Please," I sobbed.

The more I looked at them, the more I tipped over the edge of losing my sanity. Will didn't look like he gave a care about anything. He was back to his same look from the first time I saw him. What about him saving the life of that lady and her baby? What about the tears I saw in his eyes when he thought he killed both of them? Was that all a hoax to make it look like he was a good person?

Monica looked at me with a face blanker than I've ever seen. The few words she said sounded unhuman. Everything from her walk to her posture screamed different.

Wendy looked as bright as can be. She was smiling with her mouth slightly open. She looked overly happy and too bubbly. The Wendy I knew would only get like this if I'd gotten hurt or embarrassed. Although both was happening, she wouldn't be the one to do it.

And Charlotte, she had to top everything off. Sitting casually next to me with her legs underneath her. It looked so innocent. It reminded me of when we were alone at her favorite spot on the mountain. Don't tell me, Charlotte, that was fake. That's what helped me feel like I was wanted. That's what made me want to be around all of you. That event alone changed me and for that to be all crushed by you killing me?

Strange noises started coming out of my mouth by themselves. They were pleas and expressions of my innermost parts, expressing themselves on their own. My lungs had enough of the extreme amount of stress and gave way to hyperventilation, blackening my vision.

"Your days are numbered, Mark, and we're all counting," Charlotte said.

"Please, don't do this."

"I love you Mark."

She leaned in extremely close towards my face. Her eyes slowly closed and before I realized what she was doing, her lips touched mine. It put a short stop on me going insane. The warmth and softness of her lips was something I'd think about but never thought I'd have the chance of feeling for myself. It was my first kiss and it would also be my last.

A cold piece of metal tapped the front of my forehead. My eyes, never being closed, darted over and saw the gun that she placed there. She was still delved into the passion of her kiss.

I didn't know what to feel. The girl I liked became a monster then she goes and kisses me.

No, I knew exactly how I felt. I had a feeling in common with someone.

I looked at the painting on the wall. The vessel was about to sink amidst the vastness of the sea. The same was about to happen to me. The water was something the captain probably enjoyed and now it was about to kill him. My life could be summed up in one painting. How sad.

There was a white flash and a sound of a bang right before everything went black and my head caved in.

\*      \*      \*

How many people can say they lived through a bullet to the head? Not many, I know that. I couldn't believe I was standing in the middle of the same hallway I was attacked. My feet were planted in front of the bathroom door. My lungs were expanding and contracting at a rate I'd never experienced.

Where was Charlotte?

Without even questioning why I was alive, I looked all over for her.

I heard a door open on the left side of the hallway. My mind immediately went and thought of when Charlotte walked out with the gun. Hesitating to look, I turned my head and saw her stumble out of the bathroom. She was holding her stomach and limped over to the wall. I had no clue as to what she was doing, but I wasn't about to let her hurt me again.

Making a stupid and rash decision, I ran over towards her. I didn't know what I was gonna do to her, but I was furious. She had to go and ruin everything. She was the person I loved and for what, to get killed by her?

Charlotte had one hand clenching her stomach and one holding the wall in front of her. When I got to her, I turned her around and grabbed her by the neck, slamming her into the wall. Hearing the noise of her head making contact with the wood made me question what I was doing. I was hurting her, but it was better than me dying.

I looked into her eyes and saw my face, completely bloodthirsty.

"Mark, please," she said, sobbing. Tears rolled down her precious cheeks and fell on her pink shawl. I've never seen her cry before. I've never seen pain on her face, and I was the one who was causing it. "Please don't hurt me again."

"Again? What? No, what the heck are you talking about? You were the one who hurt *me*!" I yelled to her face in complete frustration.

"What...but you killed me."

I thought back to when she walked out of the bathroom and connected the two. She was obviously in some sort of pain just like I was and if I supposedly killed her just as she did to me, would that mean we both just died?

I reached down for where Wendy stabbed me and felt for the hole I expected to be there. My suit jacket wasn't pierced. The tightly knitted sewing was still placed in its correct spot.

My hands slowly released from Charlotte's neck. Red imprints of my fingers were left on her, showing my horrible act. My brain shifted into reality. This was Charlotte you did this to. Charlotte. Remember? The one you like. Your friend.

There wasn't time to react to it. We both heard a scream coming from the girl's bathroom. Both of us forgot about everything and ran into the bathroom. Even the fact that males were forbidden in there was not even acknowledged.

I barged through the door, slamming it back into the door stopper. The fancy decor was completely overlooked as I searched for the source of the scream. Wendy was hunched over the counter looking back at the stalls that were behind her. Monica had to be the only other person who was in there.

"Monica!" I yelled, hoping she'd open the door. I pulled on the knob wishing it would budge. The lock held firmly and made my efforts pointless. There was another scream, this time louder. "Monica open the door!"

Someone else burst through the bathroom. It had to be Will because the stall door was spontaneously unlocked and thrown open. Inside was a horrible sight. Monica was sitting on the toilet lid, holding her legs close to her chest.

Her face was completely lost in a daze that seemed like it couldn't be broken. Her lips were quivering as the mascara she wore was smearing all over her face. Despite it not being the form I wanted, she was showing something that all of us had never really seen. Emotion.

All of us were frozen by the effect of shock, uselessly watching her in pain. It took me a second to realize that something was missing from the top of her head. The bow I bought her yesterday was clenched in her hand, wrinkling its delicate form.

After a few moments, she finally realized we were watching her and jumped up in fright. She tried standing but fell the second her feet touched the floor. Wendy caught her right before she made contact with the ground.

"She used too much power," Wendy said, holding her up.

"You just wouldn't die," Monica said in a shaky voice, still looking completely out of it.

Was she talking about me? If she used too much of her powers then that mean she tried killing me.

"It happened to all of us," Will explained. "A slip in space or something like that."

"And how would you know that?" Wendy asked.

"How else would you explain each of us having our own separate experience?" Monica grabbed the counter and used it to help her stand. She looked in the mirror and within the snap of a finger, her face was back to its original state. The white of the cloth used for cleaning your hands was replaced with the remnant of her mascara when she wiped it off. "I don't expect that we all had identical events happen."

After checking to see if she looked how she did before, Monica walked out of the bathroom, ignoring us. We tried to call out to her but she kept her course to leave the inside of the mansion.

"Do you think she's gonna leave?" Charlotte asked.

"No. She's not just gonna leave us like that," I replied.

"I don't know about that. She just turned human for a short second," Wendy said.

"Then let's go get her," Will said.

"Yeah, sure. Let me just throw my insides out," Wendy said before running to a stall and vomiting violently.

*　　*　　*

When I was walking out of the mansion, I couldn't stop thinking about how and why we even went through this. At least I could narrow it down pretty easily. It had to be someone with powers. Will's suggestion about how it was a slip in space and time was kind of out there. It did sound like something like that could be relevant but I wasn't sure how much I could trust his reasoning. And if it was someone who had powers, it had to be someone from BloodLip. None of the ones I knew had powers like that. Whoever did have this power was surely powerful. To create a realm specifically for one person and make it so it actually felt real was not something you could just do randomly.

The next question I was supposed to ask was begging to be asked. I didn't wanna think about it but I had to. I let out a sigh and heard the voice in my head ask away like a toddler that was just starting to discover their world.

They certainly weren't trying to hurt us because we got out just fine. So if that wasn't the case, why were they trying to scare us?

Loud slow paced music was flowing out of the overly large speakers. People were carrying on with the party while

I had just died. I felt my brows curl. They think everything's just dandy. They don't have one ounce of care for anyone other than themselves and their pretty lives.

A lifting feeling started in my chest and spread to the rest of my body. Envy was taking over. I wanted my normal life back. I never asked to be tormented like I was.

While looking over the people, I noticed Monica at the punch bowl filling a cup very slowly. Just looking at the back of her head made the past couple of events flash before my eyes. Inside the bathroom when she was screaming, the incredible force and pain of her electricity, and her piercing words. And to think I was doing anything just to get out of dying, once again proving Monica's notion right. How was I any different than these people?

I still needed to apologize for not telling her about Penn asking me to join them. My feet hesitated before making their way over to her.

When I got to the table with the punch, I noticed she was still holding her bow. She tried her best to pour the punch using the big spoon while also holding the cup and the bow in the same hand. She would have to set the spoon back into the bowl to recuperate and try again because of her shaking too much.

"Need any help?" I asked.

Her whole body froze when I spoke. She stayed like that for a few seconds before again trying to reach for the spoon.

I couldn't help but feel guilty at the thought of her being scared of my voice. I was what made her freak out. Of course, it wasn't really my doing, but just in the same way as a dream, it seems way too real to find the bridge that leads back to reality.

"I'm fine," she said firmly.

"Doesn't look that way to me."

I reached over her and grabbed the spoon along with her cup. I quickly poured her some, pausing for a second, thinking I might've done it too fast. She'd think I was mocking her for being too slow right now.

"Uh...here," I said, handing her the cup. When I turned to give it to her, she wasn't looking at me. Her black eyes inspected the innermost part of the world as she lost herself in a daze. "Monica."

She snapped out of it and grabbed the cup, turning her head while she did. She avoided looking at me completely.

I hated us acting like this with each other. I needed to apologize instantly to end this.

"Monica, look. I'm sorry for what I did."

"You never did anything. It was all fake anyways." No, that wasn't what I was apologizing for. "I just—I just held everything in for too long." She held her mouth open to say more but nothing came out but her soft breath.

I reached for her bow that she was still clenching tightly. Grabbing her shoulders, I turned her to face towards me. Her eyes were still not giving in to my direction. They feared what was there; constantly focusing on anywhere but where I was. For the first time ever, I touched her soft hair. Yesterday when I'd taken the bow out of her hair, I was careful not to touch any of it, only gripping the bow. This time, I caressed the strand that she usually clipped it on in preparation to return it to the place it belonged.

When I did this, I noticed that her face was softening. It assured me what I was doing was helping her in some way. It always felt better when someone apologized in action over word. You could feel their sincerity and that they really cared about you. I only hoped that she would accept this over any small two words that I could say.

I eventually carefully clipped the bow in her hair and tidied it up to make sure it was perfect. Her chin lifted up ever so slightly.

"I was so scared, Mark," she said, holding back tears. I felt accomplished for finally getting her to talk on her own instead of always following after my words. "And I don't want anyone to see me like that."

"Believe me. I was scared too. And you have to remember, Monica, you're human just like we are. When we see you act like you did, it reminds us that you are and that's when we're our purest." I felt like she wasn't buying into what I said. I didn't expect her to anyways. I was her murderer after all. "Look. We're here for you. You don't have to worry about anyone else seeing you like that either. I'll make sure when you start to feel like that, to give a black eye to whoever's looking at you."

Her mouth budged just barely. The far corners of it tilted up slightly for a quick smirk. I needed to keep going.

"Remember when you held my hand after I fought Eli? And then you went and did it again when Charlotte and Wendy fought Penn. It's either you really liked holding my hand or you wanted to help me. I'm pretty confident it was the latter, so I want to return the favor. You made sure I wasn't held in the dark about what you knew. I'm sorry I didn't do the same. I need to make it up to you with a promise. If I ever have something I know, I promise I'll let you know, okay?"

"I'll accept your apology if allow a request," she said, looking at the ground.

"Sure," I said, confused as to what it'd be. "What is it?"

"That you and I have a dance."

She finally looked into my eyes and gave a smile. I gave a nod. Of course I'd dance with her even if Eris didn't help teach me how.

In the corner of my eye, I saw Wendy waving her hands furiously, trying to get our attention. I stuck out my elbow towards Monica so she could hook her arm in mine. It was a classic pose for dates to use. The only reason I was doing it was because she couldn't walk that well. I finally saw the effects of using too much power. They said that each of them had experienced it before. Learning you had powers, you'd probably overuse them the instant you did.

Monica slowly moved her arm in and cupped mine. She tugged in close and leaned on me for support.

"Aww, you guys look so cute!" Wendy said.

"Make the wrong move, Mark, and you'll upset Charlotte," Will said.

"Shut up!" Charlotte yelled.

"She's right," I said. "Now's not the time for jokes."

Will fiddled with his collar and tilted his head down.

"Right."

"So, let me get this straight. You think what happened to us was that we went through a split in space or something like that?"

"It's just my guess. Of course, we can't be sure about it. The only reason I suggest it is because we each had our own different experience. Mark and I went into the mens bathroom and Wendy, Monica, and Charlotte went in the women's bathroom. When I walked out of the bathroom was when everything happened; meaning the slip had to be created when we were in the bathroom."

"There obviously had to be someone who made this. For all of us to be killed in some way by Mark had to be set up," Wendy said.

"Mark was actually killed by me," Charlotte said, looking over at me to make sure it was okay for her to say it.

"Yes, there had to be," Will said, putting a finger on his chin. "There had to be a reason why yours was different from ours. As far as I know, you killed all of us. And to be honest, the fake you is a real jerk."

"Not helping," I said, glaring him down.

"Someone from BloodLip then," Will said, coming to a conclusion.

"But not one of them have powers that can do that," Charlotte added.

"We don't know that," Monica chimed in softly. "There's still the possibility that there are more of them."

"She's right." Will gave a sigh. "Now I'm kinda hoping you joined them so you could've found out who had those powers."

At that moment, it clicked.

Penn wanted me to join BloodLip. It was because she wanted me there for my safety and partly because I was the Equilibrium. I told her that I wasn't going to leave my friends like that, showing I cared a lot about them. And what does that mean to her? She'd have to persuade me into joining them by making me want to leave my friends; in this case, by having them murder me. Why else would she have me wait to tell her my answer?

My body immediately clenched up in rage. Despite Penn being a murderer, I was starting to look at her like a regular human being, but she had to go and do this. She had to make me experience this living nightmare and be scarred for the rest of my life; seeing a side of them that wasn't real. God, Penn. You're terrible.

"What is it?" Charlotte asked. She could read me well. She knew the second I got upset.

"It was BloodLip."

"How do you know?"

"Think about it. They wanted me to join them. What better way for her to convince me to leave you guys then having you murder me."

We all stood there, thinking about everything. Monica still was holding on to my arm and using it for balance. The soft and subtle presence of her calmed me a bit and prevented me from going over and punching Penn straight in the face.

"It's getting pretty hard for us to just ignore them, Charlotte," Wendy said. "These idiots are willing to do whatever it takes to get what they want."

"So what do you expect us to do?" asked Charlotte, looking at me.

"There *is* nothing for us to do." I extended my chest ever so slightly to somehow force my words on them. "We keep doing what we were doing. Not once did they hurt us today." I paused. "Physically, that is. We keep our distance and if they keep up, then we'll come back to it and think of what we'll do. For right now, enjoy the party. Penn's still expecting an answer from me today. I'll talk to her and we'll settle things." My eyes shifted over to Monica. "And I owe you a dance."

She gave a small nod. I looked back over the group and gave my own nod towards them. I made sure I followed it with a genuine smile. They took it surprisingly well. They all returned the smile, including Will and Wendy. I couldn't help but feel as if I was leading them in some way. I didn't think much of it at the time. But little did I know what this feeling was.

I made my way with Monica over to the dance floor. The slow paced music set the pace and we slowly moved in motion to it. I was just now starting to like the slow-paced beat. It gave me time to think about what happened without being overly upset. And plus, how could I when Monica was completely in sync with me. I noticed that she was starting to smile and caught herself, forcing back her blank emotionless face.

"What are you afraid of?" I asked her. "Why would you suppress a beautiful smile like that?" She took what I told her and allowed everyone to see it. She looked completely different when she was happy. It added so many layers to her and showed how complex she actually was. She giggled every time she'd mess up a step or wobble with her heel. This was the girl that was hiding all along.

Standing off to the side of the dance floor was the redhead I didn't want to see. She curled her finger towards herself, telling me to come. It was time. I signaled Will to come and take over for me as I made my way to her.

As I was getting close to her, I noticed my heart rate speeding up. I didn't really know how she would react to what I was to tell her.

"I hope I gave you enough time to think about it," she said. "I know it was kinda unexpected but I always wanted you with us. I think it's where you belong."

"What you think, huh." I had to restrain any anger I had. "What about what I think or about what my friends think?" Of course that wasn't gonna happen. "Does that mean anything to you?"

She was taken aback by my sudden anger.

"Of—of course it does. But it's you we want."

"We? I thought *you* wanted to protect me? As far as I know, the rest of BloodLip doesn't like me."

Penn stumbled over her words and tried to salvage anything left of the conversation.

"No, Penn. I'm not going to be joining BloodLip." My eyes peered into hers. "I'm no murderer and I'm never planning on being one."

I turned and walked away, making sure my last words stung. The thought of her looking back at me, hoping she would've taken things better, made me feel good about myself. I too often accepted requests with no reason to. This time I made sure I would show that I made my own decisions. No form of persuasion could change my decision but the people I loved most.

With this extra burst of confidence and courage, I walked up to Charlotte. Ever since I walked out of the secluded pit of death made for me, I've been acting different. It somehow helped me be a little more appreciative for what I had, knowing I didn't have friends that'd stab me in the back.

I'd take that new feeling and use it for something good. Something that would make both of us feel good. I met her with a compassionate smile that sparked one in return.

"This is the part where I make up some stupid line on how I want to dance with you."

She giggled and made her short hair bounce on her shoulders.

"Like the one you just now used?" she asked.

"Oh, I just did it, didn't I?"

"Yeah, but I liked yours."

Charlotte reached out and grabbed my hand, leading me to where the rest of the people were dancing. When we got to our spot, I tried my best to remember what Eris told me. Charlotte apparently had some previous knowledge on how to dance to this type of music. She went right ahead and put her hand behind my back, bringing herself closer to me. She watched as my fingers laced over her own and our hands clamped together. I went and did my part and placed my hand on her hip. I cursed in my head about how hard my heart was beating. She could for sure hear it, no doubt feel it. It was as if we were in an eternal hug, moving to an ambience that can't be seen. But gosh did it feel good.

"What'd you tell her?" she asked.

"Do you trust me enough when I say that I told her no?"

She gave a small smirk as she looked into my eyes. "Of course I do."

Looking into her dark eyes like that reminded me of what I saw earlier. I was practically strangling her. Just now did I realize what I'd done. Did I really get to a point that low?

"Charlotte…," I paused, thinking of what exactly I was trying to say.

"Hm?"

"I'm so sorry about what I did." I removed my hand from her own and traced the spot on her neck where I had grabbed her. "I didn't know what I was doing."

She reached around with her other hand and gave me a full hug, resting her head on my shoulder.

"Forget about that, Mark."

I didn't know how to respond to that. She, once again, took my words away. But I didn't really mind. She was hugging me; taking comfort in me. It gave me a feeling that I had felt nowhere else. Pure joy.

I felt her chuckle against me.

"I feel it," she said, still leaning on me. "Your happiness."

It was the same feeling Charlotte gave me on the mountain. I looked over to my left where Will and Monica were dancing. They were both looking at me, smiling. They must have felt it as well. Wendy was doing the same from the bench she sat on, stuffing her face with the four plates she tried holding in her hands. I really was connected to them in some way. Part of my powers maybe. Whatever it was, I wanted to feel it all the time. I wanted it to be in every second of my life.

And there we were. All happy, despite what happened. Why couldn't it always stay like that?

I wish I would've enjoyed myself a little more. It'd be the last time I was going to be happy in a long time.

# Chapter 7

I never knew how tiresome parties could be. Although, I guess our experience wasn't considered normal. Being murdered takes a lot of energy from you. You have the stress, the turmoil, the suspense. Must I go on?

I guess the party was fun at least. It really started to kick into gear around 10:00 when they played music everyone loved. You know, the ones with the hard hitting bass. The ones where people could get crazy with the drop of a beat. I gotta give it to Eris's "friends". Best DJs I've ever heard. They certainly knew how to please a crowd, especially knowing what got Wendy to move.

I'm not kidding you, the second we heard the music switch, Wendy ran to the dancefloor and busted moves I've never seen before. She completely ignored the fact that she was in a dress and moved about freely, holding the record time for being in the circle the longest.

All five of us walked home together. It gave us some more time to talk about what happened, not like there was much more to talk about anyways.

The party ended up carrying on late. There were still plenty people there when we left, dancing away to their hearts content. And I considered when we left late. It'd already turned the next day, passing the midnight mark.

When I got home that night, I carefully and quietly tiptoed upstairs to my room. I quickly changed out of the unusual dress clothes and into something more comfortable. My mom must've been sleeping for a few hours already. It started to dawn on me how late it actually was.

I went ahead and crawled into bed and laid there with my eyes open. The ceiling was my only friend at a time like this. It was confusing to think that everything actually happened. It happened so fast that it felt like a dream, completely a figment of my imagination.

I thought of how Penn must've felt, starting to regret my word choice. Maybe I was a little too harsh. No, what was I saying? I needed to remind myself of what happened in the hallway of that mansion. I was murdered by people I loved for some hope that I'd be persuaded into joining a group of murderers. Of course she needed it. She deserved every ounce of pain I had caused her. It still wouldn't amount to what she did to me and my friends.

I wanted to question her motives some more, but I was drawn in by the warmth of my bed and the calling of the land of slumber. I remember, just before I fell asleep, thinking of the dance with Charlotte. She was so comforting to be around, and to think that I'd gotten a kiss from her. I know it wasn't actually her, but it was still something.

A smile found its way to my face and everything went dark.

*　　*　　*

I was awoken by a creak on the wood of the stairs. My door had been closed, but because of the poor making of the house, it was heard no matter where you were inside. I figured it was my mom getting a drink of water or changing the heater temperature.

My eyes quickly resumed their closed position, not thinking anything of it. Within seconds, I returned to the unconscious state of sleep.

The doorknob quietly and slowly rattled as it turned, breaking my trance. I was facing the wall, opposite of the door. I was unable to see who the person was that opened the door and I didn't care all that much either. It wasn't uncommon to see my mom check up on me every once in a while at night. Especially in this case, she knew I'd be getting home late. She would reasonably want to see if I made it home. I, once again, closed my eyes.

What made me suspicious was that the door closed and I still felt the presence of someone. My mom had no reason to close the door and stay in the room. Just as I was about to turn around and see for myself if it was her, I was pounced on. The heavy weight on me made me wake up instantly.

I tried my best to fight the beefy hands that held me down on my bed. My whole body struggled to shimmy out of grasp but it was no use in fighting. How could I compete with him when he had the upper hand?

Just when I was starting to realize who was on top of me, another person, a girl, came over to my bedside. In her hand was a white cloth that she slowly placed over my mouth. The disgusting stench of the chemicals forced its way up my nostrils. I wanted to stop from breathing it in but that'd mean no oxygen, and with him on top of me, it forced air out of my lungs.

So this was it. I knew why they were doing what they were doing. It was expected, but never did I think it would come so soon. The effects of my decision never really dawned on me that much. They never caused a presence for anxiety. Not once.

"Shhh," Sarah whispered, putting a finger on her lips. "Have fun with her." She gave me a wink along with a wicked smile.

I looked back up into the eyes of Eli. He was too focused on his task of subduing me that he didn't bother to insult me. But somehow, hatred for me still found its way to his face, doing its job of mocking me.

The effects of the cloth she put on me were starting to take effect. I was starting to feel weak, to feel even inferior than I already was. Where I was to go after this, I didn't know. All I did know was that this was the end of my life. I was to be killed by the hand of BloodLip.

\* \* \*

My stomach was pushed in to a point where I thought Eli must've still been on top of me. I ruled that out after I realized I was sitting. Even then, it took me a while to figure that out. Everything looked and felt extremely weird. The whole room spun and I couldn't keep my eyes focused on anything. No matter how hard I tried holding my head up, it'd fall back down, slamming my chin into my chest.

I planted my feet on the floor to stand but failed to. For a while, I just sat there, waiting for all my senses to come back and figure out where the heck I was. Well, I had nothing to do but sit. I figured I'd try and maybe stiffen my neck muscles and get my head to act like it should and do as I wanted.

With the depleted strength I had left, I was able to manage it. All that was needed now was for my eyes to focus. As I sat there, I tried my best to make images in my head.

This had to be where BloodLip meets up. It had to be the place where they planned all their horrible acts. Their main place. Who knew how many people would be here. If I was so important to them, would there be a crowd watching, waiting for whoever was in charge to execute me?

But was it? Was it really their base of operations?

The more my eyes focused, the more I started to recognize the place. This was the place I went to five times a week, constantly returning with work in hand. It was the place where I met my friends. It was the place I met the very person standing in front of me.

It took me a while to see that there was someone standing in front of the desk. She would stand in front of it every day just as she did now. Her arms were crossed as she sat on the lip of it.

"Finally decide to wake up I see," she said.

It was strange to see Violet without any other students around. She seemed a little more mature this time, looking quite tired herself.

My whole body had returned to normal and I could see everything. I was sitting in my homeroom class. The desks had been stacked against the wall. We all had the task of moving them the day before we went on break for a cleaning of the floor. There was only one chair in the middle of it, and it was the one I was sitting in. I had nowhere to go. I was secured to the chair by a rope, unable to do anything but look at Violet.

Behind her on the desk was a black gun, similar to the one the fake Charlotte used to kill me. Next to it was a knife with jagged edges.

She noticed me looking at them and turned her head towards them.

"You don't have the best of grades but you're smart enough to know what this means," she said, looking straight at me. She was wearing the same clothes she did the first day of school; the white blazer and the denim pants.

"So you were one of them," I said calmly. I didn't know why I wasn't worried or surprised for that matter.

"Of course I was."

"Does Penn know about what you're gonna do?"

"No. She's sleeping soundly at home being guarded by Eli, Brittany, and Sarah to make sure she doesn't leave."

"Then I'm guessing you have powers too."

"Me?" She gave a soft chuckle "No. You don't have to have to powers to be in BloodLip. Having powers means nothing."

"So when Penn referred to others, she was talking about you? Of course you'd be the leader."

"You're wrong. I'm not. Penn is. From the moment I held her as a baby, she was the leader. I'm just here to guide and protect her."

"Then you're not her mother," I assumed.

"Penn's told you before. I adopted her when I was eighteen. Now, do you really think an eighteen year old girl would adopt a child out of her own accord? I never asked for it. I didn't want this responsibility but duties are duties and orders are orders."

"You just proved it right there. There is more of BloodLip."

She leaned in a little closer to me, letting her point be clear.

"We're all that there is."

"But you were given orders."

A longing smile came out of nowhere that faded as she started to talk.

"You think we're from here? Do you think you guys would have your powers just because? Do you really think that we have *anything* in common with *them*?!" she yelled, pointing out of the window. "How blind can you be, Mark!"

"How blind can I be? What kind of stupid question's that?!" I shook my head in frustration. I shouldn't be asking these questions. I needed to understand why she wanted me dead. "Why do you guys want me?"

"We were given orders. Either you join us or we kill you. Simple. It was the job I've had this whole time. The moment I saw you I should've just pulled this gun out of my desk and shot you to get it over with. But no, I wanted to take things slow. Do my job precisely. Then Penn met you. She liked you so much she wanted to have you join us. For a while, she was just as convinced as I was to kill you but things changed. I wanted to make her happy so I gave her time. I gave *you* time." She let out a sigh. "Mark, it's been going on for too long. We only have a couple more days and time's running out. You're too dangerous to live."

"Dangerous?! I don't even know what my powers are! What the heck does Equilibrium mean?!"

She completely ignored my question and continued on.

"I never did enjoy terminating people. Hearing them plea with all their energy made for some nasty nightmares. Let's just hope yours won't cause anymore. After all, you'd be my last target. You caused everything and I'm ready to end it."

She reached for the gun and loaded it up. Meanwhile, I sat there struggling to fight the rope that wrapped around me and held me to the chair. My breathing increased and so did my heartrate. It felt strange, though, almost like it wasn't my own adrenaline. I'd felt this once before. This shared feeling was only between me and the others. I felt exhaustion in my legs as if I'd been running for a while. It was getting closer and closer, stronger and stronger.

"It's nothing personal, Mark. Only orders," she said, putting the gun to my head.

My eyes focused on the window where the direction of the feeling came from. An extreme urge of courage and strength filled my body, knowing what was coming. Her finger was just about to press down when...

*Swoosh*

The sight of seeing people I knew increased my plea for life. Charlotte, Wendy, Monica, and Will stood in the room now holding hands. They were all out of breath and sweating. All of their eyes were quick to take into consideration what was happening, finding out that their teacher was a murderer as well.

This was my chance to change the course set out for me. I lifted the chair up and used my head to ram into Violet as she was distracted looking at them. She stumbled back and involuntarily fired the gun, making a hole in the wall. Wendy teleported right in front of her and picked her up off of the ground with both arms. She was now given the opportunity to do something that wasn't allowed. She never found Violet annoying or a pain but the sheer fact that she could fight her own teacher was probably enough to give that extra edge.

After lifting her by her collar, she threw her against the wall giving me an immense flashback to yesterday. I didn't know how much Violet was of a fighter but I knew for sure that she was absolutely caught off guard by this.

Wendy rammed a knee into her stomach before Violet could do anything and was crippled even more. I lost focus of what they were doing when I felt a tug behind me.

Will had pulled out a knife and ran behind me, quickly moving his hand up and down to cut away at the rope. Waiting for it to be cut, I looked back up and watched the four of them fight against the wall, Charlotte and Monica joining her now. Violet managed to grab her knife in time and threw it around with precision. I was finally able to see her potential in combat. She held her own against the three girls like she had done it so many times before.

I still couldn't believe that they were all here. They had come and saved me from my impending doom. If it wasn't for them, I'd be slumped in a chair with a bullet in my head. They must've felt it for sure. They had to have felt me in danger.

Knowing I had them to back me up added another layer to my buzz. Suddenly the fear of the situation was gone and I was ready to have at Violet. She saw me running towards her and managed to make it out of the human barrier in front of her, pushing all three of them out of the way. With arms pumping as fast as she did running away from the falling penthouse, she charged at me. I leaned down, hoping to take the weight of her and throw her back down to the floor, but instead, she was the one who threw me down.

She tightened her grip on the knife and raised it over her head, driving it down with a force I thought I wouldn't be able to counter. Hopelessly, I threw my hands up to try and catch it. The palms of my hand cupped the fists of Violet's, barely stopping the knife from entering my neck. But she kept persisting. She kept on with her everlasting force and threw her body weight on my hands, making me lose my strength.

There was then a gunshot and the knife flew out of Violet's hand into the wall. With the continued force of her hands, they fell down on top of my chest. She turned and followed the position of the knife and stopped. She seemed to completely freeze on top of me. Her face filled with confusion and contorted in frustration as if she were trying to remember something.

I turned to see that Charlotte had her gun in her hands, still pointing towards Violet, making sure she wouldn't make another move.

Violet grunted as she grabbed at her head and closed her eyes.

"Not now. Not now! Get the heck out of my head!" she said to herself.

Still holding her head, she stumbled towards the knife and turned to throw it at me. With Will's quick reflexes, he threw his hands out forwards, sending her flying through the window. The sound of the glass shattering echoed through the room and exposed the fresh cool air of the night.

Monica ran over to me and helped me up. Upon standing, I saw she was already getting up despite being flung through a window and getting torn by the flying shards. All of us stepped out of the window and met her in the parking lot. Violet straightened her back and readied her stance, fixing the knife so it was sticking out towards us.

"You don't think I haven't done this once before?" She threw her arm across her lips, smearing the blood that had cut up her face. "You guys don't realize I had to train four people with powers how to fight." Her eyes scanned over us. "Looking at this, the numbers appear to be about the same." Her last words focused on me, smothering the fact that I had no clue to what my powers were. And that's what drove me insane.

She grabbed Will's arm and swung him around, kicking him in the back. Once she was exposed again, Monica sent out her purple essence into her body. Monica's face contorted with pain and anger, quietly grunting. She must've still been exhausted from depleting her energy earlier. Violet fought the pain, ignoring every ounce of stinging and ran at her. Experiencing firsthand the pain of Monica's power was excruciating and Violet treated it like it was nothing.

When she was within reach, Monica stopped the flow and grabbed at her arm, bringing it down low. Once Violet was hunched over, Charlotte went over and jumped on her, throwing her to the ground. Wendy and Will ran over and joined in laying waste to her, throwing punches left and right. They all had knives but chose not to use them, wanting to cause pain but not to the point of severely injuring her. Seeing them do that made me burn. Made me fill with a rage I've never experienced. Did they forget what she did? With what all of BloodLip did to us and all we're doing is throwing punches? With madness coursing through me, I picked up Violet's gun off of the floor and aimed it towards her.

Violet kicked up her legs, launching Wendy in the air and falling flat on her back. She swept her feet and knocked all of them down. With movements faster than my eyes could keep up with, she reached for Charlotte's neck and held the knife close.

I froze, making sure I didn't cause her to swipe the knife and cut her open. Charlotte stared at me in fear, realizing what situation she was now in. Her eyes chose to focus in on me. I was the one she turned to in this moment. After the moment we just had a few hours ago, when she was hugging me and we were dancing, when she was looking me in the eyes with our shared joy, would I be left with those last moments?

My fervor to stop Violet and hurt her immensely were stopped. Anything I did now rested on the fate of her life.

This wasn't supposed to happen. This wasn't supposed to happen at all. I was the one who was supposed to get killed, not her. Things changed only because I didn't want to die. You selfish imbecile.

Violet was breathing heavily, making sure her eyes beat into mine.

"It's not her you wanted to kill," I reassured her. "You wanted me."

"You don't think I was going to let them live either, do you?"

Her tone of voice disgusted me. My hands squeezed the gun tighter. I had only felt a gun once, and I'd never used it. This time, I wasn't so sure.

The sight in front of me looked like a picture from a movie scene. There Violet was, with a hostage. Knife to her neck, waiting for someone to make the first move. She had nothing to lose. To her, all of us were dead. For me, all I had could be lost in seconds. I had worked so hard for what I didn't have. I felt the pain of loneliness. I felt the agony of envy. I felt the misery of want. All of it was now gonna be lost because of one person?

No. Like I'd let that happen. I once thought of Violet as being an awesome teacher with a good personality. All I saw now was a cruel monster with no limits and morals but that of the commands given her.

The face of Charlotte mimicked the one I saw at the party. Fear and distress weren't supposed to be on that face. Her face only knew of happiness. It was now starting to get used to the look and feel of the other feeling. If it kept up any longer, the natural smile that somehow found its way there all the time would be lost.

"Put her down, Violet," I said in a firm voice.

"Or what? You'll shoot me? You have nothing to persuade me. Just face it, Mark. You lose. I have all the cards. I have answers. I know the truth to everything. I know what's gonna happen and you don't." She gave a scoff. "Even if you were to make it to the other side you wouldn't last a day before they'd kill you."

I ignored her mess of confusion.

"There's no reason for you to kill her."

"Oh there's perfect reason to kill her. I was given orders."

"And you're letting them rule over your life? How pathetic can you be?!"

She pressed the knife into her skin, slowly slicing it open, letting little dots of blood trickle down her neck.

"Now that you gave your request, I'll go ahead and give mine. Put your gun down," Violet said.

"And what's stopping you from killing her when I do that?"

"Nothing."

Charlotte started to cry out due to the pain. The others stood idly by, frozen by the chill of their friend's pain. I'd once again, found myself leading them in some way. I was the one calling the shots. I was even surprised that Wendy wasn't saying anything. This was her best friend's life on the line and she was putting her life in my hands.

I refocused the gun at Violet's head. Why was I so hesitant? One shot and that'd be it. One shot and it'd be over. The knife kept getting deeper and deeper.

"Five seconds and I kill her."

My eyes widened. I had to do it now.

"Five."

I had to.

"Four."

The gun slipped around in my hand, trying to stay center.

"Three."

I heard scuffling on the right of me. There were people running towards the area we were at in the parking lot. I didn't look once. I made sure my focus was kept on them. Whoever they were, they'd been running. They were out of breath and they were getting closer. I couldn't do it with other people here.

"Two."

No, Mark. I don't care what kind of person you are. You know this is the only option you have. You've been tortured by these people several times now and you did nothing. Not once. You need to take action against them. Show them what lengths you're willing to go.

"One."

"Mom!"

*Click*

The weight of the gun got lighter as the bullet flew out of it and into Violet's head. The disgusting sound of the chamber exploding sounded throughout the school. Violet plummeted to the floor, letting go of Charlotte and the knife. Seeing the work of my hand made me tremble. How lifeless her body was, how cruel it looked. And it was because of me. I did this. It was me.

My head slowly turned towards the direction of the scream. God did I hate what I saw. Penn stood there along with Eli, Sarah, and Brittany. Penn's face was already starting to change. Her cheeks were squished together and the tears started to roll. They all did this on their own.

There was no sound whatsoever. Everything was dead silent. We still couldn't believe what happened—what I'd done. I continued to hold the gun but it fell out of my hand. My grip suddenly disappeared and faded away.

After the few seconds of silence, Penn let out an inhuman scream, one of complete despair and pain. She ran over to her dead mother and lifted her in her hands. The rest of BloodLip followed and let out their own expressions of sorrow.

"Mom!"

All I could do was stand there and watch.

Penn soothed the cuts on Violet's face from the window. Her tears covered her face and helped in cleaning her. None of them acknowledged us yet. None of them were hurting us. They weren't giving me what I deserved.

"I'm sorry mom. I'm sorry," Penn repeatedly sobbed. "I should've listened."

She turned and looked at me. I couldn't bear to look in her eyes but I felt obligated to do so. No matter how much I wanted to turn my head, I couldn't. The blood red eyes of hers had the same color of the blood trickling down Violet's head.

With a face as horrendous as hers, she broke me. Her whole essence chipped away at me. My soul was starting to break and it was because of her death stare. The look on her face was a look that I hadn't gotten from anywhere else. Complete disappointment. If what Violet said was true, that she did like me, I had let all her expectations down. It wasn't the fact that she had feelings for me, it was that she trusted me enough to be part of them when the rest of them thought otherwise.

"Go!" she screamed, breaking our idiotic stance. The shout was unexpected and full of heart, making me jump. "Go! Go! Go! Just leave me alone!"

Neither of them had gotten up and tried to force us to leave. They were too entrenched in their sorrow and torment to even try. All of us moved as a whole and headed slowly away from them, tiptoeing so as to not startle them.

Penn went ahead and screamed some more at us, almost pleading this time, pleading to the murderer of her mother to just simply leave. Who was I to not do this simple task and give her the privacy she wanted?

I turned and ran out of the parking lot. The others shortly followed behind.

What had I just done? I couldn't tell if it'd been reality when I had shot her. It happened all too fast. I didn't know if my decision was the right one. I could've put the gun down but there was no guarantee that Charlotte would still be behind me.

Flashes of Violet's dead body popped up in my head, displaying my horrible crime to me over and over again. *Look what you've done, Mark. Look at what pain you caused. You're now no different than they are.*

I pressed my feet into the sidewalk as hard as I could, sprinting at full speed. Charlotte called from behind me but I didn't want to stop. I didn't want to hear any of it. How could I let them see my face after what I'd done?

Tears pushed their way out of my eyes as I pushed my body to its limits. It smeared my vision but still wouldn't wash away the pictures of Violet. No matter how hard I tried to convince myself that it wasn't real, that I was just in another slip in space, I still couldn't undo what I just did.

How selfish could you be, Mark?

All I wanted was to keep what I'd been longing for this whole time. You were about to take it away, Violet. And gosh could I not go back. I don't want the pain and misery of not having friends. These were the people that found something precious in me. They dubbed me worthy of their friendship and I never had that. People looked at me like I was crazy, weird, nothing. It made me feel so insignificant. I was completely hopeless. Charlotte, Wendy, Monica, and

Will changed that for me. They gave me something I never had.

These were your orders, I know. But how long can you live by them? Look where they'd gotten you.

I'm so sorry Violet. I never meant to cause you harm. My own stupid selfish thinking got to me. I wanted to keep what I had so badly. You probably hated me for not going with Penn's proposition. I must've been causing you both a huge amount of stress. Again, it was never in my intentions.

Please Violet. Find somewhere in your heart that you could forgive me. You had a way of putting me in my place. I often thought too much of myself and thought I was better than other people. You always found a way to make me realize that I was no more important than any other person in this world. And for that I thank you. You helped in a very subtle way but I'll never be able to thank you. Even if I did, you'd probably just look at me like I was some weird person just as everyone else does.

I can't say it enough. I'm sorry. I'm sorry. I'm sorry.

I repeated that in my head so many times that night running home. There were an amount of tears that I never experienced before and I was the only person to blame for them.

"I'm sorry Violet. I'm so sorry."

# Chapter 8

There was a pit in my stomach. A hole so wide and deep that no amount of joy and comfort could fill it. It clenched to my insides and held on for dear life. It had been four days that this feeling had become a new part of me. It got to the point where I thought it had always been there, constantly eating away at me.

On the brighter side of things, I found out something new about the human body. You can actually run out of tears. My eyes had been dry for the longest time. Whenever they managed to summon the watery substance for the wellbeing of my eye, it was quickly drawn out and wasted in the use of a tear.

Whenever I'd wake up and look in the mirror, I would look like a drunk. Bloodshot eyes were a common thing now. As I stared at the murderer I was, I couldn't help but curse at myself. I threw the most insulting things I could but none of them had the impact that it needed. Any sort of words meant nothing. Sympathy was nowhere to be found and I was lost to my own pain.

I hunched over the sink and felt the need to throw up. Everything had taken a physical toll on me. My legs shook with every step. Body jittered at every thought. Chest caved in with every loud sound. It was truly a living nightmare.

Do I dare look up again?

When I met face to face with the monster in front of me, I noticed the rare chance of tears. I examined myself as best as I could.

Who are you Mark?

Are you a selfish person that only cares for himself? Is it only about you? Other people have feelings you know and you're the one that causes them pain. You hurt them not knowing it. And for what? All because you wanted to save something that you never had? You are selfish!

A picture of Violet flashed in my head.

What about her?! All she was doing was following orders. She had to protect what she loved. I'm apparently too dangerous and I had seen the very truth of that. I had the audacity to kill someone in front of their daughter. Where is the sense in that?! No matter what you do now, you're left with the guilt. You're left with the stupid decision you made. You screwed things up and it's there to stay.

"I'm so sorry Violet," I sobbed, breaking down on the floor of the bathroom.

*      *      *

I walked back to my room after finding the energy to get back up. I had no idea how long I was in there. Track of time was now something of the past. It was all horror to me, nothing else. There wasn't a point to it. I'd rather not know how long I was sulking in my own grief.

When I left the bathroom and walked back out into the hallway, I noticed my mom was there. She was holding a hamper full of dirty clothes. I didn't bother to make eye contact with her. She knew from the morning I got home that something happened. She didn't harass me on why I got home around 4 o'clock in the morning. As far as I know, she thinks something happened between me and my friends. Although that was true to an extent, she hasn't asked much.

The dinner table would be extremely quiet. She'd do her best to try and spark up a conversation like we had months before I met them. I was slowly drifting away from her and now the time I did stay away from them, I couldn't even talk to her. It'd always end up with her talking about some random topic and I'd sit and listen. I could see the desperation in her face as she tried her best to get me to react—to look alive.

Any type of food she'd make was delicious, but now, all foods tasted disgusting. The very thought of food that I hardly ate made me want to run back to the bathroom.

"Hey," she said softly.

I felt so gross standing there letting her look at me like this. My mom always found a way to make me cheer up when I was sad or upset. Now it seemed as if her charm had left.

I didn't say anything in return. I turned and walked into my room, closing the door behind me. The bed called me in for a nice long nap but I slept too much. Even though it wasn't physically possible, I probably made up for all the lost sleep in my life. My pillow was covered in my old dry tears. The blanket thrown around in the furious fits I'd have. Looking at it from afar, I saw how much of a mess I was; what all of this had done to me.

My phone placed on my desk buzzed for about the fifth time this day and that's this day alone. The past few days had been non-stop ringing and buzzing. It wouldn't let up. *They* wouldn't let up. Charlotte, Wendy, and Will had been trying to talk to me. All of them except one person. Monica.

I sat there on my bed with my phone in hand. The vibrating was quickly phased out after around the second buzz. Charlotte's name was on the screen. I didn't want to talk to any of them. How would they see me now that they saw I killed someone? I hadn't bothered to listen to any of the thousands of voicemails they left. I'm pretty sure they couldn't leave anymore because it was full.

I waited until the phone went silent to unlock it. The voicemail box was jam-packed with countless calls from them. I randomly tapped on one and listened.

"Hey idiot." It was Will. "Listen, not like I expect you to be listening to this useless message anyways. How much of a selfish jerk can you be? You're hurting them. If you think you're trying to prove some point by not talking to us then you're terribly wrong. I hope you know I don't care one bit if you rot where you stand right now. But I know of one thing. You care the most about Charlotte and if you care about anything you'd go and talk to her. She leaves early when we go out because she can't help but feel depressed the whole time. No matter what I do I can't seem to help out and I know for a fact that you're just making things worse. You wanna be a man then pick up the dang phone!"

He was right. I knew I'd worry them. But my face didn't deserve the light of the sun. It didn't deserve to be seen by anyone. And look where my selfish tendencies took me again. I was making Charlotte depressed.

I thought about what I would've said if I answered her call just now. "I'm stupid." "I'm a terrible person." "I know you hate me." Probably something along those lines.

Will said they were worried about me but what about Monica. She hadn't bothered to call. Maybe she was just smart in knowing that I wasn't going to pick up. I gave a slight chuckle. It was the only form of emotion that wasn't depressing that I've expressed in a while. She would know me best. Or maybe…maybe she was listening.

The microphone was right at the bottom of my phone. She had the ability to listen to my furious fits of rage and despair. She'd know not to call me.

The phone buzzed once more. I didn't want to even bother looking down to see who it was but I gave in and did.

*Incoming call: Monica*

What? Had they convinced her to call me just so I could talk? The middle of my chest filled with a burning sensation. They think that just because she calls, I'd talk? Who do they think I am?! Who do they think *she* is? She's no messenger. She has feelings and intentions like they do. As much as I wanted to pick it up, out of spite, I didn't. I'd just rather listen to what she had to say when she leaves a voicemail.

After the phone stopped ringing, I checked for her message and went ahead and played it.

"Mark!" She was clearly out of breath. Maybe running? "Mark get out of there. They're coming. Penn's headed your way."

I stood now, paying full attention. It brought the same feeling as when that girl on the phone called me telling me that people wanted me dead. This time they surely did want that. There was no doubt that's what they were coming for. Revenge.

"We're heading towards your house but you need to get out of there *now*."

The voicemail ended and I was left to comprehending it. The phone fell stiff in my hand. I had fought with them before but now it was different. It was personal.

I rapidly looked around my room and thought of a way to leave. I didn't know what to do. Everything caught me off guard and happened all of a sudden. I mean, I just recovered from an episode on the bathroom floor. Now I was tasked with leaving and running from my killers.

What about my mom? They were about to burst through the front door and lay waste to anything that gets in their way. How do I tell her? How do I explain and tell her that she needs to leave?

Ugh! It doesn't matter! I just needed to warn her. I was about to run downstairs but the front door was suddenly thrown open. The hinges that connected it to the wall were instantly broken with one kick from Penn's boots. My mom shouted out in surprise and yelled.

From where I stood at the edge of the stairs, I could see the four of them in front of my mom. Brittany instantly lit her hands on fire and stormed towards her. I was helpless and did nothing.

"Don't hurt her," Penn commanded.

Brittany gave a frustrated groan and gave Penn a look.

"It's what he deserves," Brittany said.

"And hurt her for no reason?"

"You're asking me that when he killed Violet for no reason?!"

The corner of Penn's mouth flared up in a snarl.

"You watch your mouth before you mention her. We're here to kill him and him alone."

"And how's that supposed to make up for our pain?" Eli said.

"Oh you want compensation for pain? We'll get him where it hurts most."

The look on my mom's face as she heard what they were saying told of fear on many levels.

"Run Mark!" she yelled.

Their heads turned towards me just as I stormed back in my room.

There were two exits. The door and the window. I had one option. I reached for my phone and ran towards the clear glass. With shaking hands, I fiddled with the lock and unlatched it as fast as I could. Pounding slammed on the wooden stairs, motivating me to move faster. I threw the window up and peeked out. There was nothing but a sheer drop. Shingles were plastered to the neighbor's roof in front of me. I either take the fall or try and reach for the roof.

I was stupid enough to actually jump out of a window two stories high. Once I was in the air, I regretted my decision. My fingers pressed against the hard clay like roofing and struggled to support me. I looked down to where my feet dangled and I tensed up. The sight of the drop was enough to make me want them to kill me instead.

With my window still open, I heard them barge into my room. Eli and Sarah had done it once before and it felt even worse that they were standing in there a second time. Penn stared me directly in the eye, scowling at me in a way I've never seen from her. The blood red eyes and the flaming hair pronounced the death sentence they had on me. They were out for blood and it was mine.

I immediately pulled up and climbed onto the roof. They didn't hesitate to do the same and followed close behind. With the view I now had, I saw the whole city. It completely encased my vision. The scarred city was still trying to grasp what happened. The famous penthouse was nowhere to be seen. It didn't look the same without it. But barely, in between two large buildings, you could see the remains of the massacre.

My feet pressed forward and wobbled against the uneven surface. I didn't really have a clue as to where I would go after this. The houses would come to an end and I'd be left with the jump into the street. I didn't bother myself with thinking about that at the moment and focused on not falling.

When I got to a new house, I hesitated. The jump looked wider than it actually was. It was only a couple of feet to some people. My eyes continued to deceive me and convinced me that it was a chasm. I turned back to see how close they were. To my surprise, they were closing the gap pretty fast. They didn't bother with trying to stay upright. It was a full sprint on top of a stranger's house.

I took the jump and continued to run. My legs burned with the overuse of the muscles I hadn't touched in days. The most I did was walk to the bathroom and back.

The chase continued on from house to house. I didn't look back anymore. They would outrun me eventually and the ground for running was dissipating fast.

Why was I even running? I'd been kept up in my room for the past couple days because I ended someone's life. The very daughter of this person was now trying to kill me to give me the justice I deserved. If I thought that I was at fault then why was I running? If anything, I should just let her kill me. I should let all of them lay waste to me and end my life in the most brutal way they see fit.

What about the others? My friends. I'd leave them in shambles. All of my efforts, all of my wrong choices leaned on the desire for me to keep them. It'd be the highest form of disrespect for me to kill Violet and let it happen for no reason at all. She'd make the same choice if she were in my position. She wouldn't give up. She would never do that.

As I pressed on, I thought of Charlotte. I haven't seen her pretty face in days. Just the day before my crime, she was hugging me. She was so close to me that she felt my joy. She felt how happy I was. Was I too blind, too wrapped up in myself to feel her sorrow and concern for me?

You're gonna make it up to her, Mark. You're gonna make it up to all of them. And the only way that's going to happen is if you keep running.

The last house was right in sight. The dull shingles had too much exposure to sunlight and were starting to chip. I started to get the hang of running on roofs, not that it'd ever help me in the future. The patterns the builders placed them in would come up too one point on the house and descend on any other side. I had to make sure that on the climb down, I would level one foot lower than the other, keeping an incline to make sure I had my footing.

The edge of the home was right above the street that lead to downtown. The black asphalt was right in sight and was tempting me with the problem that lay ahead.

"How the heck...?"

My phone that I was carrying in my hand buzzed.

*Monica:*

*Jump*

"Jump? Are you kidding me?!" I yelled at my phone.

*Yes*

I didn't have a choice. My decision was clear. I'd be getting out, and that put my reliance on them to a huge extent. With my current state of vision, I had the sidewalk in sight. No one was there. Not one person. I searched and searched for any sign of them but all I found was the occasional pigeon.

Without any heads up, the sound of guns popped. I froze up for a second before remembering that I needed to keep running. Of course, this was their opportunity. Shooting someone before jumping off a building. Thinking about it, you'd be screwed either way. From their perspective, they thought I was better off getting shot and so did I.

The more they shot, the more visions of Violet flashed. How could you run away from a sound like that? It haunted me, making the hairs on the back of my head stand up.

With a few feet away, I amplified my lunges and flung myself over the edge. I still have no idea as to why I jumped. I mean, think about it. I was in the air, flinging myself at a road that was positioned downward. The fall was way more than two stories. My suspension in the air felt way longer than it should've been, almost as if I was being held up for some reason. It must've been Will but he wasn't there.

My arms flailed and the openness of the air was tasked with writing down my wrong in doing this unnatural task of freefall. I was so free, yet, to every extent, I was controlled. The effects of gravity were starting to pull me down like I was a pebble thrown into a lake. So helpless. So small. Forced to do whatever it wanted.

I thought of what they were doing behind me. Were they watching, waiting for me to fall and break something? Was my head in their line of sight, holding the gun up towards me? I'd fallen a few inches and realized that wasn't the question I was supposed to be asking. Where were they?

Just over the horizon, where the road curved upwards, I saw a sliver of gold. What did that mean for me? The only thing that mattered at that point. Salvation. The despair and uncertainty were dissipating and being replaced with a chance.

Her pigtails bobbed up and down with incredible speed. The only dark portion of hair on her was the curved eyebrows, adding focus to her mission.

Despite me still falling, I was filled with a feeling I felt a couple times now in the past days. It was the shared feeling that connected me to them. It was coming from the direction of Wendy. The feeling of strength, courage, adrenaline. Her feelings felt way stronger than mine ever were. Adrenaline is what kept me going. It's what pushed my body to jump over these rooftops. But Wendy's, gosh, Wendy's was something on an entirely different scale. She could fight a whole pack of wolves and still have enough to rip a lion's jaw off. And boy did I love it.

I couldn't keep my eyes off of her and continued to watch her draw closer. With every second I did that, I would fall farther.

She teleported in little spurts, disappearing and reappearing at a closer position until she was close enough. This time, she jumped before teleporting one last time.

*Swoosh*

The impact she made with my body was tremendous. My left ribcage was now shattered for all I knew. I didn't want to feel or check to see if everything was actually okay. To be honest, my eyes were closed the whole time. From the second she grabbed me, I flinched for the incoming pain and waited for the time we would teleport once more.

*Swoosh*

I hated it. Hated it! How the heck could Wendy teleport so much with this feeling? Words could not describe how it felt. Alright, well I guess I'm sorta forced to tell you now although it's going to sound weird.

It first starts with your chest. Your heart is compressed while thousands of bears press against you. The ears are next. They pop to their heart's content. And when I say pop, I'm not talking about the little cheeky pop you get on a car ride or an airplane. I'm talking an implosion. They go through a process where the insides of your ear are practically ripped out and are forcefully pushed back in when you finish. Now, as for your body. Imagine having your limbs disappear. Completely gone. Once you're in between transport; that was it. Can't do anything.

When this happens, it's mere milliseconds. Still, I managed to find the time to press myself closer to Wendy. This was completely her environment; her habitat. I was turned into a child, finding rescue in someone older.

I never touched her skin before besides her hands. To my surprise, it was extremely soft. One of my hands was placed on her arm, slightly dipping into her short sleeve. The other was wrapped around her stomach, holding her back. Something about this felt so long. It felt like an entirely different universe. Maybe it involved the same sort of mechanics with the slip space we walked into. Either way, we transcended all reality into this perfect little bubble for a miniscule amount of time. I could feel her heartbeat. It must've been pumping out blood at an incredible rate to keep up with her running, but now, it was immensely calming. Soothing to listen to. It wasn't often that she teleported with me but I hated it and loved it every time. The physical feeling it gave you was absolutely wretched but the euphoria it gave you was almost worth it.

My eyes opened back up when I felt that we had made contact with the ground and I was spared the horrible consequences of taking that jump. Wendy was quick to throw me off of her.

"C'mon! Hurry!" she yelled, already taking off.

Knowing BloodLip would soon find a way down and catch up, I went ahead and sprinted with her. I not once looked back at the roof where I was just a few moments ago.

The both of us went down the road towards downtown. All I heard the whole time was the both of us panting to compensate the plea of our lungs. After some time of running, she slowed down to a jog and stared at me. I noticed her head turn in the corner of my eye and didn't bother to acknowledge it.

She shook her head and let out a groan.

"I save your life and you don't even say anything?!"

What was I supposed to say? Thank you or I'm sorry? It had to be one of the two. She had every reason to be upset but I was at a loss for words.

"Oh, I'm doing fine. Thanks for asking. Great seeing you by the way. It's like it's been days," she said in an overly cheery voice. My hatred for her annoyance had resurfaced but I suppressed it for the wrong I'd done. "Oh wait. It has!"

She shoved me to the side and threw me into the street.

"What the heck's wrong with you, Mark?! To leave us all like that? What good were you thinking was gonna come out of this?"

"Wendy, I killed someone!"

"To save a friend's life!"

"That's no excuse!"

Her hand wrapped around my shirt and pulled me close into her face.

"Then what is?! Staying at home and leaving your friends, the people that care about you, to worry?!"

That was anger if I've ever seen it. Her whole face was a complete snarl. The corners of her mouth would occasionally jitter up towards her cheek bone, showing the white canines.

"We're not doing this now," I told her in a firm voice.

"Whatever."

She let go of me and continued her jog. My interactions with Wendy aren't the best. It was a constant battle between us and always called for a winner. Despite all that, I was still incredibly happy to see her. Even the way she looked at me with disgust, I mean, sure. Who'd want to be looked at like that? But with Wendy, it was in her law, her inner code to make sure that she did that. The glint of sunlight that amplified the color of her hair and added to the prettiness of her face brought a soft smile to me.

Thanks Wendy.

"Where's everyone else?" I asked.

"Well, it's kinda long." Her mouth moved to one side of her face and scrunched up, crinkling her lips. "We were in the mall and we saw your secret lover with her friends. She thought that we'd tell her where you were." She proceeded to call Penn a variety of curse words and explained that she kept persisting in wanting to know where I was. "And then she randomly takes off. Just like that."

"So she knew I was at home?"

"Simple deduction, Mark. Anyone could put things together and figure that out. You weren't with us. You just killed someone. Do you think that anyone in that situation would be out and about?" She ended her sentence abruptly and quickly changed it. "Actually, not anyone. Just you. They know who you are and how you'd react."

"And then you followed them."

"No. We're not that much of creeps, and it actually took a while to realize where they were going. Can you guess who found out?"

"Monica."

"Aww. It wasn't supposed to be that easy of a guess! Why do you have to ruin everything?!"

"It wasn't a guess. She called me that they were coming."

"Still, that doesn't mean anything. Charlotte tried calling first."

"So you did make Monica call," I said, raising my voice.

"Eeh, kinda. Not entirely. She wanted to do it in the first place." Wendy waved her hands to get the thought out of my head. "That's not important."

"Fine. Keep going."

"Okay. So, Monica hacked into the city's surveillance system without telling us." She chuckled a bit before continuing. "We were walking around looking at bikinis for the beach and she's over here just hacking away. Yeah, anyways, she just watched where they were going. She was the only one, of course, to think that something was suspicious. Well, we all thought something was a bit fishy but not anything life threatening."

"You should know better. They killed people before."

"Shut up! Don't call me stupid!"

"I didn't!"

She pointed her finger at me in accusation.

"You were implying it. It's the same thing. Ugh! Why do you have to keep interrupting me? It's hard enough to talk right now as it is."

"But you're the…" I stopped myself before she would use it as proof to prove her point.

"As I was saying," she said, shoving her face in my own. "Monica saw they were running towards your place. She came and told us and we left. By then, they had a pretty big lead over us so we knew they'd get there before we could help you."

"That still doesn't explain where everyone else is."

"Oh yeah. I was getting there."

"Sure."

"Shut it," she said with a glare.

"And how'd you get here so fast?"

"Hitched a ride in a sporty Corvette. Well..." She stopped herself for a quick second. A nasty grin appeared as if she'd done something bad and enjoyed it. "Here." She tossed me her phone. "Go to the contacts and tell me if you recognize the first number."

I scrolled through the various numbers before realizing that I was in the outgoing calls tab. My stomach fell at the sight of the list. Practically every single call that she made was to me. I hadn't answered a single one.

It's not the time to sulk in your guilt, Mark. You can do that later. I went ahead and went to the calls tab and found a number that I'd seen once before. I memorized it, thinking one day it'd show up on my phone again.

"It's the girl," I said in amazement.

"Yup! Can you believe she gave me a Corvette to take over here? Mark! It was a Corvette! Who does that?!"

"So she just told you to take it?"

"Yeah. I was thinking I'd see her there but she wasn't. She just told me the street that the car was on and that it had the keys in it. What I don't get, though, is how she knew I needed it. But anyways, Will just told me to take it because I was the one who could save you the easiest."

"How'd he know I'd be on top of a house?"

"He didn't. Like I said, he just said I could get you out of tricky situation pretty quickly. So I went ahead and took it."

"Where's it now?"

"That's a question. Um...I was speeding. But hey, there was a logical reason for it. One of my best buds was in trouble." She jabbed her shoulder into my chest and winked at me. A sigh was released before she dropped the whole facial expression and her back hunched over. "Cops were on me."

"Wendy!"

"What?! I had to get to you fast."

"How fast were you going?"

"Mmm, about 110."

"Don't treat it like it's nothing! You could've hurt someone!"

"It's fine. No one was hurt. Never crashed. I'll have you know that my dad had me driving his car around ten. I'm pretty good behind the wheel, boy. But the cops got to me and I slammed the thing into a light post and ran off." She lifted a hand to stop me from talking. "I said I never crashed and that's true. When you crash, it's on accident. When you do what I did, it's because it was on purpose. I wasn't just gonna brake and stop the car before I run off. So I had to run for a bit and made it just in time it seems."

"How do you suppose we're getting back, then?"

"We're going to the bus stop. The rest of them are waiting there."

Oh Wendy. You still don't fail to do something stupid. Listening to her tell her little adventure of how she got here made me realize how much I missed her. I guess it is possible to want to hear the annoying bratty voice of this snob. That's when you know they're a true friend.

Pretty soon, we got to the bus stop. The blue little case that allowed for seating was occupied by the rest of them. Charlotte, Will, and Monica turned and looked at me from afar. Just that alone triggered the guilt train and hauled everything at me once again. All of them almost looked like strangers. It'd only been four days but after being used to hanging out with them every second of the day, it really changes a lot of things.

The distinct smell of the spring air and the light breeze brought a great sense of ambition. I wanted to go over and give all of them a hug. Heck, even Will. There I said it. I missed all of them.

Charlotte's hair blew around slightly with the breeze. Her hair had remained short the entire time we'd known each other. Every other month it required a trim so it never changed. I grew to love it so much that I tried to convince every other girl I knew, even my mom, to cut their hair short. Everyone gets tired of me saying it but my claim still stands. Any girl with short hair is drop dead gorgeous.

Okay, what am I gonna say? It's gonna be extremely awkward when I get to them. With Wendy it was easy. I could count on her to break the ice. A quick little smart remark from her and that was it. With them, I guess you could say they were slightly more normal. It needed more effort to chip off that resentment they most likely had for me. My reliance on Wendy had been expended. It was now my turn and my job to make sure I said something.

I thought and thought but nothing came to mind. The bus stop drew nearer and I was eventually there. My eyes scanned over them pretty quickly, making sure not to stay focused on them for too long.

Charlotte went ahead and gave me a subtle smile along with a nod. Her hands were placed in her lap, resting on top of her purple skirt. Monica didn't show any form of expression to seeing me again. It was all I needed. That told me she was fine and everything was okay. Will was leaning up against the post and raised an eyebrow at me. I'd almost accidentally scoffed at him but remembered that wasn't easily accepted at a time like this; with tension like this. You know, when I was alone, by myself in my room, I thought that I'd start to lose the feelings and connections I had with them. I proved that notion false when I wanted to punch him in the face. Nope, still had that feeling. Darn pretty boy.

A small instance of happiness resonated throughout but I still failed. I hadn't said anything at all. The big black letters that spelled out "jerk" hovered over my head. I left them for days and I said nothing in return for my absence.

"Guys," Charlotte said. Her voice crackled with uncertainty.

I was quick to focus on her like I was used to doing. Her eyes were widened at the sight in front of her, looking in the direction I just came. I didn't need to think twice about what was there. Wendy and I only had a small advantage over them in time.

Without turning around, my mind started to make up the picture in my head. Furious eyes. Quick sprinting. A group of murderers bent on the soul craving that they had for revenge.

"The bus," I said softly to myself. The bus wasn't here. Where was it? Surely it must've been running behind because of the commotion in the city. Detours and all that. But it needed to be here.

My feet felt weak underneath me. No matter how much I tried hopping on my toes and moving them around, it wouldn't go away.

They all stood now and watched them get closer.

"Where's the bus?!" I yelled this time. I wasn't about to fight them again. Not after what I did to her mom. Someone was bound to end up in the same place as Violet and I'm not risking that. Was I really going to have that depend on a stupid bus?

Monica walked over to me and looked me in the eye. She was still calm and hadn't been phased by the approach of BloodLip. It was normal for her, yes, but how could she?

It was like she saw a pack of toy poodles running towards instead of the pit bulls that we saw.

"It's right down the street. I made the bus skip a couple of stops to get here in time." Her head moved towards the rest of them to better amplify her voice. "Get ready to jump in."

Of course. Why didn't I trust her? Monica was gonna make sure we got out. After all, she was the one who saved my life by seeing where they were going.

"There's no way the bus is gonna take off that quick," Will said as the bus took a turn and appeared on the street.

"That's why you're gonna bribe him."

The bus hissed and came to a halt. I waited an eternity before the doors squeaked open. We all piled in and rushed for a seat. I was at the back and the last one to get in. With a few seconds before it'd be my turn, I went ahead and looked over my shoulder. I'm talking mere feet here. Only a few more steps and they would've reached out and grabbed my shirt.

"Go!" Will yelled at the bus driver. He threw his wallet on his lap and manually closed the doors.

The driver saw that some other people were running towards us and stepped on the gas. Good thing Monica chose a smart driver that won't ask questions.

"You got some people chasing you I see," he said.

And here we go.

"None of your business," Wendy hollered.

"Actually, you made it my business. How much are you planning on giving me? And you better make it reasonable so I don't throw you out right now."

Okay. I'll take back what I said about him. He's an idiot. A person only interested in further investing in his money. Nothing but a snob like everyone else in this worthless city.

I could tell by looking at Will's face that he badly wanted to talk back to him. Make him pay. I was right along with him but we couldn't irk him. He had the upper hand.

"Take whatever's in there."

The bus driver's moustache was lifted due to his gut wrenching smile.

"Heh. Seems like a fair trade. Go ahead and take your seat. Hey, and uh, why were those people chasing you anyways?"

"I said it's none of your business!" Wendy was starting to lose it. "So you sit your fat butt in that seat and drive us like you're supposed to!"

"I'm not much of a man for mannerism, but that's no way to speak to an adult."

"I don't care if it is or not. You should be used to it by now anyways. Hearing all kinds of junk is your job. And I'm not the reason you chose to be a lousy pig and do nothing but eat fast food and turn a freakin' circle."

There we go. Thanks a lot Wendy. Have I told you how much I appreciate you ruining everything because I don't think I do that enough. I'll start off by thanking you for having us thrown off our fastest way to getting downtown.

The man gave a hearty laugh that made his beer belly jiggle with a disgusting amount of mass.

"Right you are little girl. Right you are."

"I'm no little girl!"

Will raised an eyebrow at her.

"You aren't?" Will asked.

Wendy let out a groan as loud as a lions roar and punched him several times over in the arm.

"Shut up!"

We went ahead and let out a few breaths before sitting down. The seats felt harder this time despite us being on practically every single bus there was. The whole thing was empty besides us. Normally, there'd be a few people here and there. If we were late to get to town, there'd be more people our age making out and listening to music; that sort of thing. It must've been because of Monica.

She sat next to Will and gave him a tap on the shoulder.

"I'll pay you back."

He shook his head.

"Don't need to. I'm not upset about that. Wendy did more than I could've done already so it doesn't matter."

"You're welcome!" Wendy yelled at him, overhearing their conversation.

"You could've risked everything, idiot."

"Pshh, I knew he wouldn't do it."

"Oh yeah? And how'd you know that?"

Wendy pointed to her stomach and started to laugh.

"He's a jolly man. There's no way he can get mad."

"Wow. You really believe that?"

"Believe? It's true! My grandpa is one of the fattest people I know besides Mark and he stays true to that."

I didn't waste my breath on trying to defend myself. As I said before, I sorta missed hearing her annoying voice and I thought I'd allow myself to be the victim once more.

Wendy kept peeking over at me, waiting for a response. Her smile was fading with every look.

"What, no "Shut up!"?" she asked.

I gave a small shake of my head.

"Well, guys. Looks like we got a problem." She dragged their attention towards her. "Someone stole our Mark. This one's a fake."

She ran over to me and started to tug on my face and pull on my hair.

"What the heck are you doing?!"

"Trying to take off your mask."

"Can't you find a better time to mess around?" I asked.

Her hands released me and she flumped in the seat next to me.

"Fine."

I checked the clock on the bus for the time. It was 3:00. Generally, with not that much traffic, it'd take the bus a few minutes to get to our stop. But how much had the terrorist attack affected the city? The penthouse fell, a highway that was a common route for getting around was blown to bits, and I heard that there were some shootings also. Pretty much, no one knew what happened or why.

With what happened with BloodLip, I'd forgotten all about it. And how could I? I was in the middle of it and was nearly killed by it. Wasn't I self-indulged.

Now the question that was to be asked was what are we going to do about Penn? We can't run from her forever. School was gonna be starting back up in just a few days. We were left without a teacher and a blood thirsty girl who wanted me dead. I'd be surrounded by her at school constantly. There was no getting around that. I felt so helpless. I was stuck.

"What are we gonna do?" I asked.

I had my head down at the time, still thinking about how deep in trouble I was. I heard no response from any of them. When I decided to look up at them, I was met with all of their eyes. What I'd do? Was there something on my face?

I almost chuckled when I realized what it was. I spent all this time avoiding them and I asked a selfish question. Wendy was upset when I did the same to her earlier.

"I'm an idiot. You don't need to tell me that," I said. "You can tell me how much I screwed up and I'll agree with you the whole way, but you'll never know the feeling I had. You think I was gonna let Charlotte die?"

Will gave me a beating glare.

"You don't think we were scared too? You selfish imbecile. She's our friend too! Stop acting like everything's about you!"

He was standing now.

"I killed someone! That's never gonna change and it's gonna stay with me forever! You have no idea what the heck that feels like!"

I combated his stance with my own. Everyone was watching as we raised our voices. Though we never really got along, we've never gone to the extent of yelling at each other.

"There you go again! Can't you spare us the pain and just stop?!"

"Spare *you* the pain? You don't know pain!"

Will's face was just as ugly as mine. With my peripheral vision, I could see our reflection in the window of the bus. Both of us were throwing our lashes at each other. I swear, if he said another word I was going to tackle him.

I noticed his fists were clenched. That wasn't all I noticed. My throat felt funny. It felt like a lump of pressure was building inside it. The more his face grew numb, the harder it became to breath.

*Is he...choking me?*

I reached up to my neck and felt for the hands that weren't there.

*What?*

He was. His face twisted as he concentrated on making me suffer. Not after a few seconds did everyone else realize what he was doing. I couldn't talk. I couldn't do anything but look into his eyes. When I did, I couldn't help but feel defeated. I lost. It was never because he was the first to attack physically, no, but he made me peer into his eyes. It was his turn to assert his dominance.

*Will. What the heck is wrong with you? What are you doing?*

Once they realized what was happening, there was a unanimous gasp. Monica shot up quickly. She didn't say anything to Will but simply stood in front of him, making her dark eyes seep into his.

Charlotte ran over to me and placed a hand on my arm as she looked at me in shock. She constantly looked between me and Will. Back and forth.

Wendy slowly stood with a burning anger.

"Will," she said in a firm voice.

"Pain? I'll show you pain," Will snarled, only concentrating on me.

"Will," Wendy said once more in the same demeanor.

My vision was starting to darken and Charlotte's face became harder to see.

"Get your hands off him," Monica said, now speaking up.

She watched him continue his pressure and I witnessed her snap within seconds. She reached up and threw a bolt into his neck. He yelled out in pain but she wasn't done. Her hands grabbed just underneath his chin and threw him at the other side of the bus, flinging him against the window.

Once he opened his eyes after the initial pain, I noticed his anger wasn't present. He didn't care about me anymore, he was scared as he should've been. Monica was the one to stop him. I'm sure Wendy would've done the same just as much as Charlotte. But Monica was the one. The quietest. The calmest. The one with "no emotions".

I fell back in my seat next to Wendy and Charlotte gasping for air. My energy was depleted for the time being and I couldn't do much to him anymore despite the pleas of my soul.

"You hypocrite," Monica said. She was standing over him as he was sprawled out on the seat. "You're just as selfish as you call him."

"Who are you to call me selfish?" Will responded.

"Who are you to choke your friend?" she threw back.

Will sneaked a quick look at me, trying not to for too long.

"Alright then. You wanna be civil then we'll be civil."

Monica helped him up and he pampered his clothes, trying to take out any wrinkle in them. He took a seat in the very bench that he was thrown at. Monica went ahead and sat next to him like nothing ever happened.

"Let's go back to your original question then," he continued. "What're we gonna do? We're gonna go downtown and get as far from them as we can."

"That's not helping anything," I said, not even looking his way.

"Then please, tell me your plan because I'd love to hear it."

"..."

"Right. You don't have one. We need to give Penn some time. Hopefully she can cool off and we can talk things out."

I finally let my scoff out this time.

"Ironic isn't it," I said.

He gave a soft laugh.

"Yeah. I guess you're right."

He threw his arms out in my direction and pushed me next to Charlotte. I bumped into her and we snugged up close to the wall.

I didn't really care what he was doing. This was his way of saying sorry, I guess, so I didn't move. Charlotte gave me a look to see if I'd move and awkwardly tried to position herself better. After doing so she focused back on the conversation.

"She had four days, Will," she said. "Knowing how she is, I don't think that's gonna happen anytime soon."

"It's the only option we have right now."

"And if they decide to raid his house again?" Wendy asked, stroking her hair.

Will didn't speak again. He knew they were flaws to what he wanted to do, but he was also right. There was no better option.

There was a scratching noise on the driver's radio. He picked up the microphone and talked into it.

"Go ahead."

I couldn't make out a thing that person on the other end was saying.

"Seriously? Another one? Okay I'll be right there." He set it down and turned his head a bit. "Hate to break your little private ride but there's a problem. I need to return to station ASAP. Looks like I gotta drop you off at the nearest stop."

"But I gave you the money!" Will yelled.

"Yup, and I'm keeping it too. Sorry man, rules are rules."

There was no further arguing with him. We had to accept the fact that we were getting jipped. If nothing else, we put some more distance between us and BloodLip.

The bus driver stuck to his word and slowed at a stop at the start of downtown. It was the line where the suburban and city culture started to mix and slapped an ugly look on the residential area. It was as if the smog didn't dare go any further than that and held pity for the rest of the suburban homes. Back at home it was clear skies for days, but once you passed here, you better limit your breaths.

We hurried off of the bus and expected him to scurry off with his crafty profit, but instead, he held the door open and was deep in thought. A troubled look plastered itself on his face. After a few seconds he turned to face towards us and searched for words to express his unusual feeling.

"You guys be safe," he said with a soft voice. "I almost had my son killed in the attack. It would've killed me to hear the news but thankfully he made it out in time. You guys remind me a lot of him. So do me a favor and don't get hurt." He looked me in the eye and gave a nod. "God bless."

With that, he left us on the sidewalk and threw the gasses from the bus at our faces.

\*        \*        \*

Something about the atmosphere felt different. Maybe all humans had the same sort of connection we had with each other. Without ever needing to tell anyone that there was an attack on this city, a blind man could feel the effect of it. Or maybe we were connected to the city somehow. Living here all my life, I knew the ins and outs of this place. The longer you lived here, the more connected you are? I don't know.

The air stank. The smell of ash lingered and gently stroked the tips of your nostrils. It brought back visions of the falling penthouse. I never really got the chance to think about it, but I wondered how many people actually died from it. Hundreds of famous people lived in there and must've fallen along with it. I would often tell myself that I couldn't care less about anyone famous, but when you think about it along the lines of actual lives, they were people too. When they realized they were plummeting to the ground and had no escape, they were not acting, singing, or creating drama. They were expressing the purest of feelings and emotions: fear, anguish, desperation. Pity was not something given lightly by me, but I felt all the more sorry for making fun of their lives before.

As we walked down the busy sidewalks, I would read people's faces. Sure, there'd always be the people who'd hate being in public places or hated their jobs, but this time you could see something there. There were hardly any smiles to be seen. I'd hear the occasional laugh but it was put to death the second it was uttered as if it was a crime to do so.

It made me think; we are all different people. We have different feelings, different opinions, different lifestyles, but we all express the same human qualities. We know what is to be expected of us in certain times. No matter what race, ethnicity, or religion; when someone has fallen or is in trouble, we can't help but feel for them. The inner desire to be treated as one wishes to be treated is expressed feely.

I don't often help people even though I should do so more often, but when I saw that lady and her child running for their very lives, I was moved to do something. My mindset was switched to something I wasn't used to.

Were we, as humans, that selfish? Do we really only connect and see how similar we are when something bad happens?

I was too deep in thought and question that I didn't realize they'd been talking. They said they were hungry and wanted to get some food. It may sound stupid to get food at a time like this and I completely agree but what can I say, we were hungry. I was down with that but I just needed to call my mom first and let her know that I wasn't going to be home for dinner.

Wait. My mom. I'd forgotten all about her. What'd she think about what happened? She's heard of Penn before and on a few occasions she even came to the door to pick me up a little early to walk to school. Suddenly, her and a few others that she didn't know came barging into her house to hurt her son. To her everything must've been so sudden. I knew I was to make up an excuse for her but I didn't want to do that at the moment.

I reached in my pocket for my phone and only pulled out the clumps of lint from inside. With assurance that I had it there, I looked again but found nothing. The only sound conclusion I came up with was that I dropped it when Wendy hit me. I was holding my phone just before I jumped so that had to be it. Because of that, I lost all connections with my mother.

We found a cafe that we hadn't eaten at before. Probably family owned. It was a little run down and felt very homey. Once you walked in, you felt that everyone knew each other, kinda like we went back in time to towns in the fifties.

The aroma of the freshly cooked food calmed me a bit. I didn't realize how hungry I was until now. The five of us took a seat at an open table in the middle of the place.

Not long afterwards did someone come to our table.

"Hey guys! I didn't expect to see you here." The girl's voice was cheery with a smile that could match the length of the Great Wall of China. It was the girl that handed me my schedule at the beginning of the school year. "Usually everyone from school eats closer to midtown but I guess because of what happened you guys would be here."

"Yeah, I guess," Charlotte said with a soft smile to not ruin Aryn's pleasant mood.

Aryn had been a very popular girl in school. She talked with practically everybody. I never knew she had a job as a waitress. She seemed like the type that'd go downtown with the rest of her friends like we do. I guess maybe she's more responsible than we are.

As weird as it sounds, the clothes that the cafe made her wear made her glow. It expressed that she was a responsible young woman with a goal. What appeared to be different was that her hair seemed darker and she wore dark nail polish. Had she been slipping into the gothic look?

"Did you dye your hair?" Wendy asked.

Aryn's eyes widened at Wendy's words. Her hands flew up to it and twirled it around quickly, not even making it look natural.

"Uh...y—yeah. Dyed? Mhm. I d—dyed it."

"Oh, that's cool."

"Yeah, cool. Heh."

Aryn stood with her arm wrapped around her other, providing comfort to herself before she jumped up.

"Oh! Your orders. I'm sorry. What do you guys want?"

You bet Wendy went ahead and ordered for herself first, trying to find the most expensive thing on the menu. She probably was gonna force me to pay since I haven't eaten with them in a while.

After we ordered our food, I found myself lost in thought once again staring out the window. At the entrance of the building where the walls should be were replaced with complete facings of glass, allowing anyone outside to look inside and have someone inside make eye contact with them.

It made for some fun watching people walk aimlessly and not realize that there was a person watching them. I would pick out things that were unique in the passersby. A new hairstyle I never saw, interesting clothing, a personality that was expressed through a window.

Even though we were at the edge of downtown, there were still plenty of people walking the sidewalks doing their shopping. As Aryn was saying, I wouldn't be surprised if midtown was almost barren.

A girl and boy walked past the windows and I immediately went down and searched them with my eyes. The girl had a decent length of hair and normal clothes. Nothing that special about her. The boy looked like another average guy in high school. Just another boring couple of people.

They passed and the next group of people came up to be victim to my searching. The moment I saw a hint of red, I froze. The girl's hair swayed with her firm steps, searching for what was hers. Three other people joined her with a stampeding form. One was a walking mass of muscle and the other two had hips that moved for miles each step. A coincidence? I could only hope so.

She stopped right in her path. For some reason I could feel something. It resembled the connected feeling closely but not quite in the way I was used to. She menacingly turned her head towards the cafe. I don't know if me looking away would've done anything for me. She would've known regardless.

I was met with bloody eyes eating at me. Lust for blood made them hunger for my flesh to be torn. She went to position the rest of her body towards me and stood for a good while and made me shrink in surmounting fear. All the while, the others kept on with their conversation. I was unable to speak or move and let them know. The chains of death held me in place for my conqueror to do her bidding.

Penn's body was scrunched shoulders and twitching muscles. As she walked through the cafe door with the rest of them, she went ahead and already coiled up her fingers into a fist. With the little jingle of the bell on top of the door frame, the others noticed who walked in and stopped any form of conversation.

"Hi welcome to—"

The lady at the front counter was cut short when Eli grabbed her by her neck. There was a gurgling noise that emanated from her compressed throat that ended the sentence for her.

Penn still had her sights on me and didn't bother with giving Eli any commands on what to do with her. Her walk paced everything, telling exactly what she was going to do to me. I stumbled over my seat as I tried to get out of it, keeping my eyes on her. Without realizing what was going on, I was jumped on by her and the other were immediately pushed back by Brittany and Sarah like a pack of wolves singling out a meal.

The table that we were about to eat on now had me as its platter. My whole body was sprawled out as if I was to be dissected and taking the situation into consideration, she might've had that planned anyways.

My vision started to blur with the loss of oxygen and my chest burned. Penn had her hand around my neck as Eli had the lady.

"Stop it Eli! Please!"

It was Aryn's voice. He still had the hold of her oxygen, robbing her the pleasure of keeping her organs alive. She kept pleading with Eli to stop but he continued to stare into the ladies eyes and watch her slowly die.

"Enough!" shouted a man that stood out of the people who stopped eating.

Penn kept a hand on me and turned to look at him.

"Oh, you think we're the bad ones," she said with a hallucinatory voice. "You think that just because what you see now means anything?" She paused and lifted her chest, inhaling in for the next couple of words. "You had a murderer sitting right with you!" she shrieked. "He killed my mom and I'm only ridding you of a filthy excuse for a human."

"I'm afraid I'm not going to be able to let you do that." He raised a badge to show her his status as an officer.

Sarah walked up to the man and threw her foot into his stomach. The officer fell to the floor having the wind knocked out of him. She picked him up by his shirt using both of her hands and rammed him into a set of chairs, making sure his head made firm contact with the corner of one of the tables. There was a gasp of unison when people saw there was blood coming out from his head.

"You think we care if you're a cop or not," she scoffed as she stood over him.

A lady in the back of the cafe fumbled quickly in her purse. She wasn't even trying to be discrete in the slightest. Anyone could notice that her movements weren't fluid enough like the rest of the people there.

Brittany stormed over to her, pushing through all the chairs and tables, knocking them over with ease. With my current position, I wasn't able to really see what she pulled out of the back of her belt but I was pretty sure what it was. I'd seen it way too many times now, even being killed by it. The shape had now been implanted in my head so even if there was a series of flashing pictures, I could tell you if there was a gun in there or not. She clanked the gun up to her head and I even felt the remembered feeling of the cold chamber on my forehead. The lady froze and kept the phone next to her ear.

"Put the phone down," she said in a crooked voice. She sounded very similar to Penn at the time. Her tone of voice was tormented. I hadn't realized how much the death of Violet had affected them. She had trained them after all.

The lady unlatched the phone from her palm and let it drop to the floor, probably cracking the screen.

"You get your gun off of my wife!" said a man that stood up. He made sure he didn't reach over her to not make her pull the trigger.

Brittany's crazed face turned towards him and smiled. She let the gun off of his wife and put it away in her belt.

"Very well," she said.

There was a little sigh of relief that I let out. Had she really an ounce of kindness? Was she more hesitant than Sarah?

Brittany's hand exploded in balls of flames and put my hopes to death. The embers illuminated the room and added the wavy glow to the walls. Her shirt caught fire and started to shribble away, having the ashes add to the amount in the city. Below her shirt was the brown tank top I'd seen twice before; the flame resistant one.

The man's eyes reflected the goddess's powers. He backed up but hit the wall of glass behind him.

"Brittany! What the heck are you doing?!" Will yelled.

She still faced the man as she talked.

"Letting everyone know that they aren't strong. They think they're all heroic for trying to protect what's theirs but they have no idea what's really there. They have no idea." She said the last sentence in a small chuckle. "It's time BloodLip reaches its full potential. Make everyone cower at the sight of us. Make them fear what we truly are."

They just broke one of the biggest rules we had. It was a universal one. It was unanimous. We didn't want to tell people about our powers, nonetheless show them. Now they decide to show everyone?

Brittany reached up to the man's neck and singed it, forcing him down and begging her to stop. I'd never seen a grown man cower down as fast as him.

The skin that she touched bubbled and peeled, giving off a foul odor. I'd say burning flesh isn't on my list for good smelling things. The act was extremely foreign and taboo to cook human meat, but if there was a restaurant that served it, I'm sure this is what the inside would smell like. Absolutely foul.

Brittany watched his wife try to help care for his wound. She would laugh every once in a while and with every chuckle, her flames would burst forth even brighter.

Penn returned her focus to me and I realized, once again, that she came here for me. I was to be punished for my actions, but would she do it here? Heh, of course she would. With what they already had done, there was no doubt that she'd do it right in front of people to make it worse.

When I looked in her eyes, I missed seeing the light and soft eyes she had when I hadn't done anything wrong. Her unnatural eyes were something of pure beauty, but to see them like this, full of absolute rage, I couldn't help but to plead for the old Penn. If somehow the old Penn was to walk through that door and see the current version of her, she would fight to protect me for sure. She actually cared for me. Even Violet said it. What had I done? Was this all my doing?

"Eli, get me the leg from that table," said Penn.

He spared no time to do as she said. The lady that he was choking passed out long ago and now laid on the floor. Before anything, he touched the same material of the leg of the table and his skin was overcome with the dark metal. With ease, he pulled it off and handed it over to Penn.

She put up her hand to reject what Eli was giving her and jerked her thumb back towards Brittany.

"Brittany, I want that thing as hot as you can get it."

A wide smile spread from cheek to cheek as she yanked the metal pole from his hands.

"With pleasure."

I watched helplessly while she lit up the metal in her hand. The black slowly started to glow and gain brightness little by little.

Charlotte and the others ran over to stop them from what they knew would be my torture but Sarah simply held up a gun in their direction to stop them from moving.

"Oh you have no idea how much I wanna shoot you," Sarah said, almost bouncing in anticipation. "If it were up to me, I'd do it right now. But Penn's plan; it's way better. Pain for pain, am I right?"

Penn took the bar from Brittany and held the glowing end close to my face. The heat could be felt from any point in the building. Even with it being a foot away from my face, I had sympathized with the man that Brittany hurt. Her powers were incredibly painful.

"Kinda funny don't you think? When I saw you for the first time, I never thought I'd be killing you like this." She looked up for a quick sec. "Nah, scratch that. I never thought I'd be killing you, period. Violet always wanted to but the only reason you're still here is because of me. I protected you and how do you repay me?!" She brought the pole closer. "Answer me!"

I knew what I'd done wrong. I knew my mistakes, believe me. But something about confessing when you know you did wrong was always going to be difficult. She knew what I did and so did I. There was no need for me to say it besides the fact that I could have third degree burns at any time of her choosing.

"Answ—"

Sirens wailed next to us in the street. Penn stopped yelling and looked over to see what was there. A few sports cars zipped by and following close behind was a few set of cop cars and military vehicles rampaging in the streets.

It was an opening. I knew it the moment Wendy disappeared from my sight and I heard her infamous sound. The adrenaline from her rippled through every single one of us and so did mine.

Wendy appeared behind Penn and pulled the bar from her grip. With only mere second to react, she threw it into Eli's face. He shouted out in pain and brought everyone's attention to him.

With one opportunity comes another. Will rammed into Penn and freed me from my little prison despite our previous bickering.

I felt the presence of Charlotte come close towards me. She had her own special feeling. It gave comfort and assurance that things were going to be okay no matter what. As long as she was there.

The soft delicate hand that she lend me inflicted a strange feeling within. Once my hand made contact with her skin, I felt something pass between us. I immediately felt any sort of feeling she was feeling. When she would shift her attention to BloodLip recovering from Wendy's initiation of an attack, I could feel the same feeling I get with fear and anger. It was the strange combination of emotions that stirred this mess of a feeling. It drove some of the craziest of impulses. When she would turn back to look at me, I felt the same thing I felt when I would look at her.

I know what you're thinking. It's love. Hah! I wouldn't know the first thing to love. What I did know is that it was something far superior than that. It wasn't on the same spectrum. I'm not saying the feeling was greater than love, but it wasn't even to be compared to it. The feeling simply just was.

The thing was, though, I didn't know why I felt this way. I almost freaked out when I found out. Looking down at my feet to see my footing, I didn't see them. Well, I guess that's a lie. I was able to see them, but the only thing that was different was that they were see through. No, I couldn't see my veins or bones, I merely was able to look past myself and see everything else. The only remnant left of me was a thin outline.

I was invisible.

Charlotte held onto my hand with an everlasting grip. Not long after she hauled me away from them did our joined hands start to fester a pool of sweat.

"Wendy let's go!" she yelled.

Before Wendy could run over to Monica and Will to teleport out with them, Monica threw a wave of electricity at them. All four of them stumbled over and cried out. I knew very well what that felt like. Monica sure was a beauty of a beast.

Penn had none of it, though. She fought every nerve ending to get back up. Little flashes of purple escaped from within Penn's eyes, creating a color like no other. The dark force was still pursuing inside her, wrecking everything it found; vital organs and all.

With the very sight of seeing their leader's strength, it impacted the rest of them greatly. Brittany, Sarah, and even Eli with the searing skin mark broke the barrier of pain to stand. Wendy stalled for no one and created her pocket of space and escaped with Will and Monica.

The rest of the people from the cafe started to finally react with us leaving, knowing that the harsh cruel punishment of BloodLip was not eternal. But they wouldn't know of the pain. Not one bit. Even the men that Brittany and Sarah hurt. They could only feel the immediate effect of their powers. But me, no, us; we would be the ones to feel the full-fledged war that they would put on. We were the ones that were going to have to deal with their wrath. The dreadful thoughts, the heart wrenching decisions, and the unforgivable crimes that each and every one of us would commit. All of this was starting right before my eyes. Was I too blind to see it?

Charlotte and I burst out of the door, practically shattering the glass in the process. Both of us were still in the act of defying nature. She took on the same form as I was in; completely see through. Despite this, I was surprised that I was still able to make out the features in her face. At the time, she was all too focused. With our connected state, I could feel her determination. We'd been in a few situations with BloodLip that probably spurred this face of hers, but not once had I intently looked at it as I did then.

Her eyes moved with incredible speed, scanning the entire area for any threats or possibly a chance at safety. The eyebrows right above were egging on any opposers that she was ready to deal with them. That is if they could even see her.

As we drew further down the sidewalk, there'd be little intervals of pain that clearly showed themselves to me on her face. With every grit of her teeth, the outline that I had would flash, revealing my visible self. She told me once before that this was her limitation. It was harder for her to make others invisible as well.

Once again, I was the one who was causing pain. Ever since I found out I was the Equilibrium, it's all been trouble and pain. Not just for me too. Specifically for my friends. Heck, even I caused pain for all of the members of BloodLip. It was eternal pain for Violet and everlasting for the others. What was so special about me anyways?! Not once have my powers benefitted me. This useless power I have isn't even worth it if it's going to cause pain.

I pulled my hand away from Charlotte and revealed myself to the world. I'm not gonna cause anyone anymore pain. Charlotte doesn't deserve it. None of them deserve it.

She turned and showed her confused face as to why I let go of her. I paid no attention to it and focused on running. Wendy and the others joined alongside us, pushing ahead and fighting the drag of the air.

There was too much sound to know if Penn had made it out of the cafe yet or not. All that was heard was the constant scream from the wind and the pounding of our hearts. And when I say hearts, I mean hearts, as in multiple hearts. Each one of their chest's found their way to my ears. In the heat of the moment, I thought nothing of it. It took a few moments to realize that there were other beats besides my own. The fact that I could hear each of their individual hearts that made sure they stayed alive was something else. It was obviously linked to the force that allows me to feel their feelings, which I still didn't know all about. The only conclusion I ended up making was that the more intense the situation became, the closer I felt to them. And with what was going to happen, it was about to increase.

\*       \*       \*

We'd been running for some time now. The soles of my shoes must've been completely torn to the point where I was just running on my socks. Even then I probably wouldn't be able to tell. My feet were numb and didn't feel the hardest of steps.

My lungs were also feeling the full effect of it. There was a cold burning sensation in the pit of my lungs, if that even makes sense.

I wanted to stop. I begged for rest but I couldn't comply with my head. There was a group of murderers right behind us. No matter where we went, they still found us. We tried weaving in and out of buildings, running around the same street twice, and so many other ways. There seriously wasn't a point to it. How's your plan working out now Will? Does Penn look like she's cooled off?

There was no time to bother with stopping and trying to come up with something else to do. I wanted to avoid another fight as much as possible but it seemed like that wasn't an option anymore. If there needed to be one, which looked like it was going to end up being that way, I wanted it to happen in an alleyway or an empty lot. Somewhere where there wasn't going to be people. They ruined everything with showing people our powers but there wasn't a point in showing even more people.

In the distance, I heard sirens. The overly large buildings blocked off some of the sound and made it appear quiet, like it wasn't anywhere close when it was probably just across the street. These wailing sirens were common here. Nothing out of the ordinary. Living in such a big city, you're bound to have a lot of crimes.

A helicopter flew over our heads and let the blades chop the air to its desire, creating a strange ripple effect. What was strange about it was that it was lower than normal. Usually they fly higher than the skyline of the city. The only time that they flew this low was when they were chasing someone down and they needed light or the news filmed it for everyone to see.

I tried my best to get it out of my head, thinking it must've been nothing and kept on. Seconds later, it came back around, this time even lower. I tried to make out what kind of chopper it was but the glare of the sun prohibited any sight. It created the same effect that lunar eclipses create, darkening the object in front of it. It hovered right on the street and slightly moved around. Another joined and took its place close by it.

The others noticed too. Monica slowed down and I followed her pace. I knew that she was looking up what was going on. I thought of what way she was doing this. Maybe she was watching the news or was looking on the surveillance cameras again?

The sirens got closer and closer with every second. You could hear when they would pass by a building and the whaling would get louder.

We all slowed, forgetting about BloodLip.

"Monica what's going on?" I asked.

"I don't—"

She was cut off when cop cars swerved around the street corner. Just when I thought they were done, more kept turning onto the street. It was a continuous flow and went on without letup. Car after car. Siren after siren.

They randomly parked around the street, stopping traffic and even pedestrian flow on the sidewalk.

Military vehicles made their way through the cop cars and halted right in front of us. I was able to notice that they were from the military outpost not that far from here, a little past the mountains.

The five of us stood in a line, encompassed by these men of force. Everyone spilled out of their cars and came out with guns in hands. And where do you think they were aiming them?

Bingo! Right at our heads.

The sliding door to the truck slid open with a loud overbearing scratch and slammed at its stopping point. Inside were four people with rifles ready to shoot. I stared directly into one of the scopes and noticed the crosshairs. In the glass was my reflection. Boy did I look stupid. It was a face of confusion mixed with frustration. Reminded me a lot of Will's face, minus the confusion of course. I wanted to punch myself so hard that it'd knock the look right off.

"Don't move!"

That pretty much sums up what they were saying. They yammered all they wanted but it still couldn't get through my head. I mean, how do you expect it to get to us when we couldn't even comprehend what was going on? And not to mention, we had nowhere to go even if we wanted. The whole street was blocked off and there wasn't even an inch of asphalt to be seen. I've ran on top of houses before but never on cop cars and I wasn't about to try it. Not with all the bullets that were ready to fly into me.

"Hey that's the girl that we were chasing earlier!" yelled one cop as he pointed at Wendy. I would've been complaining about how childish he sounded but all my mind was filled with was questions. He snarled before he went on. "Filthy terrorist! I had my little girl die because of you!"

"Terrorist?" Wendy silently asked. I hadn't seen that look on her face before. It was a solemn expression. She was actually being affected by this guy's anger.

The officer in the military vehicle came out in uniform. He stood with an overly straight posture. With the many tiles he wore on his shirt, I was sure he had a long time of military service, fighting in a continuous war across an ocean. His face read of nothing, but carried the disgusting look that he felt he knew everything.

As he walked in the circle of officers, he raised his hand to stop the man from yelling at Wendy. For a while, he just stood there watching us. When he decided to speak, I was surprised to hear that his voice was quiet. Not to mention the helicopters didn't help.

"You're under arrest for destroying the penthouse and are charged with murder along with terrorism. To be honest, and the rest of the people here would agree, we don't want to bother with listing how many crimes you committed. Just don't make things complicated and not fight with us even though we'd very much like the opposite," he said, giving a small smirk.

"What the heck are you talking about?! We never did anything wrong!" I yelled.

"Oh, no?"

"We never blew up the penthouse!" Charlotte said.

"Oh but you did. Look. I'd like to believe you, trust me. You're kids and that's what ticks me off even more. I know you think you can get away with anything because of that, but sadly that isn't the truth."

Out of nowhere, Monica gasped louder than the man talked. All of us turned to look at her. Her eyes stared out into the emptiness of the air.

"I've been cut."

"Cut?" Will asked.

"I can't connect to my computer. I can't look at the news or read anything. I...I—"

The anger burned inside of me. I hated every second of what was going on. For someone to claim that we were the ones that caused this terrible crime when we were running along with everyone else when the building was falling.

I was so caught up in my anger to realize they were looking at me. Of course they were. They felt what I was feeling. They felt it all. Every last bit of rage.

I reached over to my left and grabbed Wendy's hand and on the right, Charlotte's. There'd be no way to escape the amount of people that were ready to apprehend us one way or another. The thing that we have on our side, though, is the gifts of powers. Specifically, the gift of teleportation.

Wendy knew what I wanted her to do but she shook her head with her slanted eyebrows and peering eyes.

"No Mark. I can't. You know that."

I ignored what she said. I knew well of the risk we were taking, but what other option did we have? Getting stuck in a wall doesn't seem that bad. At least I think. Meh, it's only suffocation. And maybe having your body crushed. Okay, maybe I'm wrong. But still, we needed to get out of there.

I looked out behind the row of cops. There was a shop that was worn down. The paint that was over the brick had started to chip long ago. It was an antique shop. This was the shopping district that's been here longer than any of the others. Every shop was connected to each other on the inside. I'm not one to shop at stores like these but when you have to shop with your mother on a boring weekend, you do a lot of random things.

"You see that antique shop? You're gonna take us in there."

"Mark," she sighed.

"When I tell you."

I was surprised she was the one who wanted to back out of running away. It was like we switched personalities. Normally, I'd allow them to arrest us and I'd just tell the truth. Now, things were different. This man had the audacity to claim we were the ones who caused all this pain. I could've spent more time thinking it over, deciding whether or not this was the right course of action, but time was not a luxury we had.

Monica and Will caught on to what we were about to do. They joined hands and we were all connected, waiting to be transported by Wendy's hand.

Once the man noticed we were all holding hands, he fumbled for his gun.

"You're not gonna pull any dicey tricks. You hear?!"

"Now!"

The exact little bubble of existence that I went inside earlier was occupied by all of us. As quick as we disappeared, we reappeared into the open. When I opened up my eyes, I noticed something I dreaded. Brick was the only thing I could see. With the fear that one of them had gotten stuck, I whipped my head around to check. All four of them rammed into the wall and flew back at the force of the teleport. We didn't make it into the building.

"Arrrrgh!" Wendy yelled.

That was it. We were all dead. At any second, they'd be unloading the hundreds of bullets they had ready. Complete overkill. Just for a small group of teens that they thought killed people in a terrorist attack.

I remember looking over into Charlotte's eyes. I wanted to make sure I'd see her face one last time. If I were to die at any point, I wanted it to be next to her. She'd be the only one to provide the comfort I wanted. But with the dreaded face, how could that give off any form of ease?

The cops were turning when everything started to move in slow-motion. Don't think of it as that movie idiocy either. When you're in the heat of the moment and you know that you're about to be killed, life and time itself allow you a small compensation for that. It allows you to reflect on your life. I know I hear a lot of stories of people saying that their life flashed before their eyes and I call that a complete lie. Not once in that moment did I remember a moment in my life. All I could think of was how I got to this point and if there was any way I could save them. Even if we all piled onto Charlotte, she'd still die.

In desperation, I reached out for her hand. With the jump, our hands were ripped apart from each other. I wanted to feel the warmth of her soft hands one more time.

The moment I heard bullets fly out of the guns, I flinched and closed my eyes. Call me a wimp, an idiot, or whatever you want, but I never grabbed her hand. I was left to the darkness of my eyelids and hope that I would reach it in time.

"Get up! Go!"

I opened my eyes. Standing there was a girl completely dressed in white. Her hair matched her outfit and didn't have an ounce of any other color in it. She was standing, holding her hand out in front of us. The bullets did nothing to us because of her. They simply bounced off the wall that she put up.

"Don't sit there! Go!" she yelled again.

I couldn't. How could I? She was using powers. Not just any powers, might I add, but the same powers that Penn uses. It was the pure form of energy from within her body manipulated to form the very thing that saved our lives.

The more she stood there blocking the barrage of bullets, the more her face clenched in pain. That's what it took for me to finally get my butt off of the sidewalk and run.

I helped Charlotte up as fast as I could, grabbing her underarms to throw her to her feet. The cops weren't slow on reacting to where we were going and followed right behind us, pushing and trampling one another. The girl followed right behind us with the wall still being held up.

The store we ran into had racks and racks of precious antiques that were held higher than any other form of life to the people inside. I'm talking little stupid knickknacks made out of cheap glass. But I'll tell you, when I ran in there, I felt the feeling that all little children were prohibited to do in these stores. Granted, yes, we were running for our lives, but I had now known the feeling.

The girl in white ran right behind me holding a hand on my back, pushing me forward. I'd look back to try and see who she was but I was always forced back to watch where I was going.

The old lady that owned the store started yammering at us and telling us to not run only to be ignored.

Just then, the door to the shop was ripped off of the wall and thrown on the floor and people in black uniforms created a stampede.

"Will! The racks. Throw them!" shouted the unknown girl.

"Are you kidding me?! I can't use my powers out in the open!"

"Just do it! There's no point anymore!"

He let the girl run ahead and ran at the back of us. He threw his hand out at every rack he saw and sent it flying at the cops, breaking the precious ornaments in their faces.

Their footsteps were like something I've never heard. Hundreds of boots stomped on the tile. I was barely able to hear my heartbeat crying in my ear. I tried matching my own pace to theirs but it was no use. They were faster than me. It took a form of persuasion that wasn't on the level of the mind. Pure determination.

Picking up the pace, I tried my best not to trip over my own legs. When I saw my arms pumping in front of my face, I remembered Violet. No wonder she could run so fast. From what she said at the last moments of her life, she had to have been trained physically. Everything from her run to her fighting style were all in perfect form. It was the work of someone who spent relentless amount of hours practicing.

With her in mind, I made sure I wouldn't make my mistake anymore of a burden and ran with a view to get out of there alive once again.

We barged into the next store that was connected to the antique shop and continued on to all the others. It was a high speed chase in a shopping center.

When we made it to what seemed like the middle of it, the girl turned to Monica and shouted in her ear. I couldn't make out what she was saying because of the rumbling behind us. Even if I was able to hear, I probably would've stopped running. I needed all the concentration to make sure I was running to par with them.

Monica glided her hand across the wall for a split second and emitted a tiny spark of purple that wasn't noticeable. The moment I saw what she did, I knew what would happen. It was the perfect plan for escape. Something just as close to Wendy's and Charlotte's. When you're surrounded by everything electronic and you have Monica near it, you bet she'll take control of what's there.

*Whiiiir.*

The light that everyone was so used to shriveled out and fell subject to its enemy darkness. Even though I knew it was coming, I stopped in place. My natural human instincts kicked in and I stepped with extra caution, raising my feet higher than they needed to go. I bet if the lights would've turned back on, they would've found me looking like an idiot with my knee practically all the way up to my chin.

Thank goodness for whoever reached out and tugged on my shirt. If not I would've been lost to the darkness.

"Grab Will!" shouted the girl.

Knowing he was behind me, I threw my hand around aimlessly, hoping that my fingers would grasp him. The very tips of my fingers felt the soft delicacy of his hair. I've always wanted to give it a good tug so I went ahead and yanked it as hard as I could, dragging him with me. It was enough to satisfy my vengeance for now.

I had no clue who was leading us, but not once had we bumped into anything. That is until we ran into a flight of stairs. It was the only little smidgen of light that gave itself to the benefit of us. With every dang stair we would go up I'd jam my shin into the thick wood, worsening whatever bruise I made ten times over.

The walls on both sides of us started to do its job and cancel out the shouts of the cops downstairs.

When we got to the top of the stairs I saw there was a lonely bulb that Monica must've kept on. Will, being the last one up, quickly shut the door to the flight of stairs and locked it while he soothed his head from my tugging.

I was able to finally have a decent look at the girl. As I said before, she wore only white as Monica did the opposite. But just as Penn had red hair and eyes, this girl had white hair and eyes. Even though she saved our lives, I felt uncomfortable around her.

She ran her fingers through her hair and turned towards us.

"C'mon. We have to keep going. BloodLip was chasing you guys right?"

"Stop! Shut up," I yelled. She was saying things I didn't understand. I needed clarification. "Who are you? And more importantly, how do you know so much?"

She reached in her pants and pulled out a phone that she waved in her face. Her expression hadn't changed from its serious look from the moment I saw her.

"I'm the girl from the phone."

I felt my legs start to give. I never knew her. Never met her physically. Despite all that, she knew all that was happening to us and came at the right times.

"But how…?"

I couldn't understand.

She looked all of us dead in the eye.

"You have no idea what's going on. There's more to your little quarrel with BloodLip. Okay? Way more. Now I'm expecting one thing from all of you and that's that you listen to me. I don't care if it sounds crazy or you don't believe it.

You make sure you listen. Otherwise you're gonna end up dead. And trust me, if that happens all our efforts were put to waste. So I'm not letting your stupid idiotic selfish attitudes dictate what you do. Especially you!"

She rammed her finger in my chest and gave me a nasty look.

"But you don't even know me," I said in a quieter voice, more afraid of her now.

"That doesn't matter right now." She let out a quick sigh before she continued. "We're gonna go out that door onto the roof and make our way downtown." She pointed at the white dirty door on the opposite side of the room. "Consider me your escort. I said I was gonna repay you guys for helping me and this is it."

"Seems pretty lackluster for repaying someone who risked their lives for some stupid names," Wendy said.

The girl gave a meaningless scoff and let out a small smile.

"You think you're the only one risking your lives?"

Wendy pressed her lips together, letting her know that she was sorry.

"Ready?"

"What other choice do we have?" Charlotte asked.

"Good answer."

The girl walked up to the door and went through a series of locks to finally open up the door. Its hinges squeaked after haven't being opened in who knows how long.

The surface of my eyes cowered at the sight of the sun, creating a desire for moisture to satisfy them. Everything looked so different from up here. I was now a part of this family of buildings at this height. I could see just how high these things actually were and this wasn't even that tall of a building.

Vents occupied the little space up here and roared without any second thought as to whether it'd bother people or not.

The girl pointed out towards a building not far from here.

"You see that older abandoned building?" she asked. "We have to get to there. It's faster to where we're going. And plus, I don't think you wanna go back down *there*," she said, gesturing to the street. "It's not that hard to get to. Just follow my lead and you'll be fine."

When I saw where we were headed, I knew we would be building jumping. I chuckled a bit. I'd have to do this again. Who would've thought that I'd do this twice in the same day? I sure didn't. Call it what you want, but I felt like I was stupidly destined to jump buildings from now on.

With confidence in what we were doing, I followed right behind her, trying to copy the exact steps she took. It was more complicated than I thought it was going to be. Being bigger buildings and having more things on them, it made for a more interesting feat. She would jump to grab hold of the emergency fire ladders and make it a full sprint across to make the leap to the next building.

As we ran, she put her hand up to ear. I just barely noticed that she had an earpiece firmly placed to allow her to talk to whoever was on the other end.

"Shawna, what's the position on the dome?"

With being as close as I was, I was able to hear. You'd think that because it was an earpiece, I wouldn't be able to hear what they were saying. Either the other girl was loud or the earpiece was poorly designed.

"They're heading their way towards you. Expect them soon."

"How long?"

"Until?"

"Both."

"They'll be running into you at any moment. Getting to the other side, I'd say about fifteen or twenty minutes. It depends on him and ultimately on how things go with you."

"Right."

"I'm sending Adam over to you. He'll be there soon."

"You had to send him?"

"You can't deal with him for a while? Gosh, he's only helping you."

"What about Amber?"

"She's busy with Ace."

The girl in white let out a sigh.

"She's not gonna get anywhere with him. Didn't you try telling her?"

"Of course I did, but none of us know what it's like to have a brother. You have to let her try."

"Trying's not gonna work. You can't fix someone once they're corrupted."

"You don't think I know that? Look, I know you care about her, but me being her friend, I'm obligated to try my best to make her happy."

"Well then she's gonna be disappointed."

"Either way, it's for her own good to face him."

"Yeah, I guess. You just tell Adam he better be on time. I'm counting on him."

She lowered her hand and continued on with her trek over to the abandoned building.

I kinda felt bad eavesdropping on her like that, but I felt like I deserved some understanding of what's going on. It didn't help though. I was left more confused and it created even more questions than I had before.

I kept repeating the conversation we had with this girl in my head. I never met her and only spoke to her once before. Now we were putting our lives in her hand. I probably should've been questioning why I did that more so than what I was actually thinking about. What I couldn't shake was what she said. There was more to our quarrel with BloodLip. With what she was saying in her earpiece to this girl, Shawna apparently, there was way more. She was right. I didn't know what was going on. It was when we made it to that building when the hysteria hit me hard and I realized that there was a problem I knew nothing about.

*       *       *

The six of us stepped into the abandoned building with unsettled hearts. Our steps were quiet and I had no idea why. Like the cops would even know that we jumped buildings to get here. Never liked them anyways. Yeah, whatever. You're gonna complain about how they're the reason why there isn't a crime rate as high as it should be. But gosh, have you seen the things they've done? They remind me so much of that army official who aimlessly pointed a finger at us for the attack.

"Oh I'm so smart and I know everything."

Pretty much what goes through my mind when I see them.

"This place is so gross!" Wendy shouted, her face scrunching up in disgust.

I know I said there was no reason to be quiet, but still, she didn't have to break the silence with a shout that could be heard throughout the whole dang place. Her bratty complaining voice bounced off of the walls and onto every surface inside.

"Why do you think it's abandoned?" Will told her.

The girl in white let out a soft sigh. And what was her problem? Thanks for saving our lives and stuff, but you can at least expect nothing more from Wendy. She knew everything as it was, right? So why did she think they wouldn't be any more different when there was a crisis on hand.

I tried my best to ignore her and hold back from yelling so I did my share of taking in the ugliness of the building. The place we were at was in a never ending corridor. The ceiling extended up pretty far also, allowing for hundreds of cobwebs to fester and add to the mosaic they were making.

The metal walls had splotches of rust sticking to them. The orangish brown didn't go well with the fading gray. Everything together made it reek. It smelled like human feces and old coins.

Even if I tried and looked around the whole place, I don't think I'd be able to tell you what it was. It would look like a factory in one place but the next it'd look like a stupid excuse for apartments.

I swear, some of the places downtown were so weird and creepy but no one seemed to care. It was like the old dirty piece of clothing you leave on the floor in your room and no matter how many times you see or smell it, you continue to let it rot.

Old tinted glass that was peeling ran along the upper half of the wall looking out to the alley. Even though it was well advanced in years, the tint held true to its task and darkened the world outside. The larger building that overpowered this one cast a shadow of surmounting glory over the alleyway between them.

"Alright, we need to hurry," said the girl in white.

"You never told us where we need to go," Charlotte said, peeking over at her face.

The girl was stubborn as usual and didn't tell us anything. She just clamped her mouth shut and started to jog forward. We needed to follow closely so we turned to a jog as well.

I still didn't understand what her problem was. If she expects us to follow her and do whatever she asks of us, then we're really gonna need some clarification and a heads up of what we're getting into. I don't care if it pertains to us or not, we deserve something in return.

"They're the same," I said, cornering her with my words.

"Hm?"

She looked over her shoulder and made eye contact with me. To be honest, if I had to give a choice between whose eyes were better, Penn's or hers, I'd go with the ones in front of me. Even though she was incredibly irritating, her unnatural mutations were beautiful. Her entire eye was white. Her iris was a glowing white that could pass as a silver if it wanted to. What amazed me even more was that her pupil was not black as Penn's was. This girl's was a light blue. A hue as the sky.

"Your powers. They're the same as Penn's."

She shrugged her shoulders.

"And?"

"What do you mean *and*?! That just doesn't happen; duplication of powers."

"You don't know that. You don't know anything after all. Could happen, maybe not. Who knows."

She was legitimately starting to infuriate me.

"Don't play games with me! You expect us to do whatever you say when we don't even get compensation for anything."

"Oh yes you do." She jabbed a thumb in her chest. "What do you think I'm doing?"

Will gave a scoff.

"What kinda question is that? What do you think you're doing," he said, mocking her. "You said it yourself. We don't know anything." He threw the strands of hair in front of him to the side to make sure his pretty boy eyes were looking at her. "As much as I hate to say it, you're right. We're absolutely clueless here. So when you ask a stupid question like that, don't expect a single logical answer or reaction from us."

"Believe me, I don't," she said in stark defiance to what he was saying.

Will's jaw clenched, making the balls of muscle tighten. Something about his glare was entertaining to look at. I gotta give it to him, he pulled it off. He could make himself look good and be aggressive.

I checked to my left to see if Monica was alright, not hearing her speak in forever. When I turned to see her, she was looking out of the faded window. Her black hair that came down to her lower back bounced around with her steps. In every instance she seemed calm. I guess because she's always so stiff and blank that when something does roll around, she stays the same, not needing to change anything about herself.

"They're here," she said softly.

"Who?" I asked.

The rest of us moved over to see out the window. What was there made me remember why I was running in the first place. It was never because of some cops. It was because I murdered someone. All because of my mistake.

Three girls and a guy were sprinting through the alleyway. They cleared all the junk and trash that was uselessly thrown there. I gotta say, their speed impressed me. If they were chasing us twice earlier, they should've caught up to us in no time. If that was the case, then why the heck didn't they?

The girl in white gave a shaky gasp. Her eyes widened and added to her purity.

"BloodLip," Wendy voiced in complete disgust of them.

The girl shook her head.

"I wish," she said, sounding like she was about to lose her sanity.

"He's gone!"

The voice came from the girl's earpiece. It was the same voice as earlier. Shawna.

"What do mean *gone*?!" The girl held her hand up to her ear and started to go into a full sprint and matched the pace with the four outside. She never moved her head and kept her eyes on their silhouettes.

Shawna sounded out of breath and running as we were.

"That idiot. He's so selfish. What the heck do think I mean when I say gone? He's dead," Shawna said, not even catering to the fact that someone they knew died.

She covered her mouth with her hand and let her eyes billow with the same substance I desperately needed earlier.

"How!?"

"Who do you think killed him, hm? Look, I'm sorry. If I was in your shoes, trust me, I'd be feeling the same way. But listen, we have to face the truth and fix things. So I don't care what it takes but you get those kids to the mall!"

Taking what Shawna said, she wiped her eyes and snarled at the sight of the four outside.

"The twins are here. I'll need some help."

*Twins?*

The more I looked at them, the more I couldn't help but feel like I knew them. Their shape and look, despite the darkness they were in, looked familiar. Then I noticed the only male with them wasn't as built as Eli nor as tall. The little streaks of hair bounced around in front his eyes just like...

"Adam?" Shawna called out to him in the earpiece.

"You guys can't give me break can you? I'm heading up the stairs now."

The girl took her hand off of the earpiece and looked over at us. Her glare was more intense than the first time. Her chest expanded while she took in a deep breath before telling us what to do.

"They're gonna jump in here at any second. When they do, it's pretty obvious what's gonna happen. Adam and I are gonna hold them off and you guys need to run. But the one thing I ask of you is that you don't look back. No matter what happens, no matter what you hear, you keep those legs running. You hear?! And don't you dare ask why."

*Jump?*

With a movement the five of us just did to escape earlier, the people running in the alleyway joined hands. For a few seconds they ran like that, connected and looking like they were gracefully flying.

*Bang!*

The noise was completely unexpected. The door on the right of the hallway flew open and standing there was a guy our age. He wore a black shirt that was slightly torn. His hair was scruffed up and there were scrapes on his face. It had to be only one person. Adam.

He ran next to the girl and gave her a small pat on her shoulder.

"I'm sorry," he said.

She shook her head in frustration.

"It doesn't matter. He wasn't real anyways."

"That's not true and you know it. He just wasn't the one you cared about. There's still someone that's real to you on the other side so you fight like it matters."

"But everything's done now. We aren't the ones to make it out." She gave a hopeless scoff. "We don't exist anymore."

The girl took back out her sword and readied it in her hand, holding it firmly.

"But at least we still have a chance. Right?"

His eyes met mine and he gave a smile. Despite what was happening, he was taking the death of this person they knew pretty well.

"It's a pleasure to meet all of you." He looked out the window as he said his next words. "It'll be a good last memory." He joined the girl's sight and put the ones outside in view. "Let's show those happy-go-lucky idiots they can't stop the Equilibrium."

Even if she didn't tell us they were about to fight I would've known. You have four random people that apparently weren't BloodLip chasing us and suddenly, you have another group backing you that you never knew. I thought I knew the severity of things while they were happening. That day I found out that no matter how much I think I know, I will never be fully informed. I'd constantly live at a disadvantage.

*Swoosh!*

*Wendy?*

There was no reason for her to teleport out of here. Granted, she might want to leave the corridor sooner but without us? But then I felt it. Whenever she'd teleport, there'd be a suction that absorbed all sound and gravity of some sort and created a deep sense of presence. Just then, I felt it behind me.

"Run!" they both shouted.

I picked up the pace and returned to the same speed as when we were being chased down by the sea of cops.

Behind us, the sounds of grunting and outcries due to pain along with the occasional giggle echoed throughout the filthy corridor. Both of them were risking their lives for us, letting us escape. But what kind of battle was going on behind us? Sounds that I've never heard forced questions to pounce on me.

"Go, I'll hold them off!" Adam yelled at the girl with a hearty grunt.

The scuffling of her shoes got closer to us as she was about to join us when I heard a voice I'd never forget.

"You really think you're gettin' away that easily?"

My eyes widened. My heart fell and my stomach imploded. The voice was one that I was familiar with. In fact, familiar would be an understatement. The amount of time I spent with her amounts to nothing before. It was a voice only a face of beauty could contain. Why did it sound so murderous?

*Charlotte?*

I ticked my head over, hoping that maybe she wasn't there anymore. But no, I could feel her still next to me. I didn't even need to look. In fact, I shouldn't have. Her face showed an amount of horror to the point that I would've guessed she saw her family murdered in front of her. And it wasn't just me. We all were staring at her, not giving her a moment to herself.

The horrifying sound of a gunshot left the gun of the voice behind us, lifting the dust off of everything in the building. With the girl being not that far from me, her scream was amplified as well as her thud. Sobs escaped her mouth and flew into the air.

"Don't look. Keep going!" she ordered.

Then the voice that sounded exactly like Charlotte's spoke again.

"You guys have fun with Em—"

I didn't need to look back to know what was happening. Her mouth was being covered and Adam was the one doing it. There were a few more gurgles of her trying to talk and then a snap broke the noise and ended her muffled rant. A cracking of bone and tendons. The very voice of Charlotte was put to death.

I reached for her hand to make sure that she was actually still there. The noise alone was enough to trick my mind into thinking that she was actually dead.

The end of the corridor was right in front of us when Adam killed the girl. I wanted to replace the sound of her struggled grunts and the snap of her neck with any other one. When we pushed through the door, I made sure to push it with extra force. All the rest of them did the same.

We left the abandoned building with hearing the last little bits of anger and shouting, protesting the event that just happened.

*What the heck just happened?*

When I was going down the stairs to get to the sidewalk, I found myself running, fleeing from the scene. I hadn't an ounce of what happened. My comprehension for everything was reduced to the point lower than a toddler.

I ran my fingers through my hair, scrapping my scalp carelessly.

"What's going on?" I said. The voice came out almost hysterically, on the edge of tipping over towards the pit of insanity.

They all looked at Charlotte and stared at her. She wasn't the monster that shot anyone. No. She was next to me the entire dang time.

"Who...who was...?"

Charlotte dug her nails into her head, desperately forcing the answers out.

The door we just came out of opened up and the girl in white came out with red replacing the emptiness of her clothing. Her arms clenched the left side of her stomach, suppressing the flow of blood. All we did was watch her stumble down the stairs, not finding the time for sympathy.

"Come on," she grunted.

"What was—" I tried asking.

"Stop. Just stop. We need to hurry. The rest of them will be here any second now. She dragged us down. All she was trying to do was delay us."

"Charlotte?" I asked her.

The girl from the phone darted her eyes at me, not showing aggression, but bending the bottom of her eyebrows down. What scared me was that she didn't say no.

Just when I thought my nightmares were coming true, a clamping noise turned the corner of the street. Out of all the moments, they had to choose now. The cops reappeared and massed together to end our lives. They pulled up their guns and fired once again.

The girl put up her hand in desperation and cried out when the wall was put up. It was true. Her powers were exactly the same as Penn's. It stayed true to the fact that they can't use them that effectively when they're tired, hurt, or out of energy. The bullets haven't even hit it yet and she still shrieked. I felt for her but I didn't care for the pain she was in really. All I cared about was us.

Once the bullets started to reflect themselves, the blood seeped out of her wound quicker and the wall was fading.

"Run! Please!" she pleaded with a scratching at the deepest part of her throat.

A mass further down the street revealed itself and took my attention from the cops. I, naturally, thought it was another group of them that came for backup but I was nowhere close to my assumption.

"No no no no no," she said turning around and forgetting about the cops. "It's too soon."

"What is that?" Wendy said in a troubled voice, starting to back up.

As they drew closer, I could start to visualize what made up this clump. Each piece of this group was a person. They were teenagers like us but all of them appeared the same. Black hair and gothic clothing. Some of the girls were wearing black lipstick and all of them shared the same darkened nails.

Simultaneously, all of them turned their attention towards the cops and jumped on them. Literally, all of them jumped on the cops and started to tear at them, ripping them apart.

The girl's face was full of insurmountable turmoil. She grabbed us, turned us around, and ran in awkward movement towards the end of the street.

I hadn't had a chance to turn back to see who the voice was from earlier so I seized the moment and turned to watch the massacre take place. After brutally beating the cops, they attacked random people walking on the sidewalk and ran on top of moving cars. It was a full-fledged mob. And I couldn't shake the fact that all of them were smiling when they were doing it.

We didn't bother with running on the sidewalk and ran straight into the middle of traffic. I watched the girl in white stumble against moving cars and cry out to only keep running. I was watching the whole time but in no way did I help. I was expecting any other of them to but they were still focused on what was happening. Their brains were too busy comprehending everything when we should've been doing something about her.

Once we made it to the other side of the street, she stopped. She was hyperventilating now.

"You guys need to go. Go to the mall. They're waiting for you."

"Who?" I asked.

"That doesn't matter. You'll find out when you get there."

"But what about you?" Charlotte asked.

"Be realistic here Charlotte. At the end of all this, the hospital is either going to be full or gone. I have no escape from this either way."

"It's not vital," Will tried explaining.

She let out a sigh mixed with a chuckle and managed to barely smile.

"When you're expected to fight and you're this wounded, it pretty much is." She tried her best to straighten her back and threw down her hand and appeared the white sword. Her eyes started to water and the tears rolled down. My heart began racing when she looked me in the eye. "Mark, please, and I mean please make the right decisions. We're all counting on you."

She reached up to her ear piece.

"Long live the Equilibrium."

With that, she threw it off onto the floor as the shouting expelled from it. Her foot lifted high and she rammed it down, shattering it. She gave one more teary eyed smile before running off with her sword in hand to face the crowd of death.

\*     \*     \*

No matter where we went now, people were scared, running about and the people that just got into town were wondering why everyone was behaving so strangely. As we ran to our destination, there would be the occasional rumble from an explosion not that far from where we were.

It was clear that there was another attack, but this time it wasn't so subtle. Sure, it still caught people off guard, but everyone was still kind of on end with the previous one. A series of terrorist attacks within days from each other in the same city was unheard of. No wonder they chose to attack again. No one would think of doing it in the same exact place.

And they thought it was us. It no doubt had to be the ones who were stampeding towards the cops. But all those kids? What kind of sick group was this? Even though I was barely understanding things, I kept wondering how this involved me.

There was a group I knew nothing about that had helped me twice now and two of them killed themselves for us. The weight of what really happened just started to press on me. I was indebted to them and I had no way of paying them back. There was more to them also. They knew everything from BloodLip to our powers and our names. Foreknowledge of this attack was known by them as well. But how?

The pain in my legs were growing numb and I didn't feel the exhaustion anymore. The large dome of the mall sprouted out over the small buildings around it. There were people waiting for us inside. I'd have to relate the news to them that two of their own had died on our account. I'd normally try to rehearse what I was going to say in instances like this but there was no time. Even then, I've never had the obligation to do so. So I wouldn't know the first thing to say.

We made it to the doors and we stopped in front of the entrance with hesitation burning within. Charlotte's face was firm now, flipping a switch to the correct situation.

"Did you guys hear the same thing?" she asked, dipping her head down.

"You mean your voice?" Wendy asked?

Charlotte gave a nod.

"Yeah." Wendy appeared to be completely out of it when she was starting to realize what that meant. Her face was thrown out and anger took its place. Her hands were now in fists and she threw out a yell. "What the heck are we doing?! I never asked for this!"

"You think any of us did?" Monica said, giving her a glare.

"Seems to me like everything's about Mr. Important over here," Will said, giving my shoulder a soft punch.

"Nothing we can do about it. We just need to keep going forward," Charlotte said.

She reached out and did the same as I did to her. Her soft hand grabbed mine and pulled me forward through the doors. It was sweaty like last time but it was shaking also.

The five of us stepped inside. I expected the usual look but the chaos had reached it. The staff was doing their best to try and keep control of the madness but ultimately, there was no way they could.

It was just like outside. Some were scared and running out of the mall with their bags and some were standing idly by, looking confused. Then all the TVs turned on to the news. Normally they would be playing ads or new pop songs that came out. Rarely were they used for the news. Only in emergencies or big political issues such as the election of a president.

It put a trance on people and forced them to stop what they were doing. The shot was from a helicopter that was flying over the city. You could see some smoke from recent explosions and also the remains of the penthouse. But that wasn't what they were focusing their attention on. Just below the skyline was a white, somewhat see through, material that was encasing Springfield. And it was rising, ever so slowly.

I was about to join everyone in taking a closer look at what was happening but I saw something. No, I felt something. All it took was a tick of my eye to see all of BloodLip standing in the direct center of the mall, under the dome, glaring us down.

*No. Where's the people? They said that we'd meet them here. They were waiting for us.*

Couldn't you think Mark? Wasn't it obvious? Who would be the only people in the entire population of Springfield who would wait for you in a place like this—at a time like this? Obviously, the people who wanted to get revenge from you.

All of us turned to face them now. That's what sparked the chain of aggression. Brittany exploded in flames, Eli took out something from his pocket and turned to a metal version of himself, and Sarah quickly unsheathed two knives from her belt. Penn was the only one not to move. Her upper lip was pulled to the side and her nostrils flared. Completely berserk.

We slowly walked up to them to the point where the only thing that stood between us was a few feet of tense air.

Was this even called for? It was as if I was facing them now, contesting them in some way. This whole time I agreed with them. I was a murderer and needed to pay for it. But now, the inner desire to prove them that their acts were wrong in themselves was present. It was me that they wanted so why the heck were they hurting innocent people who were doing what was right and standing up to them? You can't tell me that it was okay in the slightest.

As we continued in our stare off, the customers inside ran out to watch whatever was happening. Our locked gazes were breakable by nothing. On their way out, they would stop and marvel at the powers of BloodLip only to cower away and run, hoping that these streams of supernatural events would stop.

"Let me ask you something Mark," Penn said, making my heart skip a beat. "Why are you here? Out of all the places right now, you decide to head to the mall. You can't tell me that it was a coincidence, could you?"

"Are you telling me that you have to do with...?"

I threw my hand back to gesture everything that has gone on but she interrupted me.

She gave a scoff.

"As if. I don't care about any human affairs. It's the least of my concerns."

"Human?" Charlotte said, raising her voice.

Sarah gave a snarled smile that quickly turned into another of her sneers.

"You idiots." She twirled her knives in her hand and beckoned us with the tips. "You're so desperate for answers. No different from a mouse looking for random pieces of food. You disgust me."

I was starting to get the clue that they knew nothing about the people that helped us. That still didn't answer why they wanted us here with them.

"I was going to tell you everything. Everything!" Penn yelled. "You were given a chance to live amongst a line of rulership. But that's the least of your wants. Goes the same for me. I wanted something that no amount of convincing would force you to do. You couldn't just conform like the rest of them, could you?" She bobbed her head back towards her friends. "No, then you go and murder my mom." The whites of her eyes reflected in the synthetic light above. "She taught us to be the best killers there are. She taught us to be relentless. I hated it. All of it." A devilish chuckle found itself to escape her mouth. "But now I see why. I see why she wanted you dead so badly."

The same white sword as the girl's appeared in Penn's hand, the edges giving off a soft glow. It was her sign of having enough. She was ready for my punishment.

The four of them ran forward and caught us off guard. Penn had no other person in sight except me. I watched helplessly as she threw herself on me. My mind ran at insane lengths to allow me to keep my eyes open and not flinch at the mass of her sword. Knowing that she wasn't completely settled on me, I threw my hands into her stomach and pressed into her soft abdomen, throwing her on the floor.

With minor seconds to spare, I drew my attention to the others. By no means were they let off the hook. Eli and Wendy were at it again, fist to face, leg to stomach. She would take advantage of her powers and throw him around, being way too quick for him to catch up.

Brittany naturally went for Monica. Never knowing them or ever seeing them together, if I was a passing stranger, I'd think that they were sisters, born with countering powers of the same stature.

It was quite a sight to see. Brittany ignited her hands into flames and threw punches at Monica. For the first few hits, she shrieked in pain, a sound I never heard from her. She turned it around quickly enough to manage herself. All it took was the extending of her fingertips to expel her electricity into her. And as there's a first for everything, Monica showed anger to the point of changing her whole expression, coming close to Penn's. Seeing the amount of force Monica would put into her punches, I'd think she'd been in fights before.

Charlotte and Sarah had knives coming close to each other's necks. Charlotte's stance was off in no way. I guess the self-defense classes paid off. She held her own with her like she's done it ten times before.

I felt better about what was happening when I saw Will run over to Sarah and tackle her. He stood by Charlotte and made sure she was okay. That fool better keep watching her.

Granted, this was only a mere second or two before I was reminded I was in a fight of my own.

Letting the sword disappear into thin air, she reached up to grab my neck. Using all her force, she jabbed her knee into my stomach several times over, knocking the wind out of me.

I tried my best to do something but I wasn't used to this pain. With every breath I would wheeze. She let me go and allowed my body to fall to the floor, clenching my stomach.

When I looked up to make eye contact with her, everything felt so familiar. The sight of her standing over me reminded me so much of the haunting look of the Charlotte that killed me. She watched me sulk in my pain and asserted her dominance.

I just barely caught the sight of Will getting tackled by Eli before Penn turned me around to face her. She laid me flat on the cold hard tiles and held a hand under my chin, but her face was different. The pure rage that she radiated was swapped with a face of controlled anger. Tears started to roll down her cheeks onto my shirt.

"I trusted you!" She sniffled before she created a small dagger in her hand. "I trusted you darn it! I wanted to be your friend but you rejected me for no reason. You thought I was nothing but a useless murdering pig! I was forced to kill! And never was it randomly. We always had a reason. But I guess you don't have the same morals. You go and destroy people's lives for the fact that you think you're doing everyone a favor!"

Penn threw her hand up as if she was casting a fishing line and let it down on top of my right shoulder.

Whenever I saw the white pure form of energy from Penn, I, for some reason, thought it wasn't going to be sharp. It was one of the smoothest cuts ever. The tip of the white dagger pushed through my skin and pierced with ease. I let out a scream just as loud as when Wendy had done the same deed.

After going in about an inch, Penn stopped. Her hand held the dagger in place and stared with wide eyes. She released her hand from the dagger and it dissolved into the air. At that moment the blood started to seep out and fall to the floor.

For a moment, she sat on me in shock and watched as I screamed.

"Penn!"

We both turned our heads. Brittany called to her. I always found it interesting that you could tell what someone means just by the tone of voice. Never was she calling her. No. She was bringing her back from the state of reality she was in.

Penn shook her head as if shaking out bad dreams and her snarl returned. She was just about to throw a fist in my face when something exploded at the top of the dome we were under.

The small explosion of energy threw Penn's hair around. She turned around and her face was illuminated.

"Enough! Get off each other unless you wanna get ripped to shreds!" Penn yelled to all of us.

She got off of me and the four of them took formation as the same as they were when we saw them; standing in a line.

I stayed on the floor with an amount of pain that was halted for a few moments as I witnessed the marvel in front of me.

A bright light that had mixes of white and blue were released from a circular shape above us. It was a flat plane that floated majestically. What looked like tendons or tentacles from an octopus occasionally flew out for a split second.

When they came over to help me up, I noticed that everything got a lot colder. It wasn't just because of my wound. I could see my breath—all of ours. I looked around to see the reactions of the people inside the mall but they were all grey. Everything that wasn't inside the radius of the circle was frozen in place. Shoppers were midstep or had their mouth open in a shout.

I returned my sights on Penn and held a hand over my exposed blood. I was expecting a cold stare but instead, in her hand she held a bow and arrow made out of her energy. The pointed arrow was aimed at me. Tears still hadn't stopped their plea of persuasion within her. All she needed to do was let go of her grip on the end of the bow and the arrow would fly into my heart. But she didn't do it. She closed her eyes and let out a compressed sigh, allowing the bow to dissolve.

With her voice broken, she spoke.

"You better be ready, Mark. We're coming for you."

The picture of them still stays in my head to this day. Her tilted stance, only giving me half of her tear stricken face. The burn mark still on the side of Eli's face. The thing that made it so daunting to look at them was their glares. It showed all the pain that they went through with the death of their mentor.

Just beside Sarah's head, I noticed something at the entrance to the mall. On the floor was a girl. She was laying on her stomach and held a hand up towards our direction. I couldn't help but feel that she was looking at me. She had been calling out to someone, trying to get their attention but her voice was lost to the stillness of the unnatural state. Behind her was another girl, a shorter one, with a crooked smile and in her hand was a block of some sort.

*Huh?*

Another noise broke my curiosity. A sound of a huge gust of wind blew downwards from the multicolored circle. All of our hair blew around and the cold air was replaced with a heat that of an oven.

Just before everything went black, Penn's stare made one final push into my soul.

And with the snap of a finger, everything was gone. No more mall. No more BloodLip. No more friends. Not even I was there. Think of it as being in a room with no light source and not having a body. I would've been scared if I was able to but I had no control of anything.

Just as fast as everything disappeared, another gust of wind screeched in my ears. This time I could actually see myself. I shook uncontrollably and I covered my ears as hard as I could to suppress the sound. A barrage of glistening lights thrust itself in my eyes. My eyelids had no impact on how brightly they shined. With no unwinding or hint at it stopping, the strange occurrence vanished as if it never happened.

When I opened up my eyes, I was standing on some rubble. There was a gasp for air besides me. Desperate to find anyone I knew, I turned to see Charlotte shaken up. I didn't know how to act so I ran up and gave her a large hug.

After pulling away from her, I noticed she was confused. I knew my hug was uncalled for and was completely given on the fact that I was scared and wanted comfort in anyone I knew, but the feeling was adding to the overall hype and jitter and I didn't care all that much at the time.

"What the heck was that?!"

It was the voice of an annoying brat.

I saw the rest of them standing in the same position at the mall.

*Wait. Where was the mall? More importantly, where are we?*

It was our go to reaction. All of our heads were on swivels and searched for a clue as to where we were.

Here's what I was able to make out.

We were standing in an old and torn building. The walls crumbled like dry cookies and let the rubble grow cold with the crisp night air. The light from the moon was enough to let us see but as far as I could tell, there was no artificial light in the vicinity.

There was a whole wall that was torn down and let the elements come inside. From where I was standing, I could see tall buildings just like downtown but none of them looked familiar. There were tons of them but they all had one thing in common. One, they were very elegant looking, appearing that it cost millions to make them. And two, they were torn to bits just like the one we were in. It replicated a picture from a warzone or a post-apocalyptic video game.

Standing in front of me was someone. It startled me a bit. She was standing there the whole time, probably watching us looking stupid. She looked about our age and wore a modern jacket with a scarf around her neck. A small subtle smile wouldn't shake from her face.

Her face. Something about it reminded me a lot about my mom. Small subtle features around her cheeks and her soft eyes.

It only took two words. Two words! Two words to change everything. It changed the way I perceived information. It changed the way I thought about things. It changed the way I thought of my life, knowing that it was all a lie. I never knew anything and by the looks of it, it wasn't going to change any time soon.

You might be asking what the heck does a group of teenagers with powers and an instructor that trained them, a "terrorist" attack on the city, the falling of the penthouse, the slip space that made me get murdered by my friends, and the second attack have to do with anything. Sure that'd be a big question but nothing amounts to the one that nagged at me constantly.

What is the Equilibrium?

Heh. Ain't that a question.

She went through and greeted us silently with her eyes and let them stop on me. Her smile extended before she spoke.

"Welcome home."

# Afterword

My deepest thanks and regards to anyone who took this journey with me in reading my first novel. I'd also like to thank my mom for all the support and tolerating my pleas for you to constantly read my revisions.

You know it's funny. One year ago from when I wrote this, I first thought of the idea to make a book. The thought came around when I finished reading a well written series by an author I admired greatly for his creative and unique grasping mechanisms. But something about the ending was not something I anticipated. In no way am I saying his ending to his books were lackluster, it was just that I overhyped myself as I waited for the last book to come in the mail.

I thought of many different theories on how the book was going to end. The one I concluded on wasn't fulfilled. The specific ending that I wanted to happen had a certain element to it that I thought was great. So I thought to myself "why not just make your own story with the same concept?"

As you've seen, that's just what I did.

I hope you continue to read and finish the series along with me. Certainly, you wants your answers don't you? I'll give them to you, but I can't promise you that they'll be the truth.

\*        \*        \*

Tell me how many times you've done this. You look at someone and you pick them apart. I don't know about you, but I know it was something I did all the time. Heck, I still do it now. It may not be for the same reasons as before but I do it regardless. It's almost a habit now.

Something different about this "picking apart" of a person is that you do it because you want to find every reason you hate them. No. Not because you want to have more reason to not like them, but rather, you have absolutely no idea why you do.

You watch them pass by and your chest burns. Your eyebrows curl inward and your nostrils flare. You want to make a move but you don't know how or what to do. Once again, you're left in the same place you've been in all along.

It burns. Stings. Festers. Relentlessly ripping you apart. Devours you. Makes you someone you know you're not. Leaves you hopeless and for dead, hoping someone can give you a way out of the desire to hate.

What can you do?

Nothing. Absolutely nothing.

You now start to experience thoughts and feelings you never felt before. Pain, misery, agony. They all combine into one thing. One thing that swallows you whole.

## CORRUPTION

"Disturb the peace my friend. Spread the Corruption. Make it grow."